# Murders and Masterpieces

*A Venetian Mystery*

Rachele Modiano Mendes Investigates
Book 2

Silvano Stagni

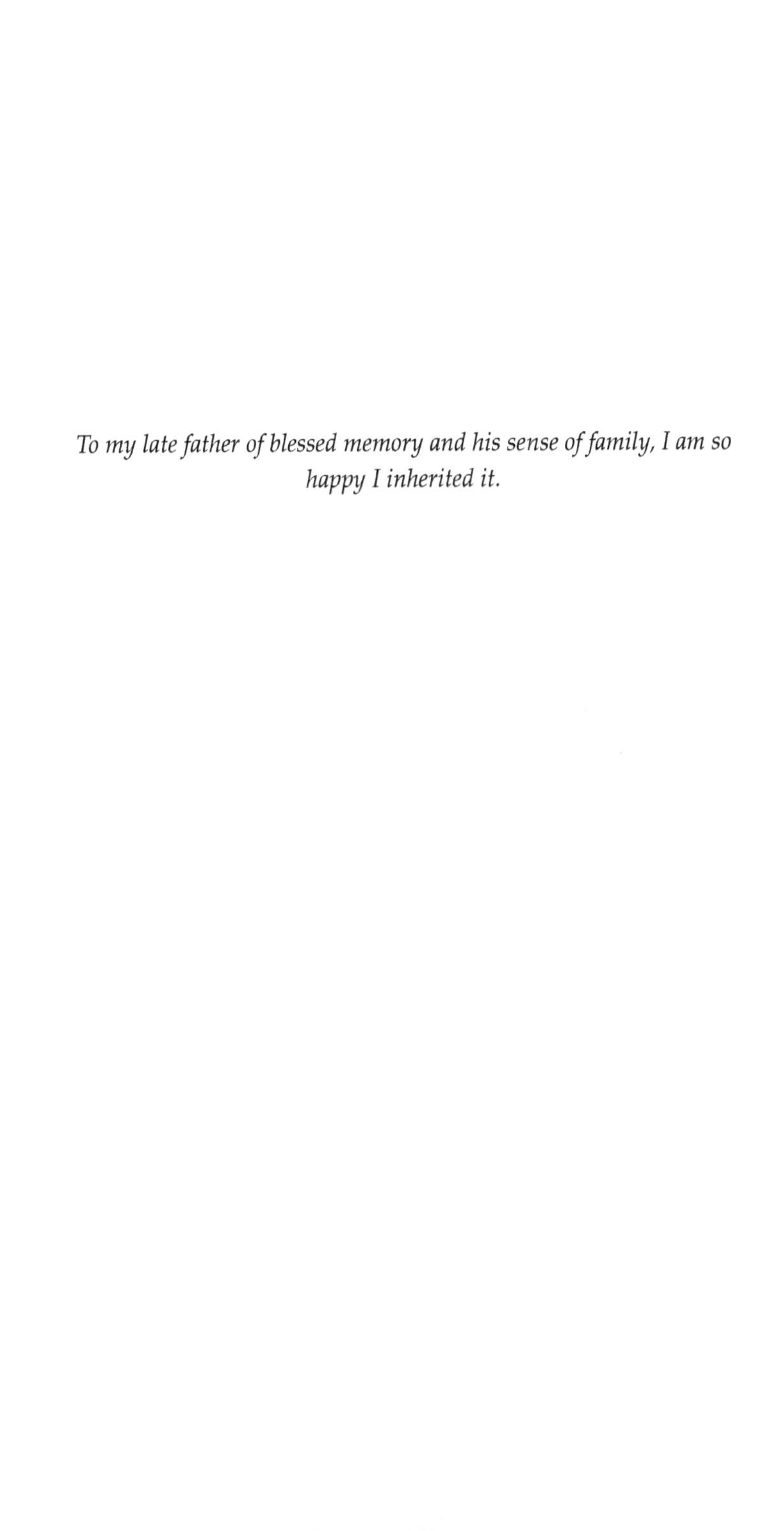

*To my late father of blessed memory and his sense of family, I am so happy I inherited it.*

# Also by Silvano Stagni

**Unconditional**

A collection of feel good short stories about acceptance, love, and memories.

**The Dressmaker's Parcels**

The story of the Modiano Mendes clan during Mussolini's racial laws, World War II, and the Holocaust. Spoiler: Rachele and her eldest daughter Emma join the resistance.

*From the series: Rachele Mendes Modiano - the early years*

### Book 1 : **Reflections in the Water**

1921. Rachele Modiano starts working for a Venetian law firm after she married Gabriele Mendes. Her first case turns into a web of fraud, blackmail, and possibly murder. Rachele must protect her client's name and win over a magistrate who dismisses her as an aristocrat toying with the law as a hobby.

### Book 2: **Villa Kalman's Secrets**

Venice 1925. Somebody shoots at two teenagers who jumped a fence to retrieve a ball from Villa Kalman's garden. A couple of months later, a young man is found severely beaten and unconscious in the shed of the same villa. Who fired the shot? Who was the young man? Why was he beaten unconscious? Were those events related?

*From the series: Rachele Mendes Modiano Investigates*

### Book 1: **Elena's Memory**

Venice, 1947. The search for the legitimate heir to a couple who did not survive the camps brings a young woman who lost her memory to Venice. The love and support of the extended Modiano-Mendes clan helps her recover her memory. They soon realise that the attempts to get rid of her had nothing to do with the inheritance.

# Foreword

The story takes place in Venice in 1950. However, it starts in 1866, when Venice was still part of the Austrian Empire. It joined Italy at the end of the Franco-Prussian War in 1870. The Franco-Prussian war is also important in the story.

Alsace and Lorraine are two regions in France on the western bank of the river Rhine. In the past five centuries, they switched between France and what is now Germany several times. They are one of those regions in Europe where different linguistic groups have lived in the same area for a long time and have alternated between being the minority and the majority several times. There is a very poignant statue in Strasbourg (the capital of Alsace) of a mother mourning two dead sons. One wears the uniform of the German Army in World War I, and the other wears a French uniform.

# Cast of Charactes

**Emanuele Cividali** (1824-1902) – A completely fictitious Venetian painter.

The **Mendes** family, not all the family members included in the list.

**Fiamma Andrade Mendes** (born 1873),

- **Gabriele Mendes** (born 1897), married to **Rachele Modiano** (born 1898)
    - **Emma Mendes** (b. 1924), **Anna Mendes** (b. 1926). **Diana Mendes** (b.1929), **Leo Mendes** (b.1932), **Davide Mendes** (b. 1934), **Mila Mendes** (b. 1943)
    - **Mario Mendes** (b. 1932), **Paola Mendes** (b. 1934) children of Gabriele's brother Emanuele. He and his wife Gemma died in 1943
- **Roberto Mendes** (born 1913)

- **Anita Torgnon** (born 1892), live-in housekeeper and Rachele's confidant. Gabriele and Rachele's children call her 'Aunt Anita'

- **Paolo Mondani** (born 1897), He and his wife are honorary member of the Mendes Clan.

- **Alex Modiano** (born 1919) – Son of Rachele's eldest brother

- **Alvise Cantoni** (born 1897) - third partner of the Cantoni-Mendes-Modiano law firm.
    - **Franco Cantoni** (born 1924).

The **Pesaro De Bonfili** family

**Deborah Camerini, Countess Pesaro De Bonfili** (born 1873)– very close friend of Fiamma Andrade Mendes, they think of themselves as sister. Their children call the other one 'Aunt'.

- **Elena Pesaro De Bonfili** (born 1932)
- **Joshua Schwartz** (born 1922) another honorary nephew of Countess Pesaro De Bonfili

The **Tron** family

**Ludovico Tron** (born 1889).

- **Tommaso Tron** (born 1922)
- **Isabella Tron** (born 1929)

The **Alcan** family (not all the family members are named in this story)

**Isaac Alcan** (born 1804)

- **Ruth Alcan Levy** (born 1824)
  - **Aaron Levy** (born 1860)
    - **Jules Levy** (born 1894)
- **Samuel Alcan** (born 1827)
  - **Raphael Alcan** (born 1864)
    - **Bernard Alcan** (born 1894)
    - **Maurice Alcan** (born 1897)
      - **Pierre Alcan** (born 1925)
    - **Chantal Alcan Klein** (born 1900)
      - **Daniel Klein** (born 1925)
    - **Isaac Alcan** (born 1910)
- **Israel Alcan** (born 1830)
  - **Philippe Alcan** (born 1871),
  - **Lottie (Charlotte) Alcan** (born 1878)
  - **Guillaume Alcan** (born 1884)
    - **Charlotte Alcan** (born 1922) – married to **Bill Campbell** (born 1920)
    - **Philippe Alcan** (born 1924)

**David Klein** (born 1920) – Chantal Alcan Klein's nephew. Son of her husband's brother.

The **Bembo** family, they own a glass blowing workshop in Murano.

**Master Antonio Bembo** (1823-1905) – Master glass blower.

- **Son not mention in the story**
  - **Antonio Bembo** (born 1894) – Master Bembo in 1950
    - **Dario Bembo** (born in 1922)

Other Characters

**Count Francesco Contarini** (born 1887) **and Countess Contarini** (born 1890) –

**Vice Commissario Umberto De Antoni** (born 1917) – Police detective,

**Alain De Lothringen** (born 1899)

**Guido Orlando** (born 1910)

**Brigitte Fontaine** (born 1926)

**Jean-Claude Ferrand** (born 1914)

# Chapter One

**Nyon, Switzerland, December 1949**

Bernard Alcan was driving to Geneva to meet Alain De Lothringen, arriving from Metz in France. He had only recently moved to Switzerland. He wanted to be somewhere boring and safe for the last years of his life, even if it meant being far away from his soulmate and lifetime companion. He had sold his share of a furniture company in Morocco and his home in Nice to fund this move. He had left almost everything behind and now wanted to get rid of the last remnant of his past, a painting his great-uncle Israel donated to his grandfather. He loved it, but it represented his old, angry self. Now that he had survived World War II unscathed despite being Jewish and an active member of the French resistance, he was not angry anymore. He wanted to end his days in peace and quiet, and maybe Alain would decide to join him when he retires. Alain was younger, and Bernard might be a Swiss citizen by then, able to sponsor Alain and make his move to Switzerland easier.

A few hours later, they were in Bernard's living room, having coffee and enjoying the view of the sunset and the lake. Bernard asked Alain to help him sell his large painting.

"Why don't you want to go on record as the owner of the painting?"

"It is a long story associated with the reason I have had no contact with my family for a long time. I need to sell it to help fund my retirement, and I am afraid somebody in my family might stop me."

Alain put the coffee on the small table in front of him, careful to put it on the coaster to avoid spoiling the intricate woodwork.

"Most art dealers I know in Switzerland are compromised with paintings stolen by the Nazis or acquired in an obscure way during the war. Are you sure you do not want me to sell it to a French art dealer?"

Alain could see that Bernard was getting increasingly stressed by the conversation.

"I prefer you didn't, for the same reason I do not want to sell it directly."

"Recently, I had an enquiry over a painting allegedly bought from our Museum during the time N azi Germany annexed Lorraine. The art dealer in Sanremo, in Italy, wanted to make sure the sale was genuine. He offered to return the painting to us if it wasn't."

Bernard could see a way out of his predicament.

"Did you ever meet face to face?"

"No, we only corresponded."

Any tension had left Bernard's face. He was smiling now.

"Perfect, I will write to him under an assumed name. We shall travel together to Sanremo with the painting, and you will take him to his shop using the same assumed name."

"I have two weeks holiday. Do you think we can manage in these two weeks? What name shall we use?"

Bernard was now in full planning mode. He had secured the help of his lifetime companion. He could sort out the rest.

"I had prepared a letter to prove the purchase of a painting from my brother. Unfortunately, I hid it in a compartment in the frame, and somebody nailed it shut. I do not remember doing it. I must ask a friend to write another letter."

"Why?"

"You already corresponded with the art dealer. I will write pretending to be Maurice Vernier, the alleged seller of the painting. I cannot write a letter and sign it Maurice Alcan, can I? Don't worry, I know who will do it. We shall have a drink with her tomorrow."

"Her? Do I have to worry?"

Bernard smiled

"Absolutely not, wrong sex to be of any interest to me."

**Sanremo, Italian Riviera, January 1950**

Count Francesco Contarini and his wife had enjoyed a holiday with all their children and grandchildren; they had escaped to the Italian Riviera to avoid the winter weather typical of the area where they lived, a small town between Venice and Padua. They just finished lunch in a restaurant near the Russian orthodox church and had decided to walk it off by the seaside. On the way, they walked past an art gallery. Countess Contarini was captivated by the painting in the window.

The light in the painting drew the viewer's attention to a young boy carrying a tray with loaves of bread. He was talking to a couple. The man was slim and elegantly dressed, a stark contrast with the shirtless and muscular young baker boy. On the right of the painting, two women wearing elegant clothes and a mask were looking at the young baker boy. On the left of the painting, children were sitting on the steps of a bridge over a narrow canal. You could see a gondola coming out of the bridge, sailing towards the Grand Canal. In the background, one could detect the Punta della Dogana.

Count Contarini did not stop when his wife did, so she had to call him back and draw his attention to the painting. The Count was also captivated by the entire scene. He liked the way the painter was aware of Caravaggio and Canaletto. In the real Venice, the canal did not exist. One would have to dig a canal demolishing a famous hotel in Riva degli Schiavoni and other buildings to have that view of Punta della Dogana. He thought the painter had used light like Caravaggio and created a Venice that had nothing to do with reality like Canaletto. On a whim, he decided to find out more and walked into the art gallery.

**Venice, February 1950**

Ludovico Tron was the world authority on Emanuele Cividali, a Venetian painter from the second half of the previous century. He was the author of the official catalogue of all Cividali's work and various books about Cividali's Venice, Cividali's portraits, and a book about Cividali and the short-lived nineteenth-century Venetian republic, the Venetian rebellion to imperial Austria. In reality, his middle child, Tommaso, wrote those books. Ludovico's eldest son was his pride and joy and his successor in the business. Tommaso was a writer and art historian at heart but a reluctant art dealer. The two brothers couldn't have been more different. The eldest was athletic, full of confidence and self-assurance. He could sell everything to everyone. He thrived under his father and was also a shrewd buyer of antique objects; his comfort zone was talking to clients in the family's art gallery or the

Piazza San Marco shop. The younger brother was slim, a dreamer, shy, and would have rather spent time with books than people. His comfort zone was in a library, buried in books.

That morning, Tommaso was trying to convince his father that they needed a new edition of the Cividali's catalogue.

"Whenever you talk about Cividali, you mention the unique situation of five identical originals. You tell people that Israel Alcan commissioned five copies of the same painting. One copy was donated to a museum in Metz when he died. The other four are lost. Yet, you have just bought a painting that you say is one of those four copies."

Ludovico was annoyed that his son was right. He had to assert his superiority, though.

"You are right. It is one of the four copies. It has the numbering on the back between the first and last name that matches what Cividali wrote to his accountant. I am not sure we need to bear the costs of a new edition of the catalogue."

For once, Tommaso did not budge.

"I think we do. Think of your reputation. Your name is associated with a publication that maintains that four 'authentic versions' are lost, and yet we have one of them in our art gallery, and we shall sell it as authentic."

Ludovico stood up and started pacing the small office in the back of the art gallery.

"Because it is authentic!"

Tommaso, for once in his life, was not budging.

"Therefore, we need another edition of the catalogue that does not say the four versions are lost. Are you sure that the origin of this version can be proven?"

Ludovico was annoyed and surprised that his shy son was being assertive for once in his life.

"Yes, I am. The seller showed me a copy of the receipt from an art dealer in Paris who bought it from Ruth Alcan Levy, sister of Israel Alcan, who commissioned the five copies. He also showed me a copy of the receipt of the purchase from the art dealer from the person who sold the painting to him. We have an unquestionable trail back to Emanuele Cividali."

"Then we need a new edition of the catalogue."

Ludovico Tron could never admit total defeat, but his son was right this time. His consent to do what his son wanted to do had to have a condition. He thought about it for a short while, then turned to his son.

"All right, prepare another edition, but you are in charge of selling it to those who bought the current one, and whatever amount of money you do not recover will be deducted from the art publication budget you manage."

Tommaso took the victory, one of the few times he convinced his father to do something he wanted to do, and his father did not.

# Chapter Two

## October 1863

Israel Alcan was a happy man. His decision to take his new young wife to Venice was brilliant. Vienna had been their first destination, visiting his wife's aunt. Then, they took the new overnight service to Venice. The new railway bridge and the new railway station made it so much easier. He will never forget the expression on his wife's face when they were in the gondola that took them to their hotel past Piazza San Marco. It was the first of many moments where his young wife had her eyes wide open, her mouth slightly open, and she could not speak.

Israel had worked hard to establish his own businesses. At 33, he owned a winery, a furniture company and was one of the three partners in a steel mill. It was not too bad for the younger sibling, who did not want to work in the family bank but loved to do things with wood. He seldom listened to his sister and his cousin, who were telling him how attractive he was. He could not believe that the young woman from Frankfurt had agreed to marry him, even though she knew he had no intention of working in the family bank.

. . .

They had been in Venice for a week and had seen all the major sights. Now, they were wandering around the city, getting lost in it and each other. In one of their morning walks along the Riva Degli Schiavoni, they went as far as the Castello area, where very few tourists ventured. They saw a painter trying to capture the 'Punta della Dogana,' the Custom House of the days of the most Serene Republic. They stopped to admire the man at work. He was capturing a detail in the background. The foreground showed a young boy carrying a tray with loaves of bread. Various other people were in the scene, but their eyes were drawn to the boy. His wife insisted he looked like a portrait of a young Israel she saw in her mother-in-law's sitting room. They introduced themselves to the artist, who said his name was Emanuele Cividali. Israel had some Italian, and Emanuele had some French, so their conversation was basic, but Israel made it clear that he wanted to buy the painting. Emanuele told him the canvas was his study for a larger piece. Israel just asked him for the address of his studio. He would come with somebody who could interpret for him. His Italian, or the painter's French, was not enough to discuss the purchase of the painting. Israel always carried a notebook and a pencil. Emanuele Cividali wrote the directions to his studio, and they agreed to meet two days later.

Israel arrived with an interpreter arranged by the hotel. He wanted to see the large painting; if he liked it, he would buy the large and small ones. When they arrived, his wife's expression when she saw the still unfinished large painting was priceless. Emanuele Cividali said the only missing part was the Canal Grande in the background with the Punta della Dogana. The section he was painting on the smaller canvas when they met. The interpreter had just finished when Emanuele, on impulse, commissioned five copies of that painting. He would give his brother and sister two versions, half the size of the large one. His parents would get the canvas the painter was using when they met. He also needed a smaller version to take with him to show his family what they would receive in due course. Emanuele Cividali was surprised; enthusiastic admirers had requested to see more of his work or had commissioned a painting. It was the first time somebody had asked him to copy his own work. The interpreter had problems translating some of the most colourful expressions in Judeo-Venetian that were coming out of the mouth of Emanuele Cividali. In the end, the painter quoted a high price. Israel only commented that he needed the small version by the end of the following week when they would leave Venice to go home. He would return the following Monday with twenty percent of the price and organise payment for the rest of the money. Before he and his wife left Metz, he had organised a letter of credit through his father's bank, putting a sizeable sum at his disposal in Venice.

That bizarre French client surprised and amused Emanuele Cividali. He had already figured out he and his wife were Jewish and was almost tempted to give them the small version of the painting for free. His wife reminded him that canvas and paint were expensive. Israel was back at the workshop on time with the agreed twenty percent in cash and a letter of credit that stipulated payment of the rest, subject to an inspection from an employee of a Venetian bank before the paintings were packed and shipped to Metz.

Israel and his wife spent the following two days touring Palladian villas. On Thursday, they were surprised to see the smaller version of the painting waiting for them in their room when they returned to change for lunch. There was also a note. "I have done one. Give me time to complete the other four". In the afternoon, the hotel had organised a visit to glass blowers in Murano. They were both impressed by the process and by the way vases, bowls, plates, and platters appeared almost by magic. At the end of the visit, they lingered in the shop. Israel's wife saw a set of dinner plates. Israel could see them having a Friday night meal with guests using those plates. He would have loved to have them yellow and light blue, the yellow for his wife's hair, and the light blue for her eyes. He decided there and then to order them. Unfortunately, they would leave the following Sunday, and he had to keep some cash for the trip back. The following morning, while his wife was waiting for the delivery of printed silk material, Israel would return to Murano. He had to think of how he could pay for the dinner plates.

Overnight, Israel had an idea. What if he could use the small painting as a part payment? If the glass workshop accepted, he would have the time to issue a letter of credit for the balance once he was back in Metz. He briefly discussed it with his wife, who thought they did not need the small painting. When he returned to Murano, he spoke to the head of the workshop, the master glassblower, and ordered 12 place settings of five plates each. Israel insisted they be the colour of his wife's blue eyes. He said he wanted the St. Mark's lion in the middle as a reminder of the three fantastic weeks in Venice. The master glass blower accepted the payment and took the painting Israel Alcan had brought with him.

On Saturday, they had lunch at the home of a family they met in synagogue the previous week. On Sunday, they packed, and on Monday, the first foggy day of autumn, they left Venice.

The master glass blower took the painting to be framed. He noticed the second signature on the back. One day, he would go to the Cividali studio and ask why he had signed it twice, once on the front and once on the back.

# Chapter Three

**Stra, February 1950**

Count Contarini and his wife walked past the art gallery in Sanremo three more times before Count Contarini decided to buy the painting. He told the art dealer to pack it securely, but he would take care of the shipment. His company had a strong relationship with a freight forwarder that had lorries making regular journeys between Padua and Nice, driving through Sanremo. He would arrange for a collection.

The day had arrived when the freight forwarder would deliver the painting to his home. His eldest son and the lorry driver had carried the boxed painting from the lorry to his study. One of the Count's employees was there with all the tools necessary to free the painting from his packaging and hang it in the study, above the fireplace opposite the Count's desk. He had won the battle with his wife, who wanted it in the living room. The Count could not hide his excitement. Three hours later, he was still sitting at his desk, contemplating the painting with a satisfied grin.

His wife walked in, holding a book they bought during a trip to Paris to celebrate her birthday. The book was a 1936 publication called "Venetian Paintings in French Museums." She passed the volume to the Count.

"Look at page 158!"

The Count took the book and opened it. It showed the same painting as part of a museum collection in Metz in 1934. He opened a drawer and took out the folder the art dealer in Sanremo had sent with the painting. His grin had gone.

"The art dealer swore by the paper trail associated with his painting."

His wife could see the disappointment on his face, but she did not like the idea of having a stolen or counterfeit painting in her home.

"I do not doubt the dealer's good faith, but what about the person who sold it to him?"

The Count was annoyed, but he had an idea.

"Let me keep it for a month, then I will instruct Rachele's firm to investigate for me. If the painting was stolen from the Museum of Metz, we shall return it. If it is not authentic, I'll ask for a huge chunk of money back from the art dealer in Sanremo. Meanwhile, we keep it to ourselves, hidden here."


**Metz, December 1863**


*Israel Alcan was trying to walk home as fast as he could without running. Running would not have been dignified. It was not an emergency after all. A messenger had delivered the news that a big crate had arrived from Venice and would be delivered in the early afternoon. His four paintings and the dinner set in Murano glass had arrived. He was excited. The paintings were presents for his parents and his siblings. The dinner set would need a big Friday night dinner to come out for the first time. He should wait until they had something to celebrate and invite the whole family.*

*When he turned the last corner, he had the entrance to his home in full view. He could see two male staff members help the delivery people unload one of two crates, the one with the paintings, judging by its size. He shouted at them to bring it in from the main hall rather than the back door. His study was just off the entrance hall, and he wanted his big painting in his study. He would use his coach to take the other versions to his father and siblings.*

*Israel was now sitting in his study, contemplating the painting. He had it hung on the wall opposite his desk. He could not stop looking at it. His wife wanted it in the living room but then relented, and it had not been hard work convincing her. The other smaller versions were leaning against furniture under his big one. He could see they were equally impressive. Israel could notice some differences in minute details. The dresses of the two masked women in the background were not the same colour, the trousers of the young baker boy were different, or the boat was not in the same position in all the versions, but that was what made them "versions" rather than copies. Emanuele Cividali had numbered them. His version was 15. He assumed the one he left in Venice as part payment for the dining set would have been 55. When his wife came to tell him he had to change for dinner, he realised he had spent most of the time looking at Cividali's work. All the other thoughts had been popping into his head while he was daydreaming of being back in Venice, on the Riva degli Schiavoni, and watching an artist painting the Punta della Dogana.*

Joshua had moved back to Venice less than two years earlier. He had not found his own place yet; he had very specific views about what he wanted, and his honorary aunt, Deborah Camerini Countess Pesaro de Bonfili, was in no hurry to kick him out. One of the first things he did as a 'returned Venetian' was to join a rowing club. Many in his 'Venetian family,' the Mendes and the Pesaro de Bonfili, were members of a rowing club near Madonna dell'Orto. He became a member as well but needed rowing mates. A week after he joined, he bumped into an old schoolmate, Dante Bembo. Their friendship picked up where they left it fifteen years earlier when Joshua's family moved to the United States. The two friends had been rowing together early in the morning three days a week.

Joshua had grown to love those mornings. He was looking forward to the summer with its earlier sunrise. That would allow them to row earlier in the morning when the commercial traffic had not started yet and they could have the lagoon almost to themselves. Dante thought Joshua was still 'In training' and did not have the stamina for real outings in the lagoon. Their usual morning trip was still rowing around the island of San Michele, the cemetery, and then returning to the rowing club. They both hoped they could go further by the summer, maybe reach one of the smaller islands.

That morning, they had just finished. Dante tied the bought to the pier and helped Joshua get off the boat, teasing him.

"The United States has killed your sea leg. You will not be a real Venetian until you can hop on and off a boat without help."

"It is not me. It is the lagoon. The boat moves, especially when another boat floats past us and creates waves."

They continued their banter, one of the things they picked up from when Joshua left Venice for the United States. They were walking along the pier to the club premises, where they hoped to shower before starting their day, when Dante noticed somebody walking towards them.

"Tommaso, great to see you. Do you remember Giosuè Schwartz? The one who moved to the United States when we were twelve?"

Dante smiled and added

"Now he calls himself Joshua."

He then turned to Joshua

"Joshua, do you remember Tommaso Tron? When we were twelve, he was the tallest in our class. He was sitting two rows behind us."

Joshua was silent for a short while, obviously thinking back to their classmates sixteen years earlier. He had been in the same class as Dante Bembo since they were six. Tommaso Tron had joined them when they were ten, two years before Joshua's family took him to Boston.

"Yes, I remember you. You used to draw very well. You were the only one of us wearing a green coat with a hood."

Tommaso Tron smiled, flattered to be remembered. They shook hands and started reminiscing about school. Tommaso excused himself, saying he had booked a boat for only half an hour. He continued walking along the pier until he stopped by the same boat Joshua and Dante had used. Dante could not help but continue teasing Joshua.

"You have an athletic body but cannot row very far. Tommaso looks like a pole but is an excellent rower. I bet he will go further in half an hour than what we could do in an hour."

"Give me time to find my sea legs again. Now I spend half of my energy just staying upright!"

Gabriele Mendes had gone to the station to meet Count Contarini, a close family friend. Gabriele and his family hid in plain sight in the Contarini estate between October 1943 and April 1945, the longest eighteen months of their lives. That day, the Count and his wife had come to Venice to seek legal advice from Gabriele's wife, Rachele, one of the three partners of the Cantoni, Mendes, Modiano law firm. His wife would visit friends, and then they would have lunch at Gabriele and Rachele's home in Campo San Giacomo Dall'Orio.

Rachele came out of her office the moment she heard her husband talk to the receptionist. They moved to the meeting room overlooking the Grand Canal and sat on the armchairs. After all, the Count was a close friend first and a law firm's client second. Coffee and pastry appeared. The Count made the usual remarks about the law firm's connection with coffee traders, Rachele's eldest brother, and with a patisserie, Rachele and Gabriele's daughter, Anna. Once the social side of the visit had been taken care of, Gabriele excused himself, saying he had to go back to his end-of-the-month billing, leaving his wife and his friend free to discuss business. The Count took an old book from his briefcase, put it on the coffee table, opened it, and took out the photo he used as a bookmark.

"Let's start from the beginning. When Laura and I were in Sanremo in January, I saw this painting at an art gallery. I knew the painter Emanuele Cividali, a Venetian active in the last century's second half. I fell in love with his use of light and shade to draw attention to the young man and with the details of the scene, so I bought it."

Rachele had taken out a notepad and a folder from a cupboard behind Count Contarini.

"I love the work of Emanuele Cividali. "

Count Contarini waited for Rachele to sit down

"As you know, I took Laura to Paris for her birthday a few months ago. In one of the stalls by the Seine, I found old catalogues of French Museums. I like the photos of some Flemish paintings in their collection, so I bought a few. This one is a book of 'Venetian Paintings in French Museum' printed in 1934. The day the freight forwarder delivered the painting, my wife was looking at it and found a photograph of 'our' painting with a caption saying that it was in the Museum of Metz."

Count Contarini opened the book on the page and showed a photo of the painting.

"The antiquarian either sold me a fake, or I just bought a painting looted from a museum in France during World War II. Do I have grounds to sue the art gallery?"

Rachele looked at the painting in the photograph.

"If the painting is half as good as the photo, I can see why you bought it. There is almost a hypnotic attraction to it. Do you want them to take the painting back?"

Count Contarini sighed

"I'd rather not, but if it is a fake, I'd like some of the money back; if it were looted from a museum, I'd like to have watertight evidence that I bought it in good faith and then give it back to the museum. So, I am asking my lawyer to establish whether it is a fake or if it was looted and then take action. I also would like you to come up with a statement that I could use as evidence of my 'watertight good faith' when I bought it."

Rachele closed the notepad, put it in a folder, and wrote 'Count Contarini's painting' on the cover

"Metz is in a bilingual part of France. If someone speaks German, we could make direct inquiries. As you know, my nephew Alex and I speak fluent German. First, we need to establish whether it could be a copy. Aunt Deborah may help with that. As you know, Deborah Camerini, Countess Pesaro de Bonfili, is an art dealer. You met her at Emma and Roberto's wedding."

～

Rachele and the Countess were having their monthly meeting at their usual coffee place past Rio della Senza. They discussed family matters first. The Countess was looking forward to Joshua's family visiting from the United States. She had not seen them since 1934 and had never met Joshua's youngest brother. After what she thought was an acceptable time, Rachele moved to business.

"Count Contarini came to see me. He bought a painting in Sanremo by Emanuele Cividali, except he now wonders whether it is a fake or art looted from a museum in France. I have a photo of the painting with me. "

She took out the photo and showed it to the Countess, expecting her reaction to the image of a muscular young man not wearing a shirt. To her surprise, Deborah Camerini was all business.

"Cividali is almost a contemporary Venetian painter. He died in the late nineteen twenties, although he stopped painting around the time when World War I ended. We have the world authority on his work here in Venice. Ludovico Tron has an art gallery in Campo San Polo and a shop in Piazza San Marco. He is a rather arrogant man who always looks down on me when we meet at an auction."

Rachele wondered who was this person who could look down on her honorary aunt and still be alive. She kept a straight face and simply said.

"Thank you. First, I want to check that the museum in Metz still has the painting Count Contarini, which was found in an old catalogue he bought in Paris. Then I'll contact Lorenzo Tron."

"Just tell whoever talks to him not to be intimidated by his arrogant ways."

# Chapter Four

## Late March 1950

Joshua Schwartz and Dante Bembo pushed the boat away from the pier of the rowing club. Joshua was still learning to row standing up. Dante had spent all his life in Venice. He was the expert. The sun had not risen yet, and the pre-dawn light revealed an unusually cloudless morning, like the ones common in January but rare in late March. The water in the lagoon was very smooth. At that time of the day, no speeding commercial boat or taxi would upset their balance and challenge Joshua's relatively inexperienced sea legs. That morning, they had not yet reached the point when Joshua stopped talking. Dante took the chance to ask a question.

"Is your aunt still an art dealer?"

"Yes, why?"

"We have a painting my father wants valued; he is not sure if he wants to sell it. He is weary of going to an antiquarian or an auction house. My grandmother used to call it her *'fornaretto,'* her young baker. The family story is that my great-grandfather, Antonio Bembo, accepted it as a down payment for a bespoke dinner set made according to the specifications of a French tourist not long after the railway arrived in Venice.

Do you think your aunt can tell my father whether the painting is worth anything or my great-grandfather made a poor deal?"

Dante could hear his friend panting like a locomotive. By then, they were in sight of the pier of the rowing club. Dante could not tell whether the 'Yes' that came out of Joshua's mouth was relief that the pier was in sight or the agreement to ask Aunt Deborah whether she minded looking at the painting.

Deborah Camerini and her adopted daughter Elena were at the Gritti Palace Hotel, one of the most luxurious hotels in Venice. They were attending a private viewing of paintings that would be auctioned the following week.

Waiters followed the guests to pick up empty glasses from wherever somebody had left them while other waiters walked around the room with trays full of champagne. Elena loved looking at art but felt intimidated by the surrounding luxury and stayed unusually close to her mother. Her daughter's reaction surprised the Countess.

"What you see in this room is not much different from what you have at home. Why do you feel intimidated by it?

"At home, everything is part of the environment. The hotel and this room are not familiar."

The Countess was not convinced.

"Look at those chairs. They are copies. We have the real thing at home. All the big paintings hanging on the wall are nowhere near worth as much money as the miniature paintings in your room. You are the same person; the room you find yourself in, or the people you are with, should not influence how you feel about yourself."

They were moving around the exhibition when the Countess stopped by a painting with an unusual scene. A muscular, shirtless young man carrying a tray with loaves of bread was at the centre of the painting. He was talking to a couple. The man was slim and elegantly dressed, a stark contrast with the shirtless and muscular young baker boy. On the right side of the painting, two women wearing elegant clothes and a mask were looking at the young baker boy. On the left of the painting, children were sitting on the steps of a bridge over a narrow canal. You could see a gondola coming out of the bridge, sailing towards the Grand Canal. In the background, one could detect the Punta della Dogana.

Elena loved listening to her adoptive mother talk about art. The Countess was in full flow:

"The painter, Emanuele Cividali, was active in the second half of the last century and the early years of this one. He loved Caravaggio. You can see it from the way he uses the light in this picture. The young man is supposed to be the centre of our attention; therefore, he is not just at the centre of the painting but brighter than the other. He plays with sunlight and shades to make sure you focus on the young man at the centre of the painting. The adults are in the shade. They are just part of the scene, almost in the background. Only the children sitting on the steps of the bridge playing are in the sun."

Elena's adoptive mother's appreciation of handsome young men was very well-known in the family. Elena was not surprised the Countess was paying a lot of attention to a painting of a muscular, shirtless young man.

Deborah Camerini was now looking at a Venetian landscape of an English artist. She told her daughter there was a lot of accuracy in the scene but next to no soul. Some modern postcards were better at conveying an atmosphere. After looking at a couple of other paintings, the Countess summoned a young employee of the auction house, asking to bring her a catalogue. She wanted to show four paintings to her client before bidding for any of them on his behalf. Elena left to go home to study and do her homework.

On her way home, Countess Pesaro de Bonfili thought about the changes in Elena in the previous twelve months. The teenager she met two years earlier who had lost her memory and was trying to find her place in the world was now a confident young woman who felt loved and, most importantly, who knew she belonged.

The Countess asked Rachele to meet at their usual coffee place past Rio della Senza; she had something to share about Contarini's painting with her.

"Two days ago, I saw the same painting at an auction. It had two signatures, one in the traditional bottom right corner and one in the back. The back signature had 35 between the first and last name. So, I called on Ludovico Tron's art gallery and was surprised to see the same painting in his shop. He showed me the signature in the back with a 45 between the first and last name. He told me the story behind those numbers. Count Contarini may have a genuine Cividali after all."

The Countess shared what the antiquarian had told her. There was a letter from Cividali to his accountant explaining the exorbitant price he charged for "the Young Baker." His client, a wealthy Frenchman called Israel Alcan, also Jewish, had ordered five copies in four different sizes. Ludovico Tron found that letter when he was an art history student in the 1930s. He did more research. Cividali was worried that somebody might copy one of them and sell it for real. Each copy has a number in the back; 35 means 3 of 5. 15 was the largest, the one Israel Alcan kept for himself; 25 is the one he gave his parents, and 35 and 45 went to Israel Alcan's siblings. When he died, the Metz Museum inherited the largest painting. When Ludovico Tron compiled the first *catalogue raisonné*[1] of Cividali's works, he mentioned all five "versions" of the painting. He also put a note stating that there was no information regarding the whereabouts of the other four paintings at the time of compiling the catalogue. If Count Contarini's painting had a number on the back, it was real. If the number was 15, it was stolen from the museum in Metz.

On the way back to the office, Rachele thought that, in a week, they would contact the museum in Metz again if they had not replied to her original query. She also thought it would help to find out the size of the painting in Metz; one of the five "authentic" copies would be smaller. The Countess also recommended checking whether the framed painting had a backboard; a backboard would have to be removed to check the back of the canvas. She decided to send Alex or Franco to talk to Ludovico Tron as soon as they could.

The countess had organised a 'school night dinner,' meaning a three-course meal. She expected everybody would leave by half past ten so Elena could go to bed early enough to wake up with no fuss the following morning. She had invited Roberto Mendes, Gabriele's baby brother and another partner in the law firm, and his wife, Leo and Mario Mendes, were also there. The dinner was an excuse to introduce Joshua Schwartz to an eligible young woman. Even Leo and Mario Mendes, who were the same age as Elena, were aware of the game and vowed to stay away from their honorary aunt when

---

1. A catalogue raisonné is a descriptive catalogue of works of art with description and comments. A deceased painter's catalogue raisonné is usually considered the catalogue of all authentic work produced by the artist.

they reached the age she thought made them suitable for a match. The conversation was flowing. The young lady was not brilliant. Elena thought being the only one not part of the extended Mendes/Pesaro De Bonfili clan might explain her problems in being part of the conversation. She whispered in Leo's ears she remembered that the poor young woman could talk.

When Joshua mentioned Dante Bembo's request to inspect his family's small painting, Elena could see what was going on in her mother's mind by looking at her face.

"You just said your friend Dante's grandmother calls the painting her *fornaretto*, her young baker boy. I wonder if it is the same young baker boy I inspected at the auction house. If it is, I need to talk to Ludovico Tron; it would be an exciting coincidence if four of the five known authentic versions of that painting showed up in Venice after years of being considered lost. I must see that painting; if it is real, I must tell Ludovico Tron. He might have to update his Cividali *catalogue raisonné*."

"Tron? Dante and I were in the same class with a Tommaso Tron in our primary school here in Venice. "

"Maybe it is one of Ludovico's children. He has two sons who could be in your age range and a daughter, Diana's age; I think Isabella Tron and Diana Mendes are both studying at Ca' Foscari. Anyway, do you have Dante's phone number? I'll call him tomorrow morning and arrange a visit to see their *fornaretto*."

When Roberto and his wife were walking their nephews Leo and Mario to Campo San Giacomo Dall'Orio, they remarked Joshua had not exchanged a word with the young woman invited to be introduced to him. Elena, Leo, and Mario talked to her.

# Chapter Five

## Early April 1950

Rachele always made a point to celebrate Anita Torgnon's birthday. She may have started as a housekeeper, but, over twenty-eight years, she had become Rachele's closest friend and confidante, the Mendes children's honorary aunt, and a much-loved family member. Over the years, she had turned the Mendes household into a well-oiled machine. During the final years of World War II, Anita protected the family home and the people who were hiding in plain sight after Gabriele, Rachele, and their children had left Venice. The whole Mendes clan loved her and considered her an integral part of the family.

Anna had baked something special before leaving for work at the usual unearthly hour. Rachele was taking care of breakfast, and Diana was making sure that her siblings and cousins were eating breakfast and later would be ready to go to school on time, dressed appropriately. Anita woke up at her usual time and had to be told to sit down. It was her special day. When the phone rang, Anita found something to do. Joshua Schwartz called to say that Alex Modiano would be late for work. He had joined Joshua and Dante in their rowing outing. Unfortunately, Alex was even less experienced than Joshua, and when Dante turned the boat, Alex ended up in the lagoon. They were now trying to dry his clothes with two hairdryers before he could go home and change for work. Anita related the message, trying to keep a straight face, then passed the phone to Rachele.

"Joshua, how dry is Alex? Can he come to the phone?"

"He is dry. We have dried his shirt. He and Dante are trying to dry his trousers. I'm afraid his jumper is a lost cause. Another member will lend him something to wear instead. Here he is."

Alex was not proud of his unintended dive in the lagoon. Rachele tried very hard to sound matter-of-fact.

"How are you? Make sure your clothes are dry enough; otherwise, you might catch pneumonia. Should I ask Roberto to bring you dry clothes?"

Alex replied with the usual tone a young man would reserve for parents or parental-like figures.

"Aunt Rachele, my mother is in Trieste. I did, but he had already left, and I did not want to check if anybody else could come. We have already managed to dry my shirt, and the trousers are getting there. I will wear the club jumper a friend of Joshua and Dante lent me."

Rachele, the aunt, was replaced by Rachele, the boss.

"Once you have gone home to change, you must go to the civil court to collect some documents. The envelope is in my name or Alvise's. On your way back to the office, drop by Tron's Art Gallery in Campo San Polo to borrow or buy a copy of Cividali's *catalogue raisonné*. Aunt Deborah told him yesterday, so he expects you sometime today."

Rachele could hear Joshua and Dante talking about the state of Alex's trousers. The aunt replaced the boss.

"Anyway, can you please ask Joshua to come on the phone?"

Rachele could hear her nephew tell Joshua she wanted to talk to him. He passed the phone to Joshua. When Rachele heard his voice, she continued,

"Joshua, please make sure that his clothes are dry enough before you let him go home."

Alex Modiano was running very late. Drying his clothes took longer than expected, and explaining what happened to Fiamma, Gabriele's mother, took longer than expected. In court, he signed off for the documents he had to collect, and the clerk added the date and time he signed on the register and initialised them, a detail that later turned out to be very important. Alex then made his way to Campo San Polo, hoping at least to look at Cividali's catalogue raisonné and take note of the dimension of the painting in the Metz Museum. When he got to the art gallery, the door was open. Before he walked into the shop, he noticed several things scattered on the floor and the pieces of a glass object that had shattered, falling from wherever it had been placed. He thought somebody had a fight not long before he arrived because they had no time to tidy things up. He did not go in; instead, he walked into a nearby café.

"Has anybody noticed if somebody has gone in or come out of the Tron's Gallery?"

People in the café shook their heads to say they did not. The cashier was the only one who replied.

"I can't tell you whether the door was open or closed when I arrived this morning, but I did not notice anybody going in or out. However, I do not spend all my time looking outside. I can be very busy when many clients are waiting to pay."

"Thank you. May I have two phone tokens, please?"

Alex called the office.

"Franco, I am outside the Tron's gallery in Campo San Polo. Can you join me? It is important. Something happened and I do not want to go inside without company. I may need a witness to corroborate what I find."

"You started talking like a lawyer. I think I'll be there in twenty minutes."

Then, he called the police and spoke to Vice-Commissario Umberto De Antoni, a friend of his aunt and uncle, who asked him to stay outside the shop and stop anybody from walking in. He could say that vice-Commissario Umberto De Antoni told him that going inside would mean interfering with a police investigation.

Twenty minutes later, Franco Cantoni arrived. Alex had barely started telling him what had happened when Umberto de Antoni arrived with two police officers. They entered the shop, asking Alex and Franco to stay outside with a police officer and stop other people from coming in. Franco took the court documents and returned to the office. Alex had to stay there because he assumed the Vice-Commissario wanted to talk to him. Inside the shop, Umberto De Antoni and the other policeman found blood on the floor. They followed the trail into the office and found the body of an elegantly dressed middle-aged man. He had blood all over his back. He was lying face down between the door and the desk with the phone in his hand. It looked as if he had died before he could make a call. The other arm was too far from the desk for him to have reached the disk and dial. Umberto De Antoni came out and told the policeman at the door to go to the nearby café and call the doctor and the homicide team, then put gloves on and looked into the pocket of the corpse, hoping to find a wallet and identification. He found them; the name of the deceased was Ludovico Tron.

He walked out of the art gallery to talk to Alex, who relayed his conversation with the cashier at the café. Umberto was standing outside the shop, and Alex was facing the shop while he was talking to him. Something caught his eye. A painting on an easel did not have the left side of the frame. He pointed it out to Umberto and wondered if the missing part was the murder weapon. They both entered the art gallery, careful not to walk on anything that could provide clues. The photographer had not arrived yet. Alex looked at the painting and realised that it could be one version of the young baker, at least judging from the description he had heard from his aunt. Umberto noticed that a thick volume on a table had a bookmark with Alex Modiano's name written on it. He was going to ask Alex why Ludovico Tron was expecting him when the doctor and the photographer arrived. Umberto told Alex he knew where to find him and could return to the office. He instinctively looked at his watch and wrote on his notepad the time when Alex left the art gallery.

The Countess had no client interested in Cividali's young baker boy, but she was thinking of buying it for herself. The auction of Venetian paintings was two weeks away. That morning, she was at a different auction. She had a client interested in buying Venetian landscapes from the seventeenth century, and there were two in the auction. She had done quite a lot of business with that client, a Swiss collector, and had an idea of what he would go for. One of the two paintings she liked came up. She started bidding. Soon she realised she was in a bidding war against somebody who looked familiar, not just because he reminded her of Cary Grant. She did not know that the husband of the lovely young American that sat next to Elena in synagogue was an art dealer. He seemed determined to get the same painting she wanted. If she did not get it, she would at least help the current owner get more money. Unfortunately, she went too close to the top limit of what she was prepared to pay. She stopped bidding. She did not like to be beaten, but another Venetian landscape would be auctioned later, and she was determined to get that one. In the end, she sought the young American who snatched the best painting away from her.

"When your wife introduced us, Mr Campbell, I did not know you were an art dealer."

Bill Campbell picked up the catalogue and the hat from the chair where he was sitting, turned around and was not surprised to see the Countess.

"I probably had one over you because I work for a New York-based art dealer who told me to watch out for you at auctions. I did not know you were Jewish or that we would meet in synagogue, Countess Pesaro De Bonfili."

They started moving towards the auctioneer. They both had to leave a check for purchases. The Countess was determined to get to know the man who took the Turner landscape away from her. She was going to invite him and his wife for lunch or dinner.

"I have seen you in synagogue. Campbell is an unusual name for a Jew."

"That is because my paternal grandfather was not Jewish. My grandmother's last name was Edelstein, and my mother's is Albahari, born in Sarajevo. I did what a good Jewish boy should do, and I married the daughter of my mother's best friend from school, except I met her in 1944 when we were both in the Navy, and I did not know who she was. After all, the last time I had seen Charlotte Alcan, she was six, and I was eight."

"Alcan? Is your wife related to the Alcan who commissioned five copies of the same painting to Emanuele Cividali in 1863?"

"She is his granddaughter, the youngest child of his youngest son. She has a print of the *'fornaretto'* that her grandfather bequeathed to the Metz Museum in his will when he passed away in 1910. She knows stories about her grandparents, but the real expert is her namesake, her aunt Charlotte, who lives in the Riviera near Nice. I would love to research Israel Alcan. Somebody who commissions five copies of the same painting because he wants to share it with his family must have been a really special person."

"Start from Ludovico Tron. He is an art dealer with a gallery in Campo San Polo. He has put together Cividali's *catalogue raisonné.* I understand there are two pages that tell the story of the five authentic copies of the same painting. It is the only case I have heard where a client commissioned copies to the artist who painted the original."

By then, they had reached the top of the queue of buyers who had to make a down payment for what they had bought. They exchanged business cards, and the Countess invited him and his wife to lunch or dinner at a date to be agreed later.

Tommaso Tron always lived in the shadow of his brother. According to his father, he was not at his level in art knowledge, sport, ability to deal with people, and more. Tommaso was taller than his brother, the only thing where he could beat him. He hated the family business. He wanted to write a book about people with his last name who lived when "la Serenissima," the most serene republic of Venice, was at its most powerful. Twice a week, he was taking advantage of his mother being in the small shop in Piazza San Marco to go to the nearby library for some research. He only felt useful when his father was organising a themed art show because he would write the catalogue. He loved writing, he loved researching, and he loved books. He dreamed of working for a publisher of art books, but he felt he was stuck with the family business, at least while his father was alive.

He had spent the morning in the small shop in Piazza San Marco. His brother was in Florence negotiating the purchase of antique glass objects from the estate of some aristocrat who had passed away the previous year. He was about to close for the long lunch break when his mother appeared looking worried. The owner of the café in Campo San Polo, which was opposite their art gallery, had called her to say that the police were in the shop. Tommaso should go and see what happened. She tried to ring the shop, but there was no answer.

Tommaso Tron agreed to check, wondering how he could manage a civilised conversation with his father.

Rachele was busy with a forensic analysis of several contracts for one of the law firm's largest commercial clients. Helping Count Contarini in his quest to find whether the painting he bought was a fake, looted art or authentic provided a much-needed respite from looking at how the four successive contracts she had on the table changed the relationship between the two parties involved. She looked at the letter of Alain de Lothringen, the curator of the Metz Museum. She wrote to the museum in German. His reply was in very basic but correct, Italian. They had the painting; they hid it when World War II started so the Germans did not destroy it when they took possession of the city. He had researched the story of Cividali's young bakers and was interested to know more about the 'versions' that had surfaced in Venice. His dream was to organise a temporary exhibition of all five versions. Maybe Count Contarini would lend the painting to the museum for a few months if it proved genuine. Rachele filed the letter in Count Contarini's folder, adding a note saying it was not looted art and they should check authenticity. Count Contarini would need to take off the backboard of the frame to establish whether it is an original or a copy.

Alex chose that moment to knock at the doorpost. The door of her office was open.

"I almost found the body of Ludovico Tron. 'Almost,' because when I arrived in Campo San Polo, I found the door open, and it was obvious from the outside that a fight had happened inside, so I did not go in. I called Franco to have a witness and then Umberto De Antoni. Things were going pretty well until he found a copy of Cividali's catalogue raisonné with a bookmark with my name written on it. I was not thrilled when he told me I could go and he knew where to find me. "

"But it is true. He knows where to find you. Can you account for your movement?"

"I have not been working around you, Roberto, and Alvise for nothing. Dante Bembo walked me home so he could testify about the time we got there. When I collected the papers at the Civil Court, they dated and time-stamped my signature. The cashier of the café near the art gallery could probably vouch that I did the two phone calls one after the other, so I think I am fine. If I really must be pedantic, though, we still do not know the time of death. If he died before 6.30 am, when Dante, Joshua, and I checked the boat out at the rowing club, I may have a problem."

"Don't worry, we know good lawyers."

"There was one bizarre thing. One of the Cividali's young bakers was on an easel. Somebody had pulled out the left side of the frame. I suggested to Umberto De Antoni that the missing part might have become the murder weapon."

∾

Two days later, Diana Mendes was coming out of a lecture on International Trade Law. She found her friend Isabella Tron sitting on a bench outside the lecture hall, looking very sombre. Aunt Anita told Diana about Ludovico Tron's death. She did not expect to see her friend. After all, they had found her father dead in his art gallery two days earlier. Diana started walking towards Isabella, who noticed her and stood up.

"Diana, I need to talk to your mother. There has been an alarming development."

"Let us not talk here. Why don't we go to Zattere? Nico's will be empty at this time in the morning."

They walked to the Ca Rezzonico vaporetto stop talking about university, the subject they were studying, and other things. Isabella Tron was the first person to speak to Diana when she returned to school after the war. Diana had been determined to join the year of high school she would have been in if it had not been for Mussolini's racial laws and World War II. She had studied for over a year to pass the admission test. The first day she walked into a class full of teenagers who had been together for three years, she felt everyone was thinking, 'Here comes the Jew.' Isabella was the first to approach her, break the ice, and show her to the empty desk beside her. That was the beginning of a very close friendship.

As Diana predicted, Nico was empty. The day was showing all the promises of spring. It was sunny and warm, for the end of March; they had kept their coats on and sat outside by the Giudecca Canal. They could talk freely without being overheard.

Once the waiter had gone, the floodgates that stopped Isabella's grief opened up.

"The police told my brother Tommaso not to leave Venice. Our father had left early. He usually did when he was organising a show. They put his time of death at 8.30. They found Tommaso's name in his diary. Tommaso told the police their father had rearranged their meeting to the late afternoon because a client asked to look at a painting around 8."

Diana was not sure what to say, but she had spent enough time around her mother.

"Did any of you hear that conversation?"

Isabella had stopped sobbing.

"No, they discussed it in the study after dinner, and my mother and I were not there. Tommaso usually takes long walks around Venice before opening the shop in Piazza San Marco. He could not think of any witness to corroborate how he spent his time between 8 and 9.30 when he opened the shop. My mother and I think he needs a lawyer, and I thought of your mother."

Diana excused herself, went inside Nico's, bought a phone token, and called the law firm to see if anybody could talk to Tommaso Tron later that day or the following day. She then went back to her friend.

"You need to tell your brother he has an appointment with his lawyer. "

"Do you mind coming with me to the shop in Piazza San Marco to tell him?"

Diana did not mind. They stood up and walked to the nearby Zattere stop to take the vaporetto to San Marco.

# Chapter Six

## April 1950

It was Joshua's family's last full day in Venice before flying back to Boston. The Countess had organised breakfast in the formal dining room with large windows overlooking the Grand Canal. Elena found her adoptive mother at her most theatrical when playing the hostess who wanted to impress. Deborah Camerini was determined to leave a memory for Joshua's parents and siblings. After all, as she had been saying very often in the previous ten days, she had known Guido Schwartz since he was born. Elena and her sister were looking at each other, rolling their eyes whenever their mother was playing the grand hostess.

Tonia walked into the room when the Countess was sharing her memories of Guido as a boy, embarrassing him in front of his children. Deborah Camerini stopped when she saw her housekeeper, who told her that Bill Campbell was on the phone. He apologised, but he needed to speak to the Countess urgently. Deborah excused herself and moved to her study to take the call. The urgency intrigued her.

The Countess sat down at her desk and picked up the phone

"Good morning Bill, what happened?"

"I had an early appointment with the auction house, the one selling the version of the Cividali's young baker. As you know, the auction is supposed to be held in three days, and I wanted to inspect two paintings included in the catalogue."

"Why did you say 'supposed to be held'? The auction is in three days."

Bill tried his best to sound matter-of-fact.

"I would not be so sure. When one of the senior executives of the auction house and I walked into the warehouse, we saw very valuable paintings pulled out of their storage slot and left all over the place. It was chaos."

The Countess understood the urgency. Now, her tone of voice matched Bill Campbell's.

"Was there a lot of damage?"

"Not really. Everything was out of place. The paintings were left on the floor as if they were looking for something specific and could not find it. When we turned the corner, we saw they had pulled out the Cividali. The strangest thing was that they had removed the left side of the frame but left everything there, including the bit of the frame they had removed."

"Where was it?"

"It was just lying on the floor next to the painting. The police are here; when they are done, the staff from the auction house will do an inventory and check if anything is missing. I volunteered to call people they knew were supposed to come to the auction. You were at the top of the list. You are the first call."

The Countess smiled at the idea of being on top of the list. She was also wondering whether Gabriele and Rachele had already left home.

"Thank you for letting me know. Tell the auction house management I am available if they think I can help with anything."

"I'll let them know. I'll see you in synagogue. It is unlikely the auction will take place this week."

After closing her conversation with Bill, she dialled the law firm's office number.

She told Rachele to tell Count Contarini what Bill Campbell told her. For once, Rachele's answer left her speechless.

"Alex told me that the police thought that Ludovico Tron died because his killer hit him in the neck with a piece of a broken frame, and one nail hit a vital part. They found the version of the Cividali he had displayed in his gallery with the left side of the frame missing."

Gabriele and Rachele were having coffee in the law firm's kitchen when they heard Alex talk to the receptionist. Rachele asked him to join her in the kitchen for coffee, and she shared her conversation with the Countess. She could see the cogs turning into Alex's mind as she talked. Alex sipped his coffee, washed his cup and saucer, then turned to his aunt.

"I think you should call Vice-Commissario Umberto De Antoni. These two cases must be connected. It cannot be a coincidence."

Rachele was washing her cup and saucer

"They are connected. I'll wait till after nine…."

They were interrupted by the receptionist, who told them that Vice-Commissario De Antoni had just called, asking to be called back as soon as it was convenient. Alex left with the receptionist, and Rachele returned to her office to call Umberto De Antoni.

"I was just talking to Alex about calling you. I was going to wait till half-past nine."

"Thank you, but I wish I had that luxury. One of the policemen who was with me when we discovered the body of Ludovico Tron was also part of the team that was called to the auction house this morning. He connected the dots. I called the Countess, asking her for help figuring out why two identical paintings from the same artist could be original. She told me the story of Israel Alcan, and you know the whereabouts of two of the four other versions."

Rachele had taken out a notepad from one drawer while listening to the Vice-Commissario.

"Indeed, I do; Count Contarini bought one in Sanremo, although we have not removed the backboard yet, so we do not know if it is one of the versions or a copy. The Countess is also aware of another one at the Bembo glass workshop in Murano. Israel Alcan gave it to the current Master Bembo's great-grandfather as a down payment."

"That is intriguing…"

"Sorry to interrupt, but it is even more intriguing because, according to the late Ludovico Tron, the expert on Cividali, the four smaller versions were lost. And yet, they are all in the area now. Three in Venice and one in Stra."

Umberto did not have time that morning.

"I called to arrange a convenient time to talk to you and the Countess. She is available in the afternoon. When are you available? I also need to talk to Alex."

"How urgent is it? In an ideal world, it would be better to discuss it after we have established whether Count Contarini's version is an original or a copy."

"I'd rather do it sooner rather than later. I think understanding the versions and figuring out why they removed the left side of the frame is the key to solving both cases."

"In that case, let us meet tomorrow afternoon at three. You can talk to Alex either before or after our meeting. By the way, we represent Tommaso Tron. Any conversation about the death of Ludovico Tron will need to take that into account."

Umberto confirmed the appointment. Rachele told him she would let her aunt know. She asked how Umberto's wife and daughter were before ending the conversation.

Once she had put down the phone, she called Count Contarini to ask him when she and the Countess could come to inspect the painting. She then called her aunt.

"Aunt Deborah, I just had Vice-Commissario Umberto De Antoni on the phone."

The Countess was eager to go back to her guests.

"He rang me before he talked to you. Just pick an afternoon you are available. I am flexible in the afternoon this week. Even today is fine."

Rachele could sense the haste in her aunt's voice. Unfortunately, she had not finished.

"Thank you. I also need to talk to Joshua. I need Dante Bembo's phone number. If his father has the fifth version of the young baker boy and the painting is in plain sight of the public, it might be at risk. I need Joshua's office number."

"Joshua is still here. It is his family's last day in Venice. Do you mind if he calls you back after breakfast?"

Rachele did not mind. She had already figured out that her aunt was in a hurry. The Countess agreed to come to the law firm the following day at 3 p.m. Rachele wrote a few notes in the 'Young Baker Boy/Ludovico Tron' notepad before moving on to another case that would keep her busy for the rest of her day.

~

The arrival of the countess always put the law firm on high alert. There was a sense of being inspected. Umberto De Antoni arrived in the middle of the 'getting ready for Countess Deborah' operation. Gabriele took him to the meeting room. Rachele appeared five minutes later.

"The atmosphere in the office reminds me of my office before the visit of the head of police."

Gabriele and Rachele laughed at Umberto's comments. Rachele put down her notepad and went to the kitchen to get the refreshment. Gabriele and Umberto sat down.

"The countess is only our honorary aunt, not our boss. That is the only difference. There is no concern for a negative opinion from your boss; we are just trying to avoid endless comments about untidiness, unprofessional attire, or something along those lines each time we meet socially, and we see her at least once a week."

The office was ready when Deborah Camerini walked through the door. Franco Cantoni came out to take her coat; his father, Alvise, remembered to kiss her hand rather than shake it. Roberto Mendes, Gabriele's youngest brother, and Aunt Deborah's golden boy, kissed her on both cheeks on his way out of the office to go to the civil court. Everybody behaved as if they were inspected. Umberto could sense relief when the countess sat in one armchair in the meeting room overlooking the Grand Canal, and Alex appeared with more refreshments. Everybody in the meeting room knew each other socially, so Umberto De Antoni immediately moved the conversation to why they were gathered.

"Before we discuss whether two crimes are connected because the perpetrators somehow took out the same part of the picture frame, can somebody explain to me, again, why there are two 'authentic versions' of a painting?"

The countess felt it was her story to tell

"To cut a long story short, a client loved a painting so much that he commissioned five versions of different sizes to the author. So, technically, each copy is not a fake because the artist himself painted it. Ludovico Tron, the expert on Cividali's work, explained how one could tell a 'version' from a fake. Emanuele Cividali had also signed the painting on the back of the canvas, adding a number between his first and last name. For instance, a 'version' would have 25 between name and last name, meaning 2 out of five; a fake would not have the signature on the back of the canvas or the number. By the way, there are only five versions in total, and they are included in Cividali's catalogue raisonné, thanks to the letter written by Cividali explaining the exorbitant fee charged to the buyer. We also know the buyer's name from the same document, Israel Alcan from Metz."

"Thank you. Now, can we try to figure out why somebody would kill and break into the warehouse of an auction house to see what is hidden inside the left side of the frame?"

Rachele had her notepad. Umberto knew that a diagram with various circles and lines connecting them would start appearing based on those notes. Rachele had shared that method with him in the past. Umberto continued.

"We can only assume it was the same person, or maybe the same people, we haven't processed the fingerprints yet."

Rachele was reading her notes. She lifted her head.

"Whatever they were after could be related to the story of those paintings. One stayed with Israel Alcan, who bequeathed it to the Metz Museum in his will. The others roamed Europe and coincidentally appeared in Venice and its surrounding area only now."

The countess had remained silent. She put down her coffee and took a sip of water before speaking.

"I met an American art dealer, Bill Campbell, married to a Charlotte Alcan, a direct descendant of Israel Alcan. Maybe she heard family stories about the painting."

Alex was collecting the empty cups and saucers.

"Diana mentioned meeting her in synagogue."

Rachele left the room. She returned a few minutes later with a copy of Cividali's catalogue raisonné.

"Here, it says that the 'smaller' versions were meant for Israel's parents and his siblings. We need to understand what happened to them and why, at some point, they felt the need to sell their version of the painting. Tommaso Tron said his father used 'version' rather than 'copy.' The interesting coincidence is that another client of mine may have bought another version when he was on holiday in Sanremo in January. So, in a way, the law firm is involved in this case. We represent Tommaso Tron and Count Contarini. By the way, Umberto, we must talk about Tommaso Tron before you leave."

The countess had been quiet too long

"And also, it turns out that the smallest and fifth copy may also be in Venice. I have an appointment to visit Master Antonio Bembo, the father of a friend of Joshua's, to establish whether the small painting in his office is the smallest of the five versions. "

Vice-Commissario Umberto De Antoni became slightly less relaxed. He assumed what he thought was an official posture, something that could be difficult when you sit on a sofa between two people he regarded as friends.

"Linking the murder of Ludovico Tron and the breaking into the warehouse is only one hypothesis we are looking into. Tommaso Tron is most definitely still a suspect in the murder of his father. Rachele, we shall discuss him at a different meeting."

The countess had an idea and, as usual, the last word in the conversation

"Why don't we ask Alex or Franco to research the Alcan family? I think that is our only way to determine if there is a reason behind the two frames being vandalised in the same way."

Once that meeting was over and the countess had left, Umberto De Antoni and Rachele moved to her office to discuss Tommaso Tron. Rachele took out another notepad and sat at the small table opposite Umberto. Umberto was reluctant to be on the opposite side of his friend; they had been cooperating since they met in 1944 when Rachele and her family were hiding in Stra, a town between Venice and Padua, and they were both active in the resistance.

"It is intriguing how the atmosphere changes after Countess Pesaro De Bonfili leaves the office. "

Rachele smiled as she was looking for the first blank page in the notepad, careful not to show her other notes to the policeman.

"Yes, try to think of your mother, or mother-in-law, who goes home, and during her visit, she did not utter a sarcastic comment or give unwanted advice. It is the same thing. By the way, I am very fond of Deborah Camerini, my mother, and my-mother-in-law."

Rachele had found the blank page, so she put the notepad on the table.

"Now, why is Tommaso Tron a suspect? As far as I know, it is all circumstantial."

Umberto felt as if he were examined, and he probably was.

"Well, we know he had a very troubled relationship with his father; he cannot account for two hours that morning, and given the time of death and the fact that death was not instant, he could have done it and then had the time to go to Piazza San Marco and open the shop by 9.30, the first time that somebody could be certain they saw him."

"And nobody saw him near the Art Gallery in Campo San Polo?"

"Nobody has contacted us. I know it is circumstantial, but I cannot write him off the suspect list. He is the only name on the list, albeit with an enormous question mark near it."

"I like the question mark. With no further evidence, I would file for dismissal of the charges if it ever went to court."

"Be patient. Ludovico Tron was murdered less than a week ago!"

"We represent Tommaso Tron. If his father's murder and the break into the warehouse of the auction house are connected, we would insist that you remove him from your list of suspects. We also represent another owner of a version of the young baker boy. I think we can work on this together. The sooner you can eliminate Tommaso Tron from your suspect list or provide evidence that could hold in court, the better."

"The only thing that annoys me is that my wife and I cannot be your guests until this is over or Tommaso Tron is cleared."

"Then, the best way to have you and your family as our guests sooner rather than later is to find out who did it."

Bill Campbell and his wife were having lunch. His wife had tried a fish recipe she had learned from Diana's grandmother, Fiamma. Charlotte told him of her shopping expedition to the Rialto fish market with Fiamma and Diana's aunt, Anita. She learnt a lot about buying fresh fish. She loved their time in Venice. Almost as an aside, she mentioned a letter from her aunt Lottie, who told her she was contacted by a cousin she had never heard of, the great-grandson of an uncle she vaguely remembered meeting. He had invited himself for coffee. She would provide more information after his visit. Bill immediately thought of the five paintings and wondered aloud when his wife's great-uncle had sold his "version" of the painting. He wondered what happened to each version before it found its way back to Venice. He thought they would make an interesting story to sell to an American paper.

The police had finished inspecting the warehouse; they had collected all the evidence, taken photographs, and allowed the auction house to run a final inventory while tidying up. The art gallery was still a crime scene. Umberto De Antoni was trying to find a link between the two crimes beyond the missing left side of the frame and the 'version' of the same painting. His guts told him there was a connection, and the frame was the key to finding the connection. The warehouse was empty, so the perpetrator did not have to kill anybody. Why did they take out the left side of the frame? What were they looking for? However, Tommaso Tron was not off the hook yet.

Assuming Tommaso's story was correct, who was the visitor that was supposed to come at 8.30 am? Umberto de Antoni wrote in his notepad, 'Find diary.' It was still too early to let the Tron family back into the art gallery.

Rachele had sent Alex back to Campo San Polo; he was supposed to find anybody who could have seen somebody enter the art gallery after Ludovico Tron or with Ludovico Tron the day he was killed. For all they knew, he could have met his client at the café and then opened the gallery and walked in with his murderer.

Franco Cantoni was supposed to talk to Tommaso Tron and try to reconstruct his walk the morning his father was killed. If they found somebody who could locate him far enough from Campo San Polo around 8.30 am, Umberto de Antoni would have to strike Tommaso Tron off the list.

Rachele had also made arrangements with Count Contarini for the Countess to inspect the painting. If Countess Pesaro De Bonfili was available on one of the days when Gabriele was travelling to Stra to help the Count's younger son with the admin of the estate, they could all make a day out of it and stay for lunch. He guaranteed Rachele they would serve fish.

Deborah Camerini and Joshua Schwartz were on the vaporetto to Murano to visit Master Antonio Bembo and inspect the painting that could probably be the fifth version of Cividali's Young Baker. The countess suspected Joshua was there to ensure she would be all right; she wondered whether one of her children had anything to do with Joshua's decision to go with her.

"Tell me again why you are coming with me. "

"I spent the morning discussing legal matters with Roberto Mendes. Going to my office in Treviso for a couple of hours was not worth my while, so I thought I could come and inspect a dinner set that Dante had described to me yesterday morning when we were rowing. I might buy it if I like it."

"I have no intention of throwing you out, but shouldn't you buy a home before buying a dinner set?"

"I am looking for the place with the right exposure, view, and… a lift."

"A lift? In Venice? That is why you have been looking for almost a year. By the way, you are welcome to stay as long as you like. I wonder what you will do with a dinner set if you do not own a dinner table. I most definitely do not need another dinner set. Even considering that Elena will have her own home one of these days, I own enough dinner sets for everybody, including you."

"Still, I was eight the last time I saw Master Bembo's workshop, and 'Master Bembo' was Dante's grandfather, not his father."

The countess was not convinced but decided that Joshua was telling the truth or lying very well. The conversation ended when the vaporetto arrived at their stop. They got off and entered a world of fire and glass. Dante and his father met them. Master Bembo took the countess into his office, where the small painting had pride of place behind his desk. He put it on his desk so the countess could examine it. The first thing she did was turn it around and look for the signature on the back. A small 55 was visible between 'Emanuele' and 'Cividali.' The painting was one of the authentic versions of the young baker.

The countess explained what 55 meant and told him of the two vandalised versions. She told Master Bembo to be very careful and keep the authenticity of his painting confidential. She would only share that information with the police and with her friend Rachele Modiano Mendes, who was representing the owner of what could be the fourth version of the same painting.

~

Two days later, the countess, Rachele, and Gabriele were on their way to Stra. Count Contarini suggested they take the train and promised that one of his sons would drive them back to Piazzale Roma[1] later that day. The countess could not help but talk about the time in 1944 and 1945 when Gabriele, Rachele, all their children, and Gabriele's mother hid in plain sight in the Contarini estate using false identities. Gabriele was not keen to talk about 'the longest eighteen months of his life' but did not dare contradict his aunt. Rachele knew her husband's silence meant he was annoyed and concentrating on something else. When they arrived at the station, Gabriele remarked that they had a car this time. Six and a half years earlier, they were met by horse and cart.

Once they arrived at the Contarini villa and greeted Countess Contarini, Gabriele disappeared with the Count's younger son and aunt Deborah and Rachele followed the Count and the Countess to inspect the painting. It was the first time Rachele had seen any version of that painting in real life; she had seen several photographs. She found Cividali's clever use of light breathtaking. It was as if the young baker had a spotlight on him, with the children sitting on the steps of the bridge under another weaker spotlight. The light drew the observer to the young baker first, then the children, then the Punta della Dogana, then to the couple near the young baker, and the last thing you noticed was the two masked, elegant women. The Contarinis and Countess Deborah allowed Rachele the time to appreciate the painting.

"I think you appreciate why I bought it."

Rachele was still taking in the scene. After a few minutes, she said,

"I am tempted to see if I can afford to buy the one for sale at

_______________

1. Piazzale Roma is the large square at the other end of the road bridge into Venice. It is as far as road traffic can go in the old city.

the Tron art gallery once the police release it and the frame is repaired. "

Countess Pesaro De Bonfili was all business. They needed to remove the backboard to see if a signature was on the back of the canvas. They sent for a farmer of the estate, somebody Rachele knew very well from her time in Stra and her time in the Resistance. He arrived with a screwdriver and a hammer to lift the nails. They removed the backboard. Much to their surprise, two pieces of paper came out, and there was a second backboard. Rachele and Aunt Deborah looked at each other.

"They must have been looking for those papers when they took out the left side of the frame in the other two paintings. Count Contarini, do you have a folder I can use to take this letter with me and show it to Umberto de Antoni? I can write a receipt for it. "

The Count took out a folder and gave it to Rachele

"There is no need for a receipt, Rachele."

"Yes, there is. Legally, this may become evidence of two crimes. The police may decide to keep it; you would want a receipt in that case. Given that the police will get it from me and not from you, I have to have a signed statement that you gave it to me, and there are witnesses who can confirm it was hidden in your painting, which makes it your property."

Rachele sat on an armchair and used the coffee table to write a receipt. She would keep it for the moment and put it in Count Contarini's file at the law firm. Countess Contarini and Aunt Deborah would also countersign as witnesses that it was hidden between two backboards of a painting owned by the Contarinis.

While Rachele was sorting out the receipt, the farmer had removed the second backdrop. They could see the back of the canvas. Countess Deborah pointed out the signature in the back with 25 between the first and last names. That was an authentic version of the young baker by Cividali, the second of five.

# Chapter Seven

## April 1950

Franco Cantoni and Tommaso Tron were walking together for the third time; they were supposed to recreate the walk of the day Ludovico Tron was killed. Franco was putting a brave face to what he thought was turning into a desperate attempt; he feared that the chances that they bumped into somebody who might recognise Tommaso or remember having seen him ten days earlier were pretty slim.

Franco met Tommaso outside the Tron home, close to the Ca Rezzonico vaporetto stop. Tommaso kept saying he took the vaporetto to the Giardini stop, walked around the Park near the Biennale building, then walked back to Piazza San Marco and the shop. He left home right after his father at about 7.45. For the third time, they met at 7.50 and retraced Tommaso's steps. Franco was hoping against all hopes that something new would happen that morning. Tommaso might remember something specific that could have occurred at a specific time, or they might meet somebody who remembered seeing Tommaso ten days earlier. That morning began like the others. Tommaso did not remember anything specific. Franco liked Tommaso. They were discussing books. He was well-read and shared Franco's love for crime stories taking place in the Victorian era, like Sherlock Holmes. They both loved the logic and the care for details. Their conversation was fragmented, interrupted by Franco asking Tommaso if he remembered any detail. They had reached the Arsenale vaporetto stop when they heard somebody calling Tommaso's name; a man ran after them. When he reached them, he said he had heard about his father, made his condolences, and then said something that made Franco almost jump with joy.

"…I cannot stop thinking I met you the morning your father died, more or less at this time…"

Franco interrupted him

"I am sorry. It is very important. Are you sure you met Tommaso Tron ten days ago at about 8.15?"

"Yes, I am sure. I remember very well because after I talked to Tommaso, I thought of inviting his father, Ludovico Tron, to a whisky tasting. I thought he would have enjoyed that. When I spoke to their maid in the afternoon, I found out that the police had found him dead in his art gallery. "

Franco wanted to be sure.

"Excuse my insistence. You remember the day. Are you sure about the time? It is very important. Would you mind talking to the police?"

"Of course, I remember the time, like this morning. I am going to my daughter's café to collect my youngest grandson. I must be there before 8.30 when her mother-in-law leaves to take the older grandson to school. My youngest grandson spends the morning with us. My wife picks up his brother from school, and they have lunch with us. Then, we take them home by 3 pm when my daughter's mother-in-law takes over. So, yes, I am sure it was after eight and before 8.30. Of course, I can talk to the police."

Tommaso was relieved. Franco almost forgot to take the name and phone number of the man they had met. Anybody who needed to talk to him could find him at his shop near Rialto bridge between 930 and 1130. Tommaso and Franco could not stop smiling; they took the vaporetto from the Arsenale stop rather than walk to Piazza San Marco.

Franco knew Alex had not found anybody who could remember seeing Ludovico Tron open the art gallery that fateful morning or anybody entering it around 8.30. That did not mean nobody was there; now they could place Tommaso Tron too far away from Campo San Polo that morning. He could not have gone to Campo San Polo, have a row with his father (that nobody heard), have caused his death between 8 and 9, and then be ready to open the shop in Piazza San Marco by 9.30.

Umberto de Antoni was having morning coffee in the law firm's kitchen, talking to Rachele and Gabriele. He was there on official police business, so nobody could have accused him of socialising with the lawyer who represented a suspect. Once they finished the coffee and the pastries, Rachele and Umberto moved to her office, where she took the letter from the safe.

"This is what we found hidden between two backboards of the version of the young baker bought by Count Contarini. My French is very rusty, but from what I understand, it is an agreement between two members of the same family that a sale was not real but a way to protect a business from the Germans. The date coincides with the early weeks of the Franco-Prussian war when the city of Metz became German."

"So you think this is what they were looking for when they removed part of the frame?"

"I do. This letter also connects the murder of Ludovico Tron with the break-in at the auction house warehouse. I also think it removes Tommaso Tron from the list of suspects."

"A list that only has one name at the moment, but I think you are right. But we need to understand more about the content of this letter to figure out who could be behind both."

Franco's voice interrupted them. He was asking the receptionist whether Rachele was available. He sounded excited, and Rachele could hear his voice from her office. She stood up, opened the door, and stepped into the corridor.

"Come here before they hear you on the other side of the Adriatic. "

"Tommaso and I met somebody who remembered seeing him the morning his father was killed."

Rachele invited Franco in. He saw Umberto De Antoni and told him about the man he and Tommaso had met earlier that morning. He took out of his pocket the note with the man's name, phone number, and the address of his shop. Rachele intercepted the piece of paper.

"Let me copy it before we give it to you. I would provide poor service to my client if I did not keep a record of this information. I trust you, Umberto, but I do not want any complaints."

She wrote the name, address, and phone number, wondered whether it was the shop selling embroidered linen by the Rialto bridge, and gave the original to Umberto.

"This witness removes my client from the list of suspects. We can socialise again. That leaves me representing Count Contarini. The evidence I am about to give you is his property."

"Yes, but now we are on the same side, and I can come here if I need help sorting out this case."

"By the way, Diana and Elena Pesaro De Bonfili told me that a Charlotte Alcan is in Venice. I wonder if she is a descendant of one of the signatories of that letter. If she is, we can organise a meeting here to see if she can help us explain the content and the possible relevance to our times."

The following Saturday, Diana introduced her mother to Charlotte Alcan Campbell when they were in Synagogue. At the end of the service, Rachele checked that nobody else had invited guests for lunch before inviting Ben Campbell and Charlotte Alcan. Rachele never discussed work on Saturdays, so she simply asked whether she was related to the Israel Alcan who commissioned the five versions of the young baker. Charlotte smiled, confirmed it, and asked why.

"In the past few weeks, I have come across three versions, and I had to check that the one in the Museum in Metz was still there. I read their stories, and I was intrigued."

Ben started talking when his wife was ready to answer, which was not lost on Rachele. He should have let his wife speak. His speaking for his wife annoyed Rachele, who had a very egalitarian relationship with her husband.

"According to my father-in-law, the family knew of their existence but thought they were lost. It is bizarre that they all appeared in Venice."

"Well, Aunt Deborah's theory is that since Cividali was Venetian, it is normal to assume that their best market would be in Venice, so owners will choose to put them up for sale here in Venice. One of them never left Venice to begin with. It was used as a part of the payment for a dinner set in Murano."

Rachele liked that Charlotte Alcan did not allow her husband to silence her.

"Those paintings have always been the subject of a family story. Allegedly, when my great-grandfather fled to Paris during the Franco-Prussian war, he took his version. The two paintings given to my great-aunt and great-uncle were never accounted for. My father is sure that they were destroyed. "

"Well, they were not. My understanding is that they are here in Venice now. Your husband and our aunt Deborah saw one."

At the end of the meal, Rachele asked if Charlotte spoke French. She needed help with translating a letter. She wondered if she could come to her office the following week. Charlotte agreed and told her that Diana or Elena Pesaro De Bonfili would know how to reach her.


*Metz 8 August 1870*


*The ethnic French population of Metz was in turmoil. The Prussian Army was approaching. Those more closely connected with the government, even the local government, were increasingly worried. Some had already left town. The conversation in synagogue the previous Saturday was about who was safe to stay and who had better go. Isaac Alcan thought that his son Israel was secure; his wife was born in Frankfurt, and he was fluent in German. Israel's business interests were separated from the family. The family bank owned a shareholding in the steel mill, but that was the bank, not directly the family. Isaac did not think he was safe; he was a major financial supporter of the local administration, lending money to the City for various infrastructure projects. He was also aware of rumours that he had funded a French army battalion, and he did not think it mattered that he did not. He, his wife, and his eldest son, together with his wife and children, ought to leave Metz and go to Paris, where his daughter lived. His wife was packing what she wanted to take to Paris. They would use carts to take them out of Metz and, hopefully, to his daughter's home. Before leaving, he was on his way to see his son to ensure that the bank and the participation in the steel mill were safe.*

### Metz 11 August 1870

*Isaac and Israel spent the morning at the office of a notaire. Isaac sold the bank and all the assets owned by the bank to his son. Later, they went to see the family lawyer to prepare another letter. Both parties agreed the sale was a way to preserve Isaac Alcan's assets from being confiscated by the Prussian authorities during the occupation of Metz. If a settlement between France and Prussia had given Metz to Germany, the sale would have protected the family's assets in the long term. They signed both copies of the letter. Isaac went home. He took out his version of the Cividali's young baker and put it on a table upside down. Then he put the letter on the backdrop and nailed a second backdrop on top of it. Israel went home and put the letter inside the family bible, ready to destroy it if he had any reason to do so.*

### Metz, 14 August 1870

*Isaac had organised two big carts with horses and two carriages for the people. He had organised the help of families who wanted to flee the approaching German army but had no means to secure transportation. He would help them once they reached Paris. They left at dawn. He hoped that nobody would think of waking up his grandchildren. They were sleeping on top of boxes that hid the cash he had taken with him. It was quite a lot of notes and a lot of jewels. The Cividali painting with the letter was safely wrapped in two blankets and tied to the roof of the carriage where Isaac was travelling. He had every intention of going back to Metz to reclaim his bank.*

*Metz, 19 August 1870*

*The siege of Metz began on the same day that Israel's wife told him she was finally pregnant after seven years of marriage.*

In the end, Countess Deborah insisted they showed Charlotte the letter in her home, a more relaxed environment than the office of a law firm. A diverse group of people was in the blue sitting room of the Pesaro De Bonfili residence near the Ca D'Oro. Umberto De Antoni had come with the letter found in Count Contarini's painting. Rachele was there representing Count Contarini. Charlotte Alcan was there to translate the letters and see if any of the family stories could help with the investigation. Her husband and Elena were there because they would have found out about it anyway.

The maid had served refreshments to everybody. Elena and Rachele looked at each other, smiling, whenever the countess acted as the perfect hostess. She followed the maid and insisted everybody had a share of refreshments she bought from Rachele's daughter Anna's kosher patisserie. Then, the countess explained why they were all here in her sitting room. She introduced Vice Commissario Umberto De Antoni to Bill and Charlotte and let him continue.

"This is the letter that Count Contarini, Countess Pesaro de Bonfili, and Avvocato Modiano[1] found hidden between two backboards of the Count's version of Cividali's young baker.

---

1. "Avvocato" (lawyer in Italian) is the formal title given to a Lawyer; Umberto De Antoni was being very formal and mentioned Rachele using her full professional title. 'Modiano' not Mendes because in Italy a married woman never officially changed her surname, she would use her husband's last name only as a courtesy or she would add it to her last name. For instance, Rachele would have three legal signatures "Rachele Modiano", "Rachele Modiano Mendes", and "Rachele Mendes".

We think it is connected with the motive behind the murder of Ludovico Tron and the break-in at the warehouse of the auction house. The letter is in French, and Isaac Alcan and Israel Alcan signed it."

He passed the folder with the letter to Charlotte, who took it without opening it.

"Israel Alcan was my paternal grandfather, and Isaac Alcan was his father. My aunt Lottie told me family stories of the time of the siege of Metz, but we both thought they were a sort of family legend. My aunt has inherited a lot of family papers."

After a while, she opened the folder and looked at the letter without touching it.

"It says that the sale of the bank owned by my great-grandfather to my grandfather was a way to prevent the Prussians from confiscating it. Isaac Alcan feared the Prussians would seize his assets because he had made many loans to French governmental organisations. He expected to get the bank back at no cost whenever he went back to Metz. If he died before he could return to Metz, his other children would be each entitled to a third of the shares in the bank."

She closed the folder and gave it back to Umberto.

"I wonder whether my grandfather destroyed his copy of the letter. There is a line under the two signatures saying that both Israel and Isaac had a copy of this letter signed by both of them. Somehow, I find it hard to reconcile the official tone of this letter with the fact that the signatories are father and son."

Rachele interjected

"Sometimes, you need official paperwork when you have a family business. My father has a good relationship with his children, and we siblings are very close. Sometimes, we have to sign documents written in a way that makes us sound more like board members than brothers and sisters. It is one joy of successful family businesses."

The room fell silent for a while, then Rachele stood up and started walking towards the window. After a while, she turned back, facing the group of people sitting down.

"Could one of the other children's descendants have heard of the letter and wants to find it to recover what was taken from his grandfather or grandmother?"

Charlotte looked as if that statement had brought her back to reality from her thoughts.

"I do not know what happened to my great-aunt or my great-uncle and their families. Maybe I could ask my aunt Lottie. I could do one better: I could ask her to come to visit us in Venice. She would love to be part of this conversation."

The Countess was back to being the perfect hostess.

"You can tell her she can stay here. I have room."

That comment meant Elena and Rachele were very busy not looking at each other to avoid any inappropriate giggling.

On their way out, Bill Campbell asked Rachele and the Countess if they could arrange for him to see the paintings at Count Contarini's and Master Bembo's workshop.

A few days later, Alex found himself in Campo San Polo. He noticed a sign outside the door of the Tron Art Gallery showing a date when it would reopen following cleaning and inventory. His companion was thirsty, and so they went into the café opposite. When he went to pay, the cashier asked him if he was there the day they found the body of Ludovico Tron.

"Yes, I was here. If you remember, I bought two phone tokens to call the police and a colleague."

"I remember. You also asked me if I noticed anybody walking in or out of the gallery that morning. Later that day, I remembered I did, but just when we opened around 7.30, I saw a woman, probably in her late twenties, tall. She caught my attention because she was blond and dressed in black. The contrast between her clothes and her hair was striking. She was walking outside the gallery as if she was waiting for somebody. Also, she was wearing trousers. You do not see many women wearing trousers around here. I did not have time to pay attention later. It was the morning rush, and I was too busy."

"I think you should call the police."

Alex searched his pockets until he found his diary. He tore a page from the back, wrote a number on it, and gave the piece of paper to the cashier.

"Here is the number. Ask for Vice-Commissario Umberto De Antoni. It is a shame you did not see that person's face, but I am sure it will be helpful."

# Chapter Eight

## May 1950

Lottie Alcan was looking forward to being in Venice again; her last time there was during her honeymoon in 1903. Two world wars later, she was sure she could still find something familiar in that city. She had packed books for the long train ride; however, the book stayed on her lap on the train heading for Genoa. She was watching the Italian coastline, but she was deep in thought. Her life, her ex-husband, who divorced her in the mid-1930s to follow his mistress to the Holy Land once their sons had jobs, her father and his love for Venice kept her company until the train arrived at Milan. She had booked a room at the Gallia, a historic hotel near the railway station, before continuing to Venice the following day. Her book became her dining companion when she had dinner in her room.

The following morning, her mood was different. Once on the train to Venice, she felt more sociable; she practiced her Italian by talking to a couple of fellow travellers, and she had lunch in the dining car. Her book stayed in her large handbag. Once the train left Padua railway station, a growing sense of anticipation made her look forward to arriving in Venice. She was eager to be in the city and see her niece Charlotte; she was very fond of her.

Countess Deborah had debated whether she should go to the station to meet Lottie Alcan, considering she would be her guest. In the end, her daughter Elena convinced her not to; Lottie Alcan and her niece had not seen each other for quite a while, and they might have liked some private moments. The countess agreed but sent her favourite porter to help with the luggage. It would also solve the problem of ensuring Charlotte could find the entrance to the building. She had only visited Countess Deborah's home twice and may have problems finding the right narrow street off Strada Nuova.

The couple of fellow travellers with whom Lottie had spent time on the train insisted on helping her with her luggage. Charlotte was not surprised to see that her aunt had enlisted the help of a young man who was now carrying her aunt's large suitcase and his smaller one, leaving her aunt and the woman Charlotte assumed to be his wife with lighter bags and their handbags. The porter sent by Countess Deborah asked which one was her aunt's and moved forward to relieve the young man of one of the two suitcases; Lottie Alcan introduced her travelling companions to her niece and thanked them for their help and their company. She turned to her niece.

"It was very nice of Countess Pesaro De Bonfili to offer me her hospitality and very thoughtful of her to send her trusted porter. Can we walk to her home?"

"Aunt Lottie, it is easier for the porter if we take the vaporetto. I do not know how many bridges we must cross, but there are at least two. Try to think of him navigating steps with his trolley."

"Do you know where we are going?"

"I have only been there twice. We see Countess Deborah on Saturdays in synagogue and have met her elsewhere. She also sent her usual porter because he knows the way. She wanted to meet you at the station, but her adopted daughter felt we wanted some private moment, so she sent her porter."

"Why did you say 'her adopted daughter'? If the countess adopted her, she is her daughter."

"I think she is about your age, and Elena is not eighteen yet. Nobody makes it a mystery that she is adopted. She is also part of a huge clan with siblings, nephews, nieces, honorary cousins, and honorary uncles and aunts."

"Intriguing. I hope I have the opportunity to learn more about her story and the clan that has embraced her as one of their own."

They had arrived at the Ca D'Oro stop; they got off and followed the porter along narrow streets that led to Strada Nuova, then more narrow streets that led to the entrance of the building where Countess Pesaro De Bonfili lived.

"I assume once upon a time, this was the back entrance. Is the building on any canal?"

"Tante Lottie. The red reception room faces the Grand Canal."

The porter rang the doorbell, walked in, left his trolley at the bottom of the stairs, took the luggage, and started carrying the suitcase and the bag to the first floor.

"Ah, Countess Pesaro De Bonfili lives in the *piano nobile*. I wonder if there is a grander staircase from what was the entrance overlooking the Grand Canal."

"I think the countess told Bill that her in-laws closed the *porta d'acqua*[1] before she married into the family. That means before World War I."

---

1. Literally, the water gate; in Venice this means the entrance from a canal, i.e. from the water. It used to be the 'grand entrance' (or grander entrance) into the building.

Once they reached the landing, Lottie Alcan started following the porter. Her niece stopped her from turning right and pointed to the door on the other side of the landing where the countess was waiting for her. Deborah Camerini was very formal when she was nervous. Reverting to old-fashioned manners was her way of coping with what she thought would have been an embarrassing moment. Her French was not good. She hoped her guest had some English. She did not dare contemplate the idea that she could speak some Italian.

Charlotte Alcan introduced her aunt. Then she looked at the two ladies standing beside each other and remarked in an accented Italian.

"Maybe it is the hairdo, but you could be sisters."

The countess thought that Lottie Alcan died her hair black, but they both had their hair in a 1920s bob, guest and hostess shared the same level of care in their appearance.

Lottie's manners made her a very gracious guest.

"I do not think it is the appearance. The countess looks so much better than I do. We had similar upbringings in terms of education, manners, and posture. That is why you see a resemblance between a glamorous countess and this old, dishevelled person who had spent the best part of two days travelling."

Much to Deborah's delight, her guest's Italian was quite good. Lottie did not miss the smile, a mixture of surprise and relief.

"Italy is not very far from Menton. I can practise Italian almost every day. "

They were talking as they were moving to the blue sitting room. The less formal sitting room everybody loved.

"That is a relief. I have some English and German, but my French is non-existent."

The art on the wall impressed Lottie Alcan. She was even more impressed when the countess opened the door and led them into the blue sitting room, where she noticed pastries on a sideboard and a teapot kept warm on a heated tray.

"I have prepared some refreshments while Tonia, my housekeeper, sorts out the porter and checks your room. I have already invited Bill and Charlotte to dinner. My daughter Elena and my nephew Joshua will both be home around six. We shall have dinner at eight. "

The countess became very apologetic. She had to leave her guests alone.

"Please excuse me. I have to call a client who wants to buy a painting the owner does not want to sell. I leave you and your niece to catch up. Please help yourself to tea and pastries. They come from one of the best patisseries in Venice. Tonia should be here to take you to your room in a moment. You are welcome to stay as long as you like, but we shall treat you as a valued family member. When it is just family, we do not change for dinner."

The countess was as good at exits as she was at entrances. Lottie remarked to her niece that she would either spend a long time in Venice because she and the countess have become close friends or leave as soon as possible because they cannot stand each other.

As usual, everybody started assembling in the blue room before dinner. Elena and Joshua Schwartz had met Charlotte many times, so she introduced them to her aunt. The countess joined them after she had sorted out both the eager buyer and the reluctant seller. By seven thirty, Tonia arrived with drinks, and the doorbell rang, announcing the arrival of another honorary nephew and his wife.

The countess stood up and introduced the new arrivals.

"This is Rachele, my honorary niece and the leader of my legal cavalry, and this is her husband, Gabriele, my honorary nephew, who keeps my finances in check."

The countess noticed Lottie did not get up but waited for Gabriele to kiss her hand. She was proud that her nephew had read the signals correctly. She felt she had to explain Rachele's role to Lottie.

"Rachele represents the owner of the young baker version, who had the letter hidden between two backboards. She and Gabriele are also close friends of Vice-Commissario Umberto De Antoni, who leads the investigations to find out who broke into the auction house warehouse and who murdered Ludovico Tron."

The countess also noticed, almost with parental pride, that Rachele had bent to kiss her guest, who felt she had to explain her presence.

"I am here to see my niece and Venice, but I am here now rather than another time to share what I know about my family. I have very vivid memories of the large painting that is now at the Museum of Metz. It used to be behind my father's desk in his study. When can we start?"

She sipped her drink and continued before Rachele could answer.

"When I was a child, I think I had a crush on the young baker. I would love to see the other versions of the painting. I remember hearing the story from my late father, who regretted that the other versions were lost."

Elena thought their guest had the same dreamy look as her mother when she explained the smaller version of the painting a few weeks ago. She added.

"When my mother and I saw one of the smaller versions, the

way the painter used the light to draw your attention to the young baker fascinated me."

Charlotte was the only one of the three ladies who had seen the painting in a catalogue.

"I went to the Biblioteca Marciana a week ago with Bill to look at a catalogue of Cividali's work. I only saw that painting in black and white. The way he used the light is very striking."

The countess brought the conversation back to the initial point raised by her guest.

"Rachele and I thought we would leave you a day to enjoy your niece and Venice, and then we could contact Vice Commissario Umberto de Antoni to arrange the first meeting. Also, Count Contarini, the owner of the version of the young baker that hid the letter, has invited all of us and the Mendes to lunch in his estate next Sunday so you can see his young baker, or, as we say here, his *fornaretto*."

The doorbell rang again, and a few minutes later, Bill Campbell entered the blue sitting room. Tonia announced that dinner was about to be served, and they moved to the dining room.

Umberto de Antoni thought it would be easier to discuss the letter with Lottie Alcan in a meeting room at the law firm rather than at the police station. He had agreed with Rachele that he would arrive half an hour earlier. They were not on opposite sides anymore.

"We have analysed the fingerprints in the pieces of frame that were removed from the two paintings. So far, we have excluded the auction house staff and Tron family members. We found two sets that do not match anyone we know but belong to people who touched the frames at the auctioneer's warehouse. "

"Have you made any progress with the identity of the mysterious blond individual wearing black seen by the cashier of the café outside the Tron art gallery at 8-830am the day Ludovico Tron was killed?"

"Yes, and no. Except somebody else with a shop on Campo San Polo confirmed that somebody dressed in black with blond hair was in Campo San Polo before Ludovico Tron opened the gallery. Whether that person has any relevance to the death of Ludovico Tron remains to be seen. I need to figure out our next step. I am sure the letter found hidden in Count Contarini's painting is relevant to the case. Beyond that, I do not know what to do."

"Let's see what Lottie Alcan can tell us about her family. Let's hope she will give us some useful information."

Countess Pesaro de' Bonfili was good at entrances. Rachele could tell that she was ready to inspect the office. They were prepared. Franco Cantoni came out of his office to receive her. She introduced him to Lottie Alcan while the receptionist took their coats. He led them to the meeting room overlooking the Grand Canal, where Rachele and Umberto De Antoni were waiting.

Umberto stood up.

"Good morning, Countess Pesaro De Bonfili."

He remembered to kiss her hand and did not smile when he noticed her reaction.

"This is my guest, Lottie Alcan. She is the daughter of Israel Alcan, the man who commissioned the five versions of Cividali's young baker."

He bowed his head in recognition and kissed her hand as well. He had done the right thing. Rachele did not miss the expression of satisfaction bordering on motherly pride on the face of the countess. He looked at the two ladies and said,

"It is remarkable. I could describe you using the same words."

The countess smiled as she was sitting down. Lottie Alcan sat next to her.

"My niece and namesake, Charlotte, thought we looked like sisters."

Once everybody sat down and refreshments were offered and declined, Umberto De Antoni took out the folder with the letter from his briefcase. Lottie picked up the letter; she recognised the handwriting before she started reading.

"I have seen other documents my grandfather wrote. This is his handwriting. There is no doubt about that. I never heard of this letter, so give me some time to read it."

The countess stood up and walked to the window, to give some space to her guest. Rachele and Umberto looked at each other in silence. They were both thinking of questions to ask based on what they knew of the content. When Lottie raised her head, the countess moved back to the table. She did not want to miss a thing.

"I inherited a lot of family documents, but I did not know this letter existed. My late father never discussed it, and I do not remember any reference to it in the family archives I inherited. After he heard the news that his father had passed away, my late father did not offer a third of the bank to each of his siblings. My grandfather did not mention the letter in the will; he just wrote that, once his wife passed away, whatever was left of their money and possession had to be divided equally among his children."

"What can you tell us of your uncle and aunt?"

"My father was the youngest. His sister Ruth married and moved to Paris. She had two sons. Jules moved to London before World War I, and his brother escaped to London with his family before the Germans reached Paris. My great-uncle Samuel became an art dealer in Paris. I suspect he used the other version of the painting and other things they had brought with them when they escaped Metz to start his business. "

Rachele was taking notes. She did not know whether anything would be helpful, but she kept writing out of habit. Umberto thought of asking Lottie Alcan if she could help somebody prepare a family tree later. He was waiting for something that he could use for his investigation.

"Jules Levy's two sons joined the RAF and fought in the Battle of Britain. His daughter had a role that nobody talks about. I am still in touch with Jules. He wanted to check who was alive after the war and came looking for me. I understand his brother moved to Haifa with his family in 1930."

Rachele interjected,

"My sister and her family also live in Haifa. They made *alyah*[2] a few years before your cousin,"

Lottie smiled

"I do not know where they are now. Three months ago, I received a letter from somebody claiming to be one of Samuel's great-grandchildren. He visited me a month ago and asked many questions about our family, especially my father and grandfather. I now wonder whether Samuel and Ruth knew of the letter. If that is the case, why did they not say anything when my grandfather died? Although by the time Isaac Alcan died, he lived in France, and Israel lived in Germany, they informed my father, and when their mother passed away, they shared whatever possessions were left."

---

2. "Make Alyah" (meaning make an ascent) is the phrase Jews use to mean move to what is now Israel.

Umberto was paying a lot of attention now.

"Can you tell us the name of the man who came to see you? Better yet, can you describe him?"

"His last name was not Alcan. He is the grandchild of my cousin Raphael's daughter. His name was Daniel Klein."

Lottie closed her eyes, trying to remember the young man.

"He is tall and athletic, with a distinctive face. Daniel reminded me of my father and Philippe, my late brother. He kept asking questions but did not share much, and he knew enough of the Alcan family to be believable."

Umberto asked if Lottie Alcan minded talking to a sketch artist to see if they could come up with sketches of her cousin. Lottie's reaction surprised everybody.

"Of course, that is why I am in Venice, to help you. Also, let me contact Jules. I wonder if he heard about the letter or if he is in touch with Raphael's family. I know he tried to reach out to see how many of his relatives survived the war. Maybe he can tell us more about the Kleins. Do you mind if I tell him about the letter?"

The countess looked at Rachele, silently asking her to intervene.

"As a lawyer, I would advise you to be cautious. If you look at it from their point of view, your father took what belonged to Ruth Alcan Levy and Samuel Alcan. I do not know whether they have an enforceable claim or if the statute of limitation is such that they no longer have one. You need the opinion of a French legal advisor, but I would rather you do not share the letter's content beyond your niece and her husband."

She nodded her head towards the countess.

"I already gave my aunt and Count Contarini the same advice. At least let us wait until we know more about why two versions of the young baker had the left side of the frame removed and why one man has died."

Lottie was perplexed and did not know what to say. She closed the folder containing the letter and gave it back to the policeman. The countess had an idea.

"Rachele, you could investigate with the French consulate to see if they can give you legal advice about the statute of limitation on this matter, and then Lottie could decide what to share with her cousin."

As he was putting things away, Umberto turned to Rachele, smiling.

"That means that now we are on the same side of this case and can work together."

Rachele nodded, inwardly smiling that her honorary aunt did not have the last word for once. The countess stood up, picked up her handbag, asked Rachele if she could use the phone to ring Charlotte Alcan. She wanted to take them to lunch at a restaurant at the Zattere.

# Chapter Nine

## May 1950

Diana and Charlotte Alcan Campbell met twice a week for a conversation in the other one's language. The two young women had discovered they had a lot of interest in common, so finding something to talk about was never a problem. They were sitting outside at a café near the Zattere vaporetto stop. It was Diana's turn to practise her English. That afternoon, they were talking about plans for the future. Charlotte had news to share with her friend.

"The New York art dealer that has sent us here has written to Bill. He wants us to consider spending another year here. Bill has sourced very important pieces for their clients, and they want him to continue. They have more requests from museums and private buyers. It looks as if we shall be here till June next year."

Charlotte and Diana had become good friends despite the nine-year age gap.

"That sounds great. Do you like the idea?"

"I love Venice. I am also excited to be in Europe. It may give me the opportunity to get to know my Aunt Lottie better, but I am bored. I'd like a job."

"You could teach English, you could write, there are several things you could do."

Diana noticed Isabella Tron walking towards them with a young man. She waved at her and told Charlotte she could be a potential client. Isabella had no intention of interrupting her friend's English lesson, but she had a quick question for Diana. She let the young man pick a table and approach the table where the two young women were sitting.

"How are you? I am sorry to interrupt. Could you ask your mother when Tommaso could come and see her? He wants to thank her; he thinks paying the bill is not enough."

"I'll ask her later this evening and call you to let you know. If it is urgent, I'll drop by the law firm and find out from the receptionist."

"It is not urgent. This evening is fine. Thank you, and once again, apologies for interrupting. "

Isabella moved to the table where the young man was sitting. Charlotte finished her ice cream.

"Access to ice cream of this quality is another reason I am happy to spend more time in Venice. By the way, Isabella had no intention of interfering with your lesson. She wanted to make sure she had no interference herself."

The two friends looked at the young man sitting with Diana's friend. They smiled at each other and continued their conversation.

Bill Campbell was in Tommaso Tron's shop. His bosses in New York were intrigued by the idea of five 'authentic' versions of the same painting and asked him to write an article for the monthly magazine they were sending to their clients and a few selected subscribers. Tommaso thought it was a good idea and suggested they worked together to research the article, provided he could use it for the Tron art gallery catalogue. An art magazine associated with the gallery could be a good idea, and he decided to talk to his brother in the evening. Tommaso knew that Lottie Alcan was in Venice.

"We could talk to your wife's aunt and ask her for her memories of the largest version hanging in her father's study."

Bill noticed a copy of Cividali's catalogue raisonné. He looked at his watch.

"Now she should be with a sketch artist at the police station to describe the face of the cousin who visited her in Menton a few weeks ago."

Suddenly, Tommaso stood up and went to the door. He opened it, went outside, looked around, and returned inside, shaking his head.

"It is none of my business, but whom do you think you saw?"

Tommaso sat down, concern was written on his face.

"I am not sure. It is more a gut feeling than a rational reaction. A man in his mid-to-late twenties walks past here every afternoon since we moved the young baker to this shop from the art gallery. He comes, stops outside looking at the painting in the window, and walks away."

Bill tried to minimise. He was interested in the five Cividali, not his wife's family history.

"This is Piazza San Marco. Lots of people from all over the world walk past. Sometimes, they stop to look at a shop window and then walk away."

"That man comes almost every day in the afternoon. At least, he has walked past every afternoon I have been here. I am not sure I can recognise him, though. I cannot see his face very well. The painting hides him."

Bill wanted to bring the conversation back to planning the article. He hoped to borrow a copy of Cividali's *catalogue raisonné* that reproduced the letter that Emanuele Cividali wrote to the person who wondered whether he had overcharged Israel Alcan.

"if you think he is here for the young baker, tell the police or your lawyer."

Somehow, the countess and Lottie Alcan had turned an afternoon with a police sketch artist into something glamorous. Deborah Camerini's original idea was to have the sketching session at Caffe Florian. Umberto de Antoni declined her generous offer, saying that, for appearance's sake, it would be better to have it either at the police station or at the law firm. She agreed but leant over her nephews and took over the kitchen. She organised a special delivery of cakes and pastries and talked her daily maid into doing extra hours at the law firm and taking over the kitchen to serve the refreshments; her housekeeper, Tonia, would take care of the maid's children for the afternoon. The staff of the Cantoni-Mendes-Modiano law firm knew it was easier to say yes to the determined lady they knew well. They liked the idea of the countess organising special refreshments for her new friend and were looking forward to the leftovers.

Umberto De Antoni was there to reassure the policeman who was doing the sketching that it was all right to eat the pastries. He would have enjoyed the experience, even if it slowed things down. It took most of the afternoon to draw the face of Lottie Alcan's cousin, but in the end, they did it.

Tommaso Tron chose that afternoon to come and see his lawyer. The receptionist knew he should not meet the Vice-Commissario or the other policeman without his lawyer being present. When he arrived, she took him to Alex and Franco's office and checked if Rachele could see him or if he had to wait. Less than five minutes later, Rachele came to collect him. He asked whether Alex could join them. If he remembered correctly, his awareness of what happened in Campo San Polo could help. Alex joined them. He did not know why.

On the way to their office, Rachele asked her aunt's maid if she could bring them some refreshments. Alex explained to Tommaso that the standard that afternoon was higher than usual. Once the maid had brought the pastries and the coffees, Tommaso explained why he had to talk to his lawyer. Then he turned to Alex.

"If I remember correctly, the cashier of the café opposite our art gallery told you about the person who was waiting outside the day my father was killed. You helped clear my name with the police. I wanted to thank you, but I also wanted your opinion on what I just told you."

Before Alex could speak, Rachele had an idea.

"Alex, after you have shared your opinion on what Tommaso told us, go to the meeting room facing the Grand Canal and ask Umberto De Antoni to join us."

Then she turned to Tommaso.

"He is here with Lottie Alcan and a sketch artist."

Alex had time to think before commenting on what Tommaso had just shared.

"I often wondered if what the cashier saw was a woman or a man wearing a shoulder-length blond wig. We associate long hair with women. Are you sure you did not notice his face?"

Tommaso closed his eyes.

"I can only tell you he has dark hair and walks fast. I am not sure why I think it is a man; I just do. He bends down to look at the painting, and by the time I walk out of the shop to talk to him, he is gone, sort of lost in the crowd. He is not as tall as I am; otherwise, I could still see his head. "

Rachele stopped taking notes.

"Why do you think you could tell his head apart from the crowd?"

Tommaso lifted his shoulders and opened his arms.

"I don't know, I just do."

"This could be very important to the police, and they can do something about it. Alex, please see if Umberto can spare us some time."

After hearing Tommaso's story, Umberto suggested he stay longer and talk to the sketch artist once he finished with the ladies. Alex agreed to wait with Tommaso in the other meeting room. They stood up and left the room. Rachele was now free to talk to her friend, the policeman.

"What do you make of it?"

"It is a possibility. I hope to show the sketches of the cousin around Campo San Polo and to the auction house staff. I also hope the sketch artist can get something out of Tommaso Tron. We may have to organise plainclothes agents to watch the shop in Piazza San Marco. The owner of the auction house has connections, and my boss is under pressure to ensure that we do not leave any stone unturned in solving this case. I need all the help I can get."

"You have ours. How are the ladies doing?"

"The countess is sketching, trying to remember people at the auction house when she inspected the Cividali. I am not sure how much it will help, but it keeps her busy and allows the sketch artist to work with Lottie Alcan without interference."

"My mother-in-law told me that Aunt Deborah wanted to be an artist before she married Count Pesaro De Bonfili. She can draw."

"Then let's hope we have some results from her memories and drawings. On another note, I think those two ladies are becoming friends. We may have to run for the proverbial hills."

Rachele smiled, thinking of those two grand dames enjoying each other's company. She was sure Venice had coped with more formidable individuals in its history.

"Since we are in Venice, we have two options: the hills or a deserted island in the lagoon."

The phone rang. Rachele picked it up. Umberto mouthed he would talk to her later and left the room.

"Good afternoon, Bill. Nice to hear from you. How can I help?"

"I had the idea of seeing if I could organise a temporary show of all the five versions of Cividali's young baker at Ca Pesaro. I have the local contacts, but I need to talk to somebody in Metz. Do you mind sharing the contact details of the curator of the Metz museum?"

Rachele took out the folder with all her notes regarding Cividali's young baker, but she could not find Alain de Lothringen's contact details.

"I have to look for the curator's address. I will leave it with the receptionist by the end of tomorrow's working day."

～

Two days later, Rachele was having coffee with the countess and Lottie Alcan. The two *grand dames* were becoming close friends. Aunt Deborah had specifically invited Rachele to discuss Isaac Alcan's letter and statute of limitation. As usual, that came after the waiter had brought their refreshments. Rachele was ready. She picked up a notebook from her handbag and looked for the correct page.

"The letter was written in 1870. The statute of limitation is thirty years. There is no risk of a valid lawsuit, whatever the starting point."

Lottie had little confidence in her Italian. She always thought she was missing something. Somehow, the countess sensed her friend's unease.

"What do you mean by starting point?"

"Well, the letter was written 80 years ago. Israel Alcan passed away 40 years ago. I do not know when Isaac Alcan died, but I am prepared to guess it was longer than 40 years ago. In other words, 30 years have passed, and the heirs of Ruth Alcan Levy and Samuel Alcan cannot sue the heirs of Israel Alcan for the share they did not get."

She turned to Lottie

"Madame Alcan, you can discuss the letter with whomever you wish. There is no risk of a lawsuit under French law."

Lottie smiled. She still had some lingering doubts.

"Could they ask for their money in other countries? In the early thirties, my father sold the bank to a larger French bank to keep everything else afloat. We don't have the means to right this wrong."

Rachele tried to be as reassuring as possible

"The letter was written when Metz was part of France. It was a contract between two French citizens. I do not see how any other jurisdiction could claim relevance to it, wherever the people involved live now."

Lottie sighed, smiled, and drank her coffee. The conversation moved on to plans to visit Count Contarini. Rachele was trying to figure out how to organise the trip; Count Contarini had invited everybody, including all the children and Anita. Depending on the weather, they were going to have lunch outside. The countess picked up her handbag and stood up. The last word was hers, as usual.

"Well, it will be a very long table. I assume they have a special arrangement with a fishing boat to have enough fish to feed us all."

# Chapter Ten

## May 1950

Anita and Rachele were planning the family holiday in the mountains. A lot of preparation was required to take three adults and six children varying in age from 7 to 21 anywhere. They were busy figuring out how much luggage they would take for two weeks in a hotel. The phone rang. Diana picked it up; a few minutes later, she appeared in Anita's office, where the transfer to the Dolomites was being planned with military precision.

"Sorry to interrupt; Joshua told me that Master Antonio Bembo surprised thieves in his office early this morning. Bizarrely, they had removed the frame from his version of the young baker. They hit him, ran away with the frame, and left the painting."

Rachele stood up

"Did Joshua tell you whether they informed the police? Do you know how Master Bembo is?"

Diana was about to reply when the phone rang again. This time, Gabriele picked it up. He appeared to tell his wife that Umberto De Antoni wanted to talk to her. Rachele took the call from the kitchen's extension.

"Joshua rang us. Diana took the call. I think Dante Bembo told him. How is Master Bembo?"

"They thoroughly checked him at the hospital today, but they sent him home. They knew what they were doing. The blow knocked him out but only caused minor damage. I do not understand how they knew he had a version of the painting and why they removed the entire frame this time."

Rachele did not know. She suggested they discuss it the following morning in her office. She and Gabriele would be there by eight o'clock as usual. Umberto agreed, and Rachele went back to planning the Dolomite campaign.

The following morning, they waited for coffee until Umberto De Antoni arrived. As usual, Gabriele was there for the social part of the visit, then he left them alone. Rachele took out the notepad marked 'Young baker.'

"There are a few questions that need answers. How did they know Master Bembo had a version of the young baker? What were they hoping to find? This time, they took the entire frame."

Umberto had an idea about the last question

"Someone explained to me that Master Bembo had the smallest version. Maybe they were not hoping to find the letter you found; maybe it is something else, something that could fit on one side of the version in Tron's art gallery and the auction warehouse but could only fit in two sides of the frame of the small one, or the whole frame."

Rachele was now leaning back in her chair, eyes closed, the two index fingers joined and touching her upper lip. The policeman knew it was a clear sign she was thinking.

"You may have a point, but I don't think they know we found the letter. However, I agree that whatever was hidden in the frame of one or the other versions may be too large to fit on one side of the small painting. The fundamental question is, who knew Master Bembo had it?"

Rachele stood up and started pacing the room, another sign that she was trying to figure out the real question.

"Also, Master Bembo's young baker never left Venice. He received it as part of a payment to his father or grandfather. If they knew about that, they might be after something Israel Alcan hid in the frame of one painting before he left Venice."

Umberto had a different theory.

"Based on what Lottie Alcan told us. Israel Alcan only took the small picture. Cividali shipped the other four versions to Metz, so he could not have hidden anything in the frames here in Venice."

Rachele stopped. She had an answer to that.

"We know the paintings were shipped from Cividali's catalogue raisonné or Ludovico Tron's research. I do not remember. Do they know? Whoever they are."

Umberto started taking notes.

"You have a point. As to the first question, I think I need to draw a list of all those who knew that Master Bembo had the small version of the *fornaretto*."

Rachele sounded a bit deflated.

"Have you been to his workshop? Joshua told me it was in his office. A glass structure separates Master Bembo's office from the showroom. Anybody walking into his showroom could have seen the painting; granted, they might not have known that it was not a copy or a poster."

Umberto had to go. They promised to talk again soon or whenever one of them had thought of something. Joshua Schwartz and Dante Bembo showed up about half an hour after he left. Rachele heard Joshua ask the receptionist if she was available; she walked out of her office and told them she was. They join her in the kitchen for coffee.

"Dante, how is your father?"

"Worse for wear, but not too bad, considering what could have happened. Joshua suggested I talk to you to discuss what legal action my family could take. Would you represent us?"

Before Rachele could answer, Joshua said he had just come in to support his friend; he had to go to his office near Treviso. He thanked Rachele for the coffee and left. Rachele and Dante Bembo moved to her office. He sat on the other side of her desk.

"At the moment, there is very little you can do. I know you informed the police. Is your father injured in any way? I struggle to find a reason to add a civil lawsuit to the criminal investigation."

Dante had an answer for that.

"Neither my father nor any of his children is a lawyer. Last night, my father was determined to make sure the police would not give up looking for the thieves. I think it goes beyond the material damage, which is a broken glass door and a picture frame. He thought of looking for a lawyer to retain. I discussed it with Joshua, who recommended you."

Rachele smiled, flattered.

"At the moment, you have no reason to retain me. However, you are a close friend of Joshua, who is family, at least emotionally. Why don't we go through the motion of acquiring you and your family as a client? We charge you a token amount to establish a lawyer-client relationship, and our conversations are privileged. We see how things develop, and we act as and when it is necessary. The firm will not charge you anything more until that moment."

Dante Bembo agreed. Rachele rang the receptionist and asked her to bring the form a new client had to sign. She then called Gabriele. When he came in, she introduced him to Dante Bembo and told him there would be no billing besides the initial token amount until further notice.

Once Dante Bembo left, she opened the notepad that had been on her desk the whole time and wrote 'Why?' and 'Who knew?'. An hour later, she called Umberto De Antoni to inform him that the firm was representing the Bembo family.

The day in the country was a great success. Gabriele and Rachele and their children were perfectly integrated into the Contarini family. They spent the last eighteen months of World War II hidden in plain sight as the Conti family in one house on the estate. The friendship that developed flourished after the war, partly because Mila, Gabriele and Rachele's youngest child, had become a close friend of the Contarinis's grandchild who was just a few months younger. The countess, Elena, and Lottie Alcan had never experienced a meal with the two families together. It was loud, funny and warm. Elena remarked it reminded her of her childhood when her birth family met up with other relatives in the countryside in Rhodes. At the end of the meal, Count Contarini took Lottie to his study to show her his version of the Cividali. Rachele used the time to talk to Count Contarini's sons to explain why they should ensure some level of protection for the Cividali. After all, they could break in for the painting and decide to help themselves to something else. Before leaving, Rachele told Count Contarini an American gentleman called Bill Campbell would call him during the week to discuss borrowing the Cividali for a show he wanted to organise.

Umberto De Antoni loved Venice; he had not dismissed the idea of trying to convince his wife to move from the mainland to the real Venice. In the meantime, he enjoyed taking the vaporetto every morning from Piazzale Roma, where the bus from the mainland left him. It was a sunny spring day, not too hot. Umberto moved to the back of the vaporetto to sit outside. On the way, he noticed a headline in a newspaper, 'Family almost burnt grandpa's inheritance hidden in an old table.' He decided to drop by the law firm at Riva De Biasio on the odd chance Rachele was there. He had something he wanted to discuss. When he got off the vaporetto, he saw Gabriele and Rachele turn into the Riva. They greeted each other, and Umberto asked if Rachele had ten minutes, maybe over coffee. Gabriele went ahead to prepare the coffee while his wife and the Vice-Commissario started talking. By the time they reached the half-landing, Umberto had come to the point.

"What if something else is hidden in one of the frames?"

Rachele stopped and turned toward him

"What do you mean?"

Umberto was eager to share his idea

"Let us assume they know about the letter. Let us also assume they do not know we have it. The letter would have been small enough to fit inside one side of the frame of Mr Bembo's painting, even if it was the smallest version; what if they were looking for something else? Something not hidden by Isaac Alcan."

They had now reached the door of the law firm. They walked in. Rachele felt she had to buy time. She talked to the receptionist and picked up the mail; then she turned to Umberto with doubt written all over her face.

"Like what?"

"I do not know, but when they broke into Master Antonio Bembo's workshop, they took the entire frame, not just the left side. A letter would have fit in the left side of that version, although it is the smallest."

They were now in her office; Gabriele appeared with two cups of coffee and some pastries and left them alone. Rachele still had doubts.

"That painting never left Venice!"

"We know it from the catalogue raisonné and the story passed on to Master Antonio Bembo; they may not know it. Whoever 'they' are."

"What could be hidden in the frame other than a letter?"

Umberto had no answer for that. He just had an idea from a newspaper headline. Sometimes, those intuitions are breakthroughs, sometimes just false dawns.

"I do not know. I just saw a headline that some inheritance hidden in an old table almost went up in flames, and that made me think."

Rachele was considering his hunch.

"I don't think I am yet prepared to dismiss your intuition. Tell you what, I will ask Count Contarini if we can remove the frame of his version of the *fornaretto*. *After* all, it is the only one they have not touched yet. If there is nothing in that frame, we either have to think of something else or write to the museum in Metz and ask them to check the frame of their Cividali. Something may be hidden in plain sight."

Umberto somehow felt better. Rachele had considered his idea. He left her to get on with her day. On his way out, he knocked at Gabriele's door, waved to him, said goodbye to the receptionist, and left.

~

Throughout her day, Rachele kept reflecting on what she discussed with Umberto De Antoni. Mid-afternoon, she decided to talk to Lottie Alcan. She rang the Pesaro De Bonfili household. Tonia told her their guest would be home in the late afternoon. The countess had invited Lottie's niece and her husband for dinner. Rachele told Tonia she would drop by after work. She put down the phone and called the extension of Alex and Franco's office to ask whoever was around if he could come to her office. Five minutes later, Franco appeared.

"Could you check with the Tron gallery and the auction house to see if the broken frames had anything unusual?"

Franco stopped writing on his notepad

"Unusual like what?"

"Umberto had a hunch this morning. Maybe the person, or the people behind the murder and the break-ins, did not know about the letter and were looking for something else hidden in the frame of a painting."

"Like what?"

"If I remember the story correctly, Israel Alcan loved a painting so much that he commissioned five versions of it, one for himself, one for his parents, and one each for his siblings, and a smaller fifth version to take with him to show his family while they were waiting for the bigger ones. He was the only one who stayed in Metz. The family fled to Paris before the Prussian Army could start the siege of Metz. They took the paintings with them. What if they hid something to protect it in case somebody stopped them on their way to Paris?"

Franco was silent, his hands joined, touching his chin. Then he picked up his pen again.

"It could be coins, jewellery, or another document, but why not remove them once they arrived in Paris? What if somebody hid them later?"

He smiled before continuing

"Or what if one of them was a spy, and they had hidden the code in the frame of one version?"

Rachele took the last assumption as a joke. She smiled.

"What are you reading? Jokes apart, we are talking about something that happened 80 years ago. According to Lottie Alcan, her uncle started his art dealership selling the painting; why didn't he remove what was in the frame before he sold it?"

Franco smiled because he had the answer to that.

"Because he did not know there was something hidden in the frame. In the same way, he probably did not know about the letter hidden in Count Contarini's version. Also, that version was the only one with a backdrop. What if Lottie Alcan's grandfather did not hide the letter in the frame before they left Metz but put it between the two backdrops once they were in Paris, but he, or somebody else, hid something else in the frame?"

Rachele kept writing notes

"That could be a possibility, so we are still ruling out the version in the museum in Metz. One of the four versions here in Venice must have the answer. Get in touch with the auction house and the Tron art gallery. "

Franco closed his notepad

"Who do I have to bill for this?"

Rachele was putting the notepad she had been writing on back in her top drawer. She lifted her head.

"Tell Gabriele to keep your time separate. We do not have a specific client for this, but we may end up with three. Depending on how things turn out, it could be Count Contarini, the Bembo family, the Tron family, or myself. I'll deal with Gabriele."

Franco smiled at the last remark. He took the piece of paper where Rachele had written the phone numbers of the Tron Art Gallery and the auction house and left the office.

Rachele was waiting for her aunt at the café where they had their chats twice a month. She did not expect to see Deborah Camerini arrive with Lottie Alcan. The two ladies had become good friends. Lottie had a specific question for Rachele. As usual, they engaged in small talk until the waiter brought their orders. The countess insisted Lottie ordered a taster's plate. Lottie loved the cakes.

"These cakes are amazing."

Rachele simply nodded. She was eating her husband's favourite, a slice of pistachio pie. The countess smiled and put down her fork.

"They come from the kosher patisserie run by Rachele's daughter, Anna. Most of her recipes come from Rachele's family. Rachele is a great baker, and Anna takes after her mother."

Deborah Camerini has spoken with a lot of pride in her voice. Rachele smiled to acknowledge the compliment. The moment Lottie stopped eating, the countess stopped talking, almost passing the conversation to her new friend.

"I was wondering, do you think Count Contarini will let me have the letter once the police have finished with it?"

Rachele was sipping her coffee. The question was straightforward, and answering it allowed her to ask what she wanted to ask.

"You need to ask him. He 'bought' it when he bought the painting. I have another question for you. Could it be possible that your grandfather, uncle, or aunt had hidden something in the frame? Could it be that the letter was put between the backboards of your grandfather's version of the painting once they were in Paris, and they hid something else in the frames before they left?"

The countess adjusted the way she was sitting. Lottie appeared lost in thought for a while. She took a sip of her coffee, buying time.

"I do not know for sure, but thinking back. Ruth and her painting were already in Paris. Master Bembo's painting never left Venice. My grandfather's and my uncle Samuel's were the only two paintings where the frame could hide something. Samuel started his art dealership selling his painting. It is reasonable to think he took out whatever they had hidden in the frame before selling it."

Rachele and the countess were both listening. The countess could not help but comment.

"This is true, and they found nothing in the frames so far. The only one they have not touched is your grandfather's, the one Count Contarini owns."

Rachele had taken out her notepad.

"You both have a point. I need to call Count Contarini to ask him whether he has any problem if we look at the frame of his painting. I must inform Vice-Commissario Umberto De Antoni. He may want to be there when we do it."

Lottie could not place the Vice Commissario. The countess had an easy way to explain who he was:

"The one who looks like a young Gary Cooper."

Rachele had a problem keeping a straight face. Lottie had identified him from Deborah Camerini's description.

Tommaso Tron had agreed to speak to the police about the person who kept looking at the Cividali they had in the shop's window in Piazza San Marco. The conversation was pretty relaxed. Tommaso was no longer a suspect but had asked Alex Modiano to go with him. They agreed that a plainclothes policeman would be at the shop with Tommaso Tron for a couple of weeks until they had a clear description of the person. Alex pointed out that it would probably be better if a plainclothes policeman sat at a table at the nearby café at some point. It would have been a better position to see the face. Umberto did not think he had the budget for two plainclothes policemen. They decided that the one staying inside the shop would move to a table outside once they were sure of the time of the day this person showed up. It was important to see the face. At the moment, they did not have enough material for a sketch artist.

Tommaso kept thinking he should have reacted faster and gone out before that person could walk away. Alex had been trying to calm him down as they returned to Piazza San Marco and the shop. They had just walked into the square from the ark at the end of Merceria Orologio when Tommaso stopped.

"Look at the person leaning on a column, three arches before our shop. I think it is him."

Alex looked at the person wearing a Panama hat and a loose jacket, making it difficult to describe him. He also heard somebody call him. Bill Campbell and his wife were sitting at a café in the square; the stranger was in the perfect position to watch them. Alex waved back and turned to Tommaso.

"He could watch Bill Campbell and his wife, Charlotte Alcan. She is a granddaughter of Israel Alcan and Lottie Alcan's niece. "

Alex failed to reassure Tommaso.

"I still think he is there for me, a shame that we cannot describe his face, given how he wears a hat. "

Alex Modiano thought the man wanted to hide his face. He asked Tommaso Tron to stand outside his shop and wait for him to wave, then he approached the table where Bill and Charlotte were sitting and sat next to Bill, who was facing the Procuratie and therefore could look at the pillars without the need to turn his head. He pointed out Tommaso Tron, but he was telling Bill that somebody was watching them. Alex and Bill waved to Tommaso Tron, who approached them. When he joined them, sitting next to Charlotte, Bill told him he saw the person Alex pointed out but did not know who he might be. He could not see his face.

# Chapter Eleven

## May 1950

Leo and Mario Mendes had developed a strong bond since Mario and his sister, Paola, started living with Gabriele and Rachele. A neighbour saved them from being rounded up with other Venetian Jews in December 1943 and took them to synagogue after the end of the war to see if they could find some survivor of their family. Later, it transpired that their parents had died trying to escape from the place where they took them. The two cousins were only six months apart. They were in the same class and had the same group of friends. That morning, they had an agenda to discuss with Gabriele and Rachele. Mario was getting closer to 18 and wanted to learn to drive. Leo was a bit more sceptical about the need to get a driver's licence; there were no cars in Venice. Still, he was giving his full support to his cousin.

They appeared at breakfast a bit earlier than usual and were all dressed. Anita knew there was something they wanted.

"You are bright and early this morning. You look like Rachele when she has to appear in court. What is the problem?"

Leo and Mario looked at each other, wondering how Anita

knew they wanted to discuss something. Leo had just started with "Aunt Anita…" when Gabriele and Rachele appeared.

"Good morning, parents. Did you sleep well?"

Diana and Anita looked at each other and smiled. Gabriele and Rachele did the same.

"Good morning, children. What can I do for you?"

Mario wondered whether he had something written on his forehead.

"Uncle Gabriele, when can we talk about driver's licence?"

Gabriele, Rachele, Anita, and Diana exchanged smiles. The younger children appeared in the kitchen, kissed their parents and guardians, and sat down for breakfast.

"Your birthday is not far away. We'll discuss it the night before you turn eighteen. Is there a driving school at Piazzale Roma[1]?"

"I have already done my research, Uncle Gabriele. There isn't one. There is one in Mestre[2] near the railway station. I can go there after school. Uncle Roberto told me we can use his car for extra practice on Sundays."

Rachele looked at her watch.

"I have an early meeting, so I'll let you finish this conversation and see you at the office. "

She kissed all the children, said goodbye to Anita, and left. Gabriele closed the subject

"Mario, I am happy you have done your research. I promise we'll discuss it the night before you turn eighteen. Now, if you

______________

1. *Piazzale Roma* is the Venetian end of the road bridge from the mainland. It is the hub between road transport from the mainland and water transport in the lagoon. It is the only place in the old city of Venice reachable by car.
2. Mestre is mainland Venice.

excuse me, I need to check if your aunt has left yet. If she has not, we'll have our morning walk together. I will see you all at lunchtime. Anita, they are all yours."

He smiled, kissed all the children, said something encouraging for their day, and left, hoping to catch up with his wife.

~

Rachele had an early meeting with Umberto De Antoni. Count Contarini would arrive later that day, and she wanted to be sure she had all the information and, therefore, would know which questions to ask. Gabriele caught up with her, so when their friend rang, he opened the door while Rachele sorted out coffee and the pastries Anna's bakery had delivered a few minutes earlier.

Once they were settled in Rachele's office, with notepads near them and the tray put to one side of the small table, they started listing what they did not know and where Count Contarini could help. Umberto started.

"I wonder if there is a way to establish whether somebody put the backboards behind the Contarini's painting before the family fled to Paris or after. If we could establish that, we would also know whether Isaac Alcan thought he would return to Metz or had given up."

That comment surprised Rachele. She looked up at her friend, who knew her well enough to read her question in her face. He had an answer for that.

"Think about it. Isaac Alcan thought transferring the bank to his youngest son would save it from being seized by the Prussian authorities. The provision in the letter we found is a request to give his other children their shares in the bank after his death if he died without going back to Metz. So, why hide it?"

Rachele had an answer to that.

"If he hid the letter before they left Metz, it was a way to stop the Prussian authorities from confiscating the bank because the sale was not real and Isaac Alcan was still the owner; you have a point. Why keep it hidden later? I can understand why Lottie Alcan did not know about it. She is Israel's daughter, but why keep it hidden once they reach Paris? Hidden from whom?"

Umberto had no answer to that.

"I do not think we shall ever know that unless we find letters, which is hardly likely. Europe has had further upheavals between 1870 and 1950. We only have access to the archive of Israel Alcan, which we do not need."

Rachele was not so sure.

"We could ask Lottie to see if the boxes she has inherited show some correspondence between Israel and his siblings. If we follow the other assumption that something else was hidden in one frame, what could it be, and who could have hidden it?"

Umberto was ready for that.

"The version belonging to Israel's sister was already in Paris. The small version never left Venice. It could only be in the version belonging to the parents or the one belonging to Israel's brother Samuel."

"But Lottie told us she knew that Samuel Alcan started his art dealership in Paris selling family heirlooms. He would have removed whatever he hid in the frame before he sold his version of the Cividali. That leaves us again with Count Contarini's version."

Umberto looked at his notes. He took out another notepad and looked for the right page. He found what he was looking for. That brought a smile to his face.

"Except Lottie Alcan showed me a copy of her grandfather's will. Her niece asked her to bring it to Venice. There is no mention of the painting in the inventory. He must have sold it before writing the will."

Rachele was deflated.

"So, asking Count Contarini to remove the frame may be futile, after all."

"Unless somebody else put something in the frame and Isaac Alcan did not know it was there, or somebody hid something after Isaac Alcan died."

Rachele stood up and started walking around the room, a sign she was thinking. Umberto knew her better than to interrupt her silent conversation with herself.

"Let us recap. Isaac Alcan felt he and his eldest son had to leave Metz because they were too involved with the French government. They organised a convoy of carts and carriages and left with faithful members of staff who had agreed to follow them. They hide something, something that would have been dangerous if found by the wrong Army in a roadblock. I assume the paintings were wrapped in blankets to protect them during the journey."

Rachele was moving around the room. Umberto felt he had to say something to remind her he was there.

"In a way, if they hid something in the frame of a painting, it was hidden twice. The blanket was hiding the painting."

Rachele looked at him as if she had forgotten he was in the room. She sat at the table before continuing.

"Why hide the letter? It was only saying that the sale of the bank was not real. The French Army would not have cared. They left a few days before the Prussian Army closed in on Metz. It must have been something small, something precious that a soldier could easily pocket."

Umberto had an idea.

"Given how you describe it, it could only be cash, gold, or jewels."

"This leaves us with two further questions. Why does somebody think they are still there? Who is that somebody?"

Umberto had another idea.

"Unless it was not them who hid it."

Rachele stopped writing on her notepad.

"What do you mean?"

"Follow me. Isaac Alcan and his two other children sold their paintings. At the moment, the only identifiable one is Isaac's. The other two have the same dimensions. Let us assume that somebody who owned one of the paintings hid something in the frame before the Nazis arrived wherever they lived. Based on what I have read, it was not just Jews that fled from the advancing German Army in 1940."

Rachele liked the idea.

"I wonder if we can find out where the Tron art gallery, the auction house, and the art dealer in Sanremo bought their versions of the paintings. It may help us identify the who rather than the what. Still, I will use generic terms when I discuss with Count Contarini why the police want to look at the frame."

"Agreed. I am not sure we have clarified anything, but I am now confident that asking Count Contarini for help is the right move. "

Umberto put his notepads in his briefcase, thanked Rachele for her time, and left the law firm.

Count Contarini arrived a couple of hours after Vice-Commissario De Antoni had left; he had an appointment with Gabriele to ask his opinion about an investment his sons wanted to make but was not so sure. He agreed to spend half an hour with his favourite lawyer before meeting his favourite bookkeeper. Rachele asked him for permission to remove the frame from his Cividali and if he could give her the details of the art dealer in Sanremo. Count Contarini had only one question.

"Why are you asking me? Shouldn't the police ask that question?"

Rachele smiled, thinking of how often she and Umberto had worked together.

"Umberto wanted to try the friendly route first. I must remind you they have enough motive to seek an injunction from the court, but it is better if it stays friendly. If you are concerned, I shall be there as a friend."

The idea of Rachele's presence reassured Count Contarini.

"Maybe we organise an outing with Gabriele as well. Speaking of a visit, when are you sending Mila? My granddaughter is asking for her."

"Tell your granddaughter that Mila will come when the school holidays start."

Two days later, Umberto De Antoni was on his way to meet the countess and Lottie Alcan on his way home. Deborah Camerini had asked Rachele to be there. She had invited her, Gabriele, Roberto Mendes, and his wife to dinner. Rachele had to be there a couple of hours before the others. Umberto De Antoni arrived with the names of those who sold the version of the young baker to Ludovico

Tron and the one who had given it to the auction house for sale.

Lottie Alcan also had news

"My niece has contacted my cousin Jules asking him if he remembered anything his mother told him about the painting. Jules wrote back. I do not read English very well, but Deborah can."

She handed over the letter to her host. The countess translated it as she read:

"Jules is saying that he only remembers a black-and-white print. His grandmother sold the painting through her uncle's gallery when he and his brother were young. He is sure she did not know about the letter; she thought Israel had bought back the bank after the Prussian seized it because of the rumour their father, Isaac Alcan, had used the bank's capital to fund a battalion of the French Army."

Once Deborah had finished reading, Lottie added.

"It is interesting that my aunt did not know about the deal between my father and my grandfather."

Rachele had two comments.

"I wonder why Isaac told his daughter and eldest son that story. We shall never know why he did not want to tell his two older children about the letter and the deal. That tells me two things. He hid the letter between the two backdrops of the painting after they left Metz. Isaac Alcan forgot about it by the time he sold the painting. So, maybe Umberto, you were right. Somebody else hid something in the frames after all."

The countess added.

"They took out the left side of the frame of the two paintings of the same size, the one sold by Ruth Alcan Levy and the one sold by Samuel Alcan. They did not know which of the

Cividali's versions had something hidden in the frame. It must be in Count Contarini's."

Umberto De Antoni was one step ahead of the countess.

"We have already asked Count Contarini when we can look at his version's frame."

Rachele smiled. This time, the countess did not manage the last word.

Tommaso Tron and Bill Campbell were walking under the arches of the Procuratie in Piazza San Marco. Bill was sharing his idea of organising a special exhibition of the five versions of the Cividali. He had contacted the Metz Museum curator to see if he could lend their version of the Cividali for a few months. He wondered if the Tron family would display their version with a notice 'available for sale' through the art gallery. Tommaso loved the idea and asked if he could write the catalogue. Suddenly, he stopped talking.

"Bill, look ahead. Somebody is looking at the Cividali in the window of our shop. I wonder if the policeman who is inside with my mother has noticed."

Bill looked ahead. He saw somebody come out of the shop, probably the policeman. The mysterious individual noticed it and started walking fast in their direction. Bill excused himself. He had an idea, started walking faster, and aimed at the stranger. They collided, and the stranger fell. Bill apologised and helped him up. He picked up the hat and gave it back to him. The plainclothes policeman had stopped at a reasonable distance, smiling. He had figured out what Bill was up to. When they crossed paths, Bill simply said.

"I had a good look at his face. I can describe it to a sketch artist."

The policeman smiled and continued following the mysterious man.

When Bill and Tommaso entered the Tron shop, Bill asked to use the phone to call the police. He asked to speak to Vice-Commissario Umberto de Antoni. They put him through to his office.

"I have seen the face of the mysterious man who stops every day to admire the Cividali. I can describe it to a sketch artist. Let me know when you want me to come. By the way, I think your plainclothes agent is following him. "

Lottie Alcan sat at a café along the Strada Nova with Charlotte and her husband, Bill. He was discussing how he had the idea of showing all five versions of the young baker at Ca Pesaro and the story of how they came about. A story that Lottie had heard many times from her father. Four of the five versions were already in Venice or near Venice. He had written to Alain de Lothringen at the Museum in Metz to see if they would lend their version to Ca Pesaro for three months. Lottie was interested. He hoped that his wife's aunt would be more excited.

"I do not know your plans, but you could return to Venice when the show opens. "

Lottie was less responsive than he expected.

"How long do you think it will take?"

"It all depends on the Museum in Metz. They are the ones that need to go through a long process before they can lend anything out. The Trons and the auction house would have no problem if we put a notice with their paintings stating they are for sale. The show dedicated to Cividali would enhance their value. Tommaso Tron volunteered to write the catalogue. He would like to talk to you to build a profile of Israel Alcan."

Lottie started showing some interest. She put down her drink and was lost in thought for a few minutes, remembering her father.

"I assume you already contacted Ca Pesaro."

"A three-month slot is coming up in the autumn, or we must wait a year. It all depends on how quickly the Metz Museum can move."

Bill looked at his watch and sat more upright.

"I have an appointment with Vice-Commissario De Antoni and a sketch artist in half an hour. I am the only one who saw the face of a mysterious man who spends about fifteen minutes every day looking at the Cividali in the window of the Tron shop in Piazza San Marco."

Lottie was curious. Charlotte had heard the description at least twice.

"Aunt Lottie, I'll tell you later. We do not want to delay Bill."

Bill left to go to the police. Once he was out of earshot, Charlotte shared the description with her aunt. Then she added,

"I did not tell Bill, but he could have described my father's face when he was in his mid-twenties."

Lottie's reaction was interesting

"I wonder if it is a coincidence. Everybody said that my brother looked like his uncle Samuel. I wonder if the mysterious person is a relative."

Charlotte was intrigued.

"But if he is, he can only be a grandchild or a great-grandchild. He would not have seen the painting."

"Yes, but he could have heard stories about it. "

Charlotte had a meeting with a real estate agent. If they were to spend a year in Venice, she wanted to rent a proper home, not the studio they were renting. Her aunt had agreed to go with her. The two women paid and left the café.

# Chapter Twelve

## May 1950

**B**oth Rachele and Anita were past fifty. Rachele and Gabriele had a check-up with their doctor once a year. She always insisted that Anita had one, too. Her housekeeper was her closest friend and confidante. She was also the hub around which the whole Mendes household rotated. Rachele and Gabriele thought it would make a lot of common sense if she had the same medical checks they had. That was why Rachele worked at a contract from her study at home when her younger children were doing their homework.

The document required her full concentration, and she could not help but dedicate only half of her focus to her work. She was listening to the sounds coming from her home, alert to any possible disruption from homework. She picked up a letter from the pile of documents she had brought home from the office the previous evening. The Sanremo art dealer who sold the painting to Count Contarini had written a letter clarifying the origin of the painting. He had bought it from the Vernier family. They had bought it from Maurice Alcan in 1938. Maurice claimed it was a gift from his great-grandfather, who received it from his son Israel, who had bought it from the painter himself. He also added that Count Contarini should have a letter stating the provenance of the painting, including his purchase.

She had a timeline for the Contarini version. If what the Vernier family told the art dealer was true, Maurice Alcan, a cousin of Lottie Alcan, had sold the painting in 1938. Since it was not in Isaac Alcan's will, he probably donated it to his son Samuel before his death. Samuel, the art dealer, kept it. Could he have found out about the letter? Did he have any other reason to hide something in the frame? The sale to the Vernier family happened in 1938, so by the time World War II started, the Alcan family did not own it anymore. What if the Vernier family had any reason to hide anything? Could they have misstated the year they bought the painting? She put the letter and the notepad page with her note in the 'Young Baker' folder.

Suddenly, loud music was coming from Leo and Mario's room. She went to check whether they had finished their homework.

Only Vice-Commissario Umberto De Antoni, Rachele, and Gabriele travelled to the Contarini estate to check what was in the frame of his version of the Cividali; Gabriele did not have to be there but was tagging along to check the tax return that the count's son was preparing. It was a pleasant spring day. Gabriele would have preferred to travel by train. He did not like cars very much, but Umberto was on official police business, so they were travelling to Stra in a police car. Stra was also the town where Umberto De Antoni had served as a police inspector during the final years of the war and met Rachele; he was a member of the resistance, and so was she. When the car passed through the town's main square, the café owner recognised Rachele and waved. Gabriele noticed it.

"I give you half an hour, and the whole town will know we drove to Count Contarini's in a police car. "

Umberto smiled.

"I shall ask to call Guido Orlando and tell him to have a coffee to manage the rumours."

Rachele had a better idea.

"Do that, but we also ask Count Contarini to send somebody he trusts to have a cup of coffee, and then on our way back to Venice, we drop and see Guido. After all, I was his secretary when we were hiding here."

Gabriele did not like remembering when they had to hide, although they had become close friends with those who helped them. The town also had some good memories.

"Rina von Moden Conti was Guido's secretary."

Rina von Moden Conti was Rachele's 'real fake identity' between November 1943 and the end of April 1945, when the Allied army reached Stra. She laughed and said,

"Of Course, Mr Gino Conti,"

Gino Conti was the name Gabriele used when they were in Stra. Umberto laughed.

"Guido Orlando and I are the only ones who used our names."

Rachele had the last word.

"Yes, but we referred to you as the Prince, after Prince Umberto, the heir to the throne."

By then, the car had reached the gate to the Contarini villa. Gabriele remarked they had gone back to leaving it open during the day. The police car stopped at the end of the drive. Count Contarini was already outside to welcome them. Somebody had telephoned from the town.

After refreshments, the driver went back to waiting by the car, and Umberto, Rachele, and the count moved to the study with the police photographer who had travelled with them. Gabriele went looking for the count's son to discuss the tax return. The most trusted farmer of the estate was waiting in the study with the tools to remove the frame that had already lost its backboards. The photographer took a few photographs of the framed picture, just in case they had to establish the connection between the painting and the frame.

Once the farmer removed the frame, Count Contarini remarked that the painting almost looked better without the heavy frame. Umberto De Antoni asked the photographers to take photos of the frame from all angles. While the photographer was busy, Umberto asked if he could call Guido Orlando. He explained to the lawyer why they were in Stra and asked him to get something in the café and manage the wild rumours. They would drop in on the way back and go to the café together.

Once the photographer had finished, Umberto started feeling the frame for any hinges, openings, or hollowness. When he reached the left side of the frame, it was hollow. The left side could be removed and put back, but somebody in the past had nailed it in position; they removed the nails and pulled it out from the rest of the frame. An envelope and a small bag appeared. The envelope had a letter from an antique dealer in Paris who had agreed to backdate a sale to 1938. When they opened the bag, they saw several precious stones or, at least, they looked like precious stones.

They all were flabbergasted. Count Contarini had his mouth wide opened looked at Umberto first and then Rachele. After a few minutes of silence, he managed only,

"A few small rubies, two small emeralds, and quite a few diamonds."

Umberto couldn't stop looking at the stones on the desk.

"I don't think they are coloured glass."

Rachele was the first to recover the ability to speak complete sentences.

"This painting contained the secret of two fictitious sales. The people who organised this had to know about the sale of the bank and decided to have a fictitious sale of their own. Umberto, we need to have an inventory of what we found. Technically, it belongs to Count Contarini. Whoever sold the painting to the art gallery in Sanremo used the Vernier name. I wonder if there is a Vernier family somewhere."

Something did not add up. Umberto was not convinced they had the whole story.

"Let me see if I got this right. Isaac Alcan gave this painting to his grandson Raphael before his death; either he or his son Maurice orchestrated a fictitious sale to the Vernier family, who could be the name they used to escape capture. Somebody with the last name Vernier sold the painting to an art dealer in Sanremo. What happened to the person who put the bag inside the frame? The person, or persons, we are looking for, did not know that the small treasure was hidden in this version because they vandalised all the others."

Rachele interrupted him.

"Let us not forget he killed one person. The irony is that, at the moment, Count Contarini is the legal owner of the small treasure."

Upon hearing his name, Count Contarini acted as if they had caught him daydreaming.

"I think those precious stones morally belong to the Alcan family."

Rachele was there as his lawyer.

"They are yours, but which bit of the Alcan family? The one we know did not put them there."

Count Contarini was not convinced.

"Legally, they may be mine, but morally they are not. Rachele, please try to figure out who put them there. Meanwhile, I think of what to do if you don't find out. "

Umberto De Antoni was not sure they should discuss the details of what they found with Charlotte Alcan, her husband, and her aunt until they identified the person looking at the Cividali in the window of the Tron shop in Piazza San Marco. He did not know whether it was a suspect. At the moment, it was the only clue he had.

Rachele did not miss her husband's pensive mood on the journey back. Gabriele was not very talkative during dinner. She noticed Anna and Diana kept looking at each other, then looking at their father, trying to engage him in conversation and only getting a few words out of him. After dinner, she suggested a walk.

Once they were out, they made their way to the Giudecca Canal. They would walk along the Venice Gabriele loved. The one with narrow canals and 'normal' buildings. The Venice that surprises you when you turn a corner. Gabriele knew the history of Venice very well and pointed out a detail about a building and the story behind it. Rachele was waiting for him to bring up what had been bothering him. They reached the Giudecca Canal, and Rachele could sense that her husband had started to relax. Almost halfway through the Fondamenta, Gabriele took a deep breath, stopped, and looked at his wife.

"I am sorry. I don't like talking about the war. Earlier today, it brought back memories I'd rather kept buried."

Rachele tightened her grip on her husband's arm, hoping he would take it as the sign of support it was meant to be.

"I figured it out. We've made it. We were lucky and went back to our home. We survived."

Gabriele asked her if she wanted a drink or something. She took it as a delaying tactic and declined; she did not want to stop the flow. Gabriele was silent for a few minutes.

"Yes, we survived. We also lost family members, but that is not what made me sulk for ours. Do you know what it means to be constantly worried because you know your wife, your eldest daughter, and your youngest brother are in the resistance? If you got caught, you could have been arrested, shot, or deported. If that happened, there was nothing I could have done!"

"You were making sure we stayed ourselves. Emma and I had double fake identities. In our authentic false papers, we were part of the Conti family and had another name in the resistance. Actually, Emma had another name; I had a nickname. Anyway, you made sure we stayed ourselves."

Somehow, the idea of his wife having another nickname amused Gabriele, who smiled for the first time since lunch.

"You mean they were not calling you General Radetzky?"

"They called me 'the stylish biker' because they claimed I looked stylish even when riding my bicycle."

They had reached the end of the Fondamenta.

"You are always stylish. Let's walk to Palazzo Barbarigo, take a vaporetto to San Stae, then go home."

Rachele agreed. Venice had worked its magic once again. Walking together never failed to improve their mood.

When they got home, Diana and Anita were the only ones awake. It was a school night, and Anna had to wake up at an unearthly hour to go to her bakery. They looked at Rachele, who smiled to reassure them. Gabriele said he was tired and would go to bed. Rachele needed a hot drink and joined Anita and Diana in the kitchen.

Umberto and Rachele had agreed to share that they found the papers but would not say anything about the precious stones yet. They had organised to meet with Lottie Alcan at the law firm in the late afternoon on the day following their discovery. Lottie arrived early. Countess Deborah was with her. Rachele was not surprised to see her, but the rest of the firm was; her unexpected arrival had everybody wondering whether they had passed the inspection. Franco Cantoni showed the two ladies in the meeting room overlooking the Grand Canal and told them that Rachele was with a client, but the receptionist had informed her they were there. Twenty minutes later, Rachele showed up with her notepads. She put them down on the coffee table, apologised that they had to wait for her, and started small talk, waiting for Vice-Commissario Umberto De Antoni. Her "small talk" was targeted. She wanted to understand more about the Alcan extended family. How many people Lottie knew, how many she knew of, and how many there were. It turned out that Lottie never met her cousin Raphael's children, but she thought there were three. Jules Levy had mentioned only Maurice Alcan.

Rachele was trying to sound as casual as possible, but she hoped she would remember to draw the family tree of Isaac Alcan's descendants based on the information she had. It may be helpful later. She had arranged with the receptionist that when the Vice-Commissario arrived, she should let her know in a way that her two visitors could not guess. She wanted a word with him in private.

The receptionist came in with a note, adding that it was urgent. Rachele showed she was reading the note, stood up, and got ready to leave the room.

"I apologise, but I have to see to this. I will be back in less than ten minutes."

Lottie moved to the window overlooking the Grand Canal.

"Don't worry, take your time. I can look at the boats in the Grand Canal for hours. "

The Countess picked up the tray with the refreshment.

"Don't worry, I will look after our guest."

The receptionist intercepted the tray, asking the two visitors what they would like.

Rachele took her notepad; Umberto was waiting for her in her office. Rachele spoke as she updated her notes.

"Maurice Alcan is one of the three children of Raphael Alcan. We need to establish who the others are. Also, I do not want them to think I came out to talk to you."

Umberto interrupted her.

"Why? It is exactly what you did."

"Yes, but they should not know. If you do not want to share much of what you found at Count Contarini's, they must tell us more than what we plan to share. The receptionist will now take you to the meeting room, and I'll follow in ten minutes and greet you as if I had just seen you."

Umberto left Rachele's office, and Rachele took the opportunity to ask Alex Modiano to do some research for another case and then went back to the meeting room. As she walked in, she apologised for being detained and greeted Umberto as if she had not seen him a few minutes earlier.

Umberto had already taken out the sketch, and Lottie Alcan was looking at it.

"I know that my younger brother is in the States. I was with Charlotte when she called him. This face looks a lot like him. He is family, but I am not sure I ever met him. Sorry, I cannot help more."

Umberto was disappointed he could not get a name, but maybe he could get an agent to look in the hotels' daily reports to see if they had a guest called Alcan or Vernier. He wanted to check if he could get more information.

"Can you help us with your family tree? It would be helpful to put a name to that face."

Lottie looked sad and frustrated

"I do anything I can, but I know very little about my uncle and aunt and even less about their grandchildren, but I could ask Jules. Based on what Bill told me, I think the person may be a grandchild of one of my cousins, and I do not know how many there are."

Diana and Charlotte were having one of their language lessons. This time, the conversation was in Italian. Charlotte wanted to share Bill's news.

"Bill received a letter from the curator of the Metz Museum who said they agreed to lend the version they had of the young baker by Cividali. He also suggested they have the exhibition in Metz after the one in Venice closes. The decision has not yet been formalised, but the curator is coming to Venice. He has asked Bill to organise visits to the other versions."

Diana corrected a couple of grammar mistakes before continuing

"I think that my mother was already in touch with the curator when she was trying to establish if a family friend had unwittingly bought a painted looted by the Nazis from a museum."

Diana had learned from her mother to share the minimum amount of information in a casual conversation. Charlotte had more news to share.

"We found a place to rent for a year. It is near you, in Ruga Bella. We shall move at the beginning of June. I am looking forward to living in a home again. As much as I love being in Venice, I have had enough of living in one room, even a large one."

Diana was happy for her friends. Her face lit up.

"You will be round the corner from us, across a bridge. Once you move in, ask Anita where the best shops are, or go shopping with her one morning."

Diana was her mother's daughter. She had taken a mental note that the curator of the Metz museum would arrive soon; she would drop by the law firm later to tell her mother.

# Chapter Thirteen

May-June 1950

They had not identified the person who regularly stopped to look at the version of Cividali's young baker in the window of Tron's shop in Piazza San Marco. Umberto De Antoni had three plainclothes men in and around the shop, ready to move. Lottie Alcan said she could not identify the man, but he looked like family. In the end, Isabella Tron had the honour of getting the whole story with no drama. She was outside the shop talking to somebody working in another shop nearby when the stranger appeared. When he stopped, Isabella acted as if she had nothing to do with the Tron's shop.

"It is a captivating painting, isn't it? I love how the painter used light to make you look at the young man first."

The stranger did not expect somebody to talk to him. His Italian was tentative.

"I have always loved it. We had a larger copy in our living room when I was a child. I had forgotten some details."

Isabella noticed that the plainclothes policeman inside the shop was ready to move. She thought she would seize the moment.

"Just look at the contrast between the young baker, who is only wearing trousers, and the elaborate, elegant, and expensive outfit of the man talking to him. By the way, I am Isabella."

She extended her hand, offering him the opportunity for a handshake. He took it and shook her hand.

"Nice to meet you. I am Pierre Alcan. My Italian is not good enough to understand everything you said. Do you speak French or English?"

Isabella repeated what she had just said in English. Pierre replied in English,

"I also love the details of the children playing. That was the thing I remembered most. My parents sold the painting when I was five, but I remember it very well. I only thought it was bigger."

He then switched to Italian.

"Do you mind if I try to speak to you in Italian? I want to improve my Italian. "

Isabella did not mind.

Tommaso Tron and the plainclothes policeman came out of the shop. Pierre Alcan was talking to Isabella and looking at the painting. The policeman had agreed to let Tommaso speak and only intervene if the stranger started moving away from the shop. He started in English because he had overheard the end of Pierre and Isabella's conversation in English.

"That is because your parents probably had the bigger version. The buyer, Israel Alcan, commissioned Cividali to paint five versions of the same scene."

Now it was Tommaso's turn to introduce himself

"By the way, I am Tommaso Tron. May I ask you why you have been coming almost every day to look at the painting?"

"Was I that obvious? I always dreamt of coming to Venice. I wanted to see if I could find the canal with the bridge where the two children played. When I was a child, I once dreamt I was playing with them. My parents sold the larger version of this painting when I was five. A lot has happened since then, but I still remember the dream. When we were hiding from the Nazis, I dreamt of being in Venice, sitting on the steps of that bridge talking to the two children in the painting."

Isabella and Tommaso exchanged looks. Tommaso translated for the benefit of the plainclothes policeman. They had noticed that the two other plainclothes policemen were walking towards them. In the meantime, Pierre repeated his request to speak Italian to him. Tommaso tried to control his voice.

"When did you arrive in Venice?"

"I arrived about ten days ago; walking around Piazza San Marco was the first thing I did. I noticed the painting, and since then, I have been trying to see if I can find the bridge. I come here to check it every day to see if I found the spot."

Tommaso smiled

"I am afraid this is a made-up scene. The canal would have to be where the Hotel Baglioni is to have that view of the Punta della Dogana."

The plainclothes policeman intervened

"I wonder if you can help us. If you are a member of the Alcan family, we would like to talk to you. There have been incidents around three of the five versions of the painting. The fourth is in the area but is in a private home, and the fifth is in a museum in France. As far as we know, they are intact."

Pierre did not expect to hear that. He became more nervous. The others could tell because his French accent became stronger.

"I am sorry to hear that. Israel Alcan, the person who commissioned the five paintings, was my father's great-uncle, his grandfather's younger brother. I'll help in any way I can."

Tommaso replied

"The police would like to talk to you. I'll pass on your details if you tell me where they can reach you. Please come inside the shop where I have pen and paper."

By then, the other two policemen had reached them. Tommaso went back into the shop with the agent who was inside with him before they came out to talk to Pierre. Isabella stayed outside. She had not shared with Pierre that she was Tommaso's sister. The other two plainclothes agents remained outside the door, ready to stop Pierre if he was trying to leave in a hurry.

Once Pierre had left, followed by two agents, Tommaso rang Vice Commissario Umberto De Antoni, who sent the agent that was with Tommaso to the hotel mentioned by Pierre to check and leave him a message to contact the police the following day. The policeman had to tell the concierge that Pierre was an important witness. Everything checked. Pierre arrived at the hotel early to change for La Fenice Opera House. He tried to see if Umberto was still in the office. He was, and they agreed to meet the following morning.

Count Contarini had instructed the law firm to find out as much as possible about the Alcan family to see if they could find the original owner of the diamonds, rubies, and emeralds they found in the frame of his young baker.

Charlotte and Lottie Alcan had spent two hours with Alex Modiano, but the descendants of Samuel Alcan were still a mystery. They knew there was a son, Raphael, who had a son, Maurice, but they did not know whether he had siblings or children. Alex was contemplating the question mark in the family tree of the descendants of Isaac Alcan when Rachele walked into their room.

"Umberto De Antoni rang. He has just spoken to Pierre Alcan, the son of Maurice Alcan. He is in Venice. If you want to talk to him, call Umberto in the next half hour to arrange a meeting. He is still there."

∽

Pierre Alcan and Lottie Alcan were at the law firm. Pierre and Lottie met for the first time the previous afternoon, a day after Umberto De Antoni had told him everything that had happened to the other versions of Cividali's young baker. Alex walked into the meeting room with his notepad, followed by the receptionist with a tray of pastries. The receptionist took their order for drinks and left them.

Umberto and Rachele had briefed Alex.

"We asked you to come because our client, Count Contarini, instructed us to find the origin of what we discovered hidden in the frame of his version of the painting you both know very well. We think we need to find as much as we can about your family in order to find answers for our client."

Pierre and Lottie looked at each other. Lottie was the first one to react.

"You mean there was something beyond the letter found between the two backboards?"

Pierre did not know what his cousin was talking about. His face betrayed a mixture of confusion and curiosity. Alex continued.

"The police asked Count Contarini's permission to see if they could remove the frame of the painting. They knew that somebody had vandalised the other three versions in Venice

125

and found nothing. What they were looking for must have been inside the frame of one of the other two paintings. Count Contarini's was the obvious first choice. The other one is in Metz."

Alex paused for effect. He noticed that Lottie's and Pierre's facial expressions had changed. They were curious. He thought their reaction was genuine, and neither knew what was inside the frame.

"When they took out the left side of the frame, they found a handwritten note stating that Maurice Alcan had sold the painting to the Vernier family in 1938, and we also found a fortune in precious stones. Although Count Contarini is the legal owner of the diamonds, rubies, and emeralds, he asked us to find out who hid them in the frame. He would like to return them to their legitimate owner."

Pierre interrupted him

"I was thirteen in 1938. I remember my father sold the painting after my fifth birthday. My mother has a photograph of me blowing five candles with the painting in the background. My fifth birthday was February 1930. Why did it say 1938? Something does not add up."

Alex started taking notes, then he added,

"Are you sure? Does the name Vernier mean anything to you?"

"Pierre Vernier was my father's business partner. In 1940, he arranged false papers for all of us, replacing Alcan with Vernier. We escaped from Paris before the German army arrived and moved to Carcassonne, where Pierre Vernier had found a home for us. We lived there until the end of the war; I was Pierre Vernier, and my father was Maurice Vernier."

Alex was more and more intrigued. Maurice Vernier sold the

painting to the art gallery in Sanremo, where Count Contarini bought it.

"As far as you know, was there a Maurice Vernier?"

"Maurice Vernier was my pretend cousin, Pierre Vernier's son. He is older than I am, about five years."

Alex kept writing. The Vernier family was more and more interesting.

"By any chance, do you remember who bought the painting in 1930? Could you possibly find out?"

Pierre looked at Lottie.

"Don't look at me. I only had a vague idea that my cousin existed. I can't help."

After his cousin's comment, he was silent for a while, clearly thinking.

"I could ask my mother. My father passed away two years ago. I could also ask my aunt just in case she might remember."

It was Alex's turn to be confused.

"Do you mind calling them from our offices? That would be the easiest way to pay for the calls. Something does not add up. We have a copy of the receipt for payment to Maurice Vernier for the sale of Cividali's painting in 1950. We also have a letter stating that Maurice Alcan sold the painting to the Vernier family in 1938. Your recollection dates the sale of the painting to 1930, but we do not know who bought it. The letter we found inside the frame makes us think somebody used it as a hiding place sometimes during World War II. Based on that, we think whoever sold it in 1950 did not know they were there."

Lottie summarised it better

"Still, you do not know who bought the painting and who sold it. Until you have answers, you do not know who hid diamonds, rubies, and emeralds in the frame."

Pierre had been quiet for a while. He reached for the bottle of water, poured himself some, drank it, and sat back down.

"I wonder if my mother has some answers. I would like to know why the painting I thought they sold in 1930 was sold by my father in 1938 to the family of his business partner. If the paper found in the frame represents a fictitious sale, why was my father's name in it?"

Alex felt the need to keep control of the meeting

"Count Contarini wants to know who hid the precious stone in the frame and whether the rightful owner sold the painting to the art dealer who sold it to him. He bought it in good faith, but he feels that the precious stones do not belong to him, regardless of the legal position; he also hates the idea of buying a painting that was not sold by the legitimate owner. I asked you to come here to determine what might happen."

Once again, Lottie was very concise.

"We already discussed the family I know. I am afraid I cannot help you with Raphael's family. I only knew he existed. I only met Daniel or David Klein, who claimed to be his grandsons."

Pierre lit up

"When did you meet my cousin? By the way, did you meet Daniel or David? David Klein is Daniel's cousin on his father's side."

"He came to see me a while ago. Alex, I can only help you with very generic information. By the way, Pierre, Daniel (or David) Klein looks very much like you."

Alex turned to Pierre

"How much do you know about the rest of your grandfather's descendants?"

Pierre stood up and started pacing the room

"Daniel Klein is my aunt's son. He is more or less my age. I used to see my cousins a lot when we were children. We lost touch when we hid in Carcassonne. We met again in 1946. They were in Nice during the war. I know nothing of my uncle Bernard. He moved to Morocco when I was three. My youngest uncle is the hero in the family. He was thirty when the war started. I am not sure I remember all the details, but he was an agent for the Free French in Paris and was involved in the uprising against the Germans in 1944. He lives in Paris, and I think he has a two-year-old son."

Alex was taking notes, trying to be accurate. He tried to draw some conclusions. His aunt and boss wanted to see action points at the end of each meeting.

"Pierre, do you mind asking your mother if she knows anything about the sale of the painting to a member of the Vernier family in 1938? That would help us."

"Madame Alcan, are you in touch with Jules Levy? Can you find out if he knows anything about your cousin Bernard Alcan? You said he tried to contact the whole extended family after the war to see who was still alive. Also, can you ask him more about his children? Especially his daughter, who played a role in WWII nobody talks about."

That closed the meeting, and Alex thanked them for their cooperation. On their way out, they stopped by the receptionist.

"Please let Madame Alcan and Pierre know when they can come to make phone calls from the office. They need to find out information relevant to a case. We can charge the cost of the calls to Count Contarini."

Alex left Pierre and Lottie with the receptionist and went looking for his aunt. He did not have the answers she was hoping for. He had more questions.

Rachele listened to Alex and read his notes. She leant back in her chair, her eyes closed, the tips of her index fingers touching her lips. Alex recognised her thinking pose. After a few minutes of silence, she opened her eyes.

"Bernard Alcan is an interesting figure. He is the only one nobody can locate. We need to find out what happened to the painting after February 1930 and the sale to the Vernier family in 1938, if it happened. The most important thing would be to find the Maurice Vernier who sold the painting to the art dealer in Sanremo, who sold it to Count Contarini. Let me ask our client if he agrees to fund a trip to Sanremo."

Lottie Alcan was enjoying her stay in Venice. Being a guest of a Venetian household gave her the chance to experience the city as if she lived there. She sat inside in the vaporetto. She smiled when she noticed her cousin Pierre standing outside, looking at the Grand Canal. They were going to the law firm and alighted at Riva De Biasio stop. Pierre had found a contact number for Maurice Vernier, the son of his father's best friend. He had arranged to call him to ask questions. Lottie was there to interpret; Pierre's Italian was not good enough.

The receptionist took them to the meeting room overlooking the back, a much quieter place. Alex, Rachele, and Umberto De Antoni joined them, and Pierre called Maurice Vernier and explained the reason for the call. During the social side of the conversation, the receptionist returned with refreshments. Rachele had the first question:

"Can you ask him if he remembers the painting?"

Pierre asked. Lottie helped him with the translation. Maurice remembered seeing the painting in the Alcan household. He also added that his father was in the room to help.

Lottie told them that Pierre asked if they remembered when his parents sold the painting. The answer surprised everybody, Pierre included. He tried to translate it with the help of his cousin.

"Pierre Vernier told his son that my parents never sold the painting. My uncle Bernard came back from Morocco and asked for it. He said it was compensation for being cut off from my grandfather's will. How could he know about the will? My grandfather died five years after the painting disappeared, and Bernard was not mentioned in his will. I remember the grandchildren inherited money, and my aunt Chantal said we got Bernard's share of the cash."

Alex was taking notes, and Rachele was looking at a page in the notepad, creating a new circle, following her tried and tested method. Umberto was the first to say what was on everybody's mind.

"So, the painting was not sold in 1930. Bernard Alcan took it. Can you ask Maurice Vernier if his family ever had the painting? Does his father remember ever meeting Bernard Alcan?"

Pierre seemed to be lost in translation. Lottie took over. She introduced herself and explained that her Italian was better than Pierre's, and she had fewer problems understanding what the Vice-Commissario was asking. The answer made Rachele drop her pen and look at her diagram in frustration.

"Monsieur Vernier claims he never had the painting. He does not know what happened after Bernard took it in 1930. Maurice Alcan was annoyed and sad when that happened. He never mentioned the painting again."

Rachele recovered from her frustration.

"Did anybody outside the immediate family circle know that Pierre Vernier was a business partner of Maurice Alcan? Also, could they know that the Vernier family had helped the Alcan family during World War II?"

Lottie translated, after a few minutes, a more intriguing answer came back

"Bernard Alcan must have known that my father and Maurice Alcan were business partners. They were also very close friends from a very young age; I am named after Maurice Alcan, and Pierre is named after my father. I do not know who could know that the Alcan family used our last name to protect themselves during the Nazi occupation."

Maurice Vernier stopped for a minute, talking to his father, then continued.

"My father is sure he and Maurice never told anybody. We never discussed it, even after the end of the war. By the way, my father also said that he never met Bernard Alcan."

Rachele asked what was on everybody's mind:

"We have a record of a Maurice Vernier selling the painting to an art dealer in Sanremo, Italy. Do you have any idea who sold it?"

Alex stopped taking notes. He expected the answer; the others were not surprised either.

"I remember the painting from visiting the home of the Alcan before 1930. I have never seen it since; I do not know any art dealer in Sanremo. If it helps you, I can tell you where I was when the alleged Maurice Vernier sold the painting to the art dealer in Sanremo."

Umberto felt he had to talk as the person in charge of investigating one murder and two break-ins.

"That would be very important. Can we call you back next week at the same time? That will give us time to ask the art dealer in Sanremo further questions."

Maurice Vernier said that he would make a point of being available next week. He then spent a few minutes talking to Pierre, and the conversation ended.

Rachele looked at her diagram, shaking her head.

"So, who is the Maurice Vernier who sold the painting?"

Alex had a crazy idea, which he thought Lottie or Pierre could validate.

"Follow me for a second. Bernard Alcan had Isaac Alcan's version of Cividali's young baker. He knew that Paul Vernier was his brother's closest friend. He needed to sort out the provenance of the painting. Therefore, he created a letter stating it was sold to the Vernier family. He then took the letter to the art dealer in Sanremo, introducing himself as Maurice Vernier."

Lottie had the last word.

"That still leaves the precious stones hidden in the frame without an explanation. Who hid the precious stones in the frame if Bernard Alcan sold the painting?"

Everybody else in the room looked at her with a facial expression that betrayed the question mark in their minds. Finding out would be the key to figuring out who owned them.

# Chapter Fourteen

## June 1950

Lottie Alcan had convinced her hostess, Countess Deborah Pesaro De Bonfili, to walk around Venice with her early in the morning. The countess needed the exercise; she also needed her sleep. Her habit of never leaving her room without make-up was not conducive to lingering in bed. She knew her routine. She did not have to be awake for that. The two ladies had taken to walk around part of Venice off the tourist tracks, stop for a coffee, and maybe take a vaporetto home, depending on where they were. The countess' face was made up, her trademark bob perfectly combed, and comfortable clothes were her only concession to the early hour, not her idea of going out, but still elegant according to most people's standards. Lottie was more utilitarian. She was neat and tidy, but a scarf covered her hair, and a pair of oversized sunglasses hid a face with no make-up. The two women had become friends and teased each other over their appearances. That morning, Deborah showed her friend the back of the lagoon. They had ended their walk at the Fondamenta Nove for their morning coffee.

They were sitting down at a café close to the vaporetto stop. It was a very clear morning. You could see the snow-capped mountains of the Alps, a sight more common in the winter than in early June. The countess was pointing them out to her guest when Lottie interrupted her.

"Look at the woman dressed in black that just got off the vaporetto. Without her shoulder-length blond hair, I would have mistaken her for a man."

The countess looked at the people coming out of the vaporetto stop. She found the person Lottie meant.

"I think it is a wig. She just turned toward us; her face would have very masculine lines if she were a woman."

Lottie's curiosity was triggered. She looked at her friend with a naughty expression.

"Do you think…"

The countess was quick.

"No, I do not think there is anything funny. She is dressed like a man. She wants to confuse somebody, and she is wearing a wig. Somehow, I can picture that face with a moustache and a beard."

Lottie laughed.

"A sort of blond D'Artagnan[1]?"

"That would be possible, but I still think it is a wig. "

---

1. Charles de Batz de Castelmore, also known as d'Artagnan and later Count d'Artagnan (c. 1611 – 25 June 1673), was a French Musketeer who served Louis XIV as captain of the Musketeers of the Guard. He died at the siege of Maastricht in the Franco-Dutch War. A fictionalised account of his life by Gatien de Courtilz de Sandras formed the basis for the d'Artagnan Romances of Alexandre Dumas père, most famously including The Three Musketeers (1844). The heavily fictionalised version of d'Artagnan featured in Dumas' works and their subsequent screen adaptations is now far more widely known than the real historical figure. [Courtesy of Wikipedia]

Two days later, early in the morning, Tommaso Tron was on his usual walk across Venice. The sun had just risen, and the temperature was still pleasant. Today, he was walking along the Giudecca Canal, a change from his usual route. When he reached the San Basilio vaporetto stop, he decided to take a vaporetto to the station and then walk to his shop in Piazza San Marco. While he was sitting waiting for the waterbus to arrive, he noticed a person dressed in black with shoulder-length blond hair. Somebody who matched that description was seen outside their gallery in Campo San Polo the day his father was murdered. He looked at his watch to remember the time; when the waterbus arrived, he noticed the person got on the vaporetto as well. Tommaso thought he'd better try to remember his face to describe it to the police or Rachele. The person had blond shoulder-length hair and wore black trousers and a black long-sleeve shirt. From the back, he almost looked like a woman, but his face was masculine, very angular. They both got off at the station, and the blond person walked toward the entrance. Tommaso started walking towards Piazza San Marco. He would call Rachele and Umberto de Antoni later from the shop before he opened it.

The blond person walked into the station. He was meeting somebody due to arrive on the night train from Paris. When the woman arrived, she was also blond, had shoulder-length hair, and was dressed in black. She was a woman. From behind, they looked identical. They started walking towards his bed-and-breakfast, speaking French. The early hour meant few people were around once they passed Ponte degli Scalzi.

"Are you anywhere closer to finding the jewels?"

"Not really. I know the art dealer in Sanremo sold the painting to somebody from Venice. I found three versions of Cividali's

Young Baker, but one of the frames did not have the secret compartment your brother and I nailed shut, the other was too small, and the left side of the frame of the third had been used to kill the art dealer that had it in his shop. The person I talked to told me she had never heard of a secret compartment. I am sure that none of them were the versions that man had in his home."

The lady was frustrated.

"You helped my brother hide the jewels so we could start a new life after the war. The problem is that somebody sold the painting under our nose."

"We hid the jewels in the painting the man from Casablanca had brought with him when he was fleeing the Nazis. The painting did not belong to the owner of the house. Also, why did you wait so long to retrieve them? The painting was sold a few months ago."

"We thought the painting was safe in the small home the man from Casablanca rented. The art dealer in Sanremo told me the name of the person who sold it to him. The man from Casablanca did not sell it; somebody else did."

Alain de Lothringen arrived in Venice in the late afternoon. It had been a long train journey with too many changes. The train from Milan was the best part, with an enjoyable meal in the restaurant car. He wanted to shower, change, and relax. Find a café with a view and be a tourist. Organising meetings with Bill Campbell, Rachele Modiano Mendes, and Vice-Commissario Umberto De Antoni would have to wait till the following morning. He needed a few hours for himself after a long journey. His close friend Bernard Alcan was due to join him for a few days the following afternoon. Alain did not know that Bill Campbell was married to the daughter of one of Bernard's cousins; he had never heard his friend mention his family or even met any of them.

~

'Ship passing in the night' could be an overused metaphor in Venice, where people end up on some sort of vessel every day. When Alain de Lothringen was standing outside in the vaporetto that was taking him to his hotel, he noticed a water taxi going in the opposite direction. Rachele Modiano Mendes was on that water taxi; she had just flown back from Rome and was heading to the office for an hour before walking home with Gabriele. She was sure her husband did not mind carrying her suitcase for the short walk home. It was not heavy. She had only been away for two nights. The bag with the contracts and previous court documents that a Roman client had asked her to examine was heavy, which was her main reason for going to the office.

Franco Cantoni came down to help her. As they were walking the two flights of steps to the first-floor office of the law firm, she updated him on what he would have to work on, with all the relevant information in the heavy bag he was carrying. When they entered the office, she saw her son Leo and nephew Alex waiting for her. They were eager to share something with her, something they felt could not wait. Gabriele came out of his office, kissed his wife, and took her suitcase. He was smiling

"These two have something important to tell you. They can't wait. We'll talk on our way home."

Leo looked at his father with the air of complacency that only an eighteen-year-old can have towards his parents. Rachele smiled and started walking towards her office. Her son followed her; her nephew made a detour to fetch her brother-in-law and fellow partner in the law firm, Roberto Mendes. When everybody was in her office, Leo asked her to get the

138

notepad with all her circles. They had something important to share. Roberto nodded to Alex.

"You may remember that the cashier of the café near the Tron art gallery in Campo San Polo had mentioned a very slim woman with shoulder-length blond hair dressed in black walking outside the gallery the day Ludovico Tron was killed. Well, the woman, or should I say that person, has re-appeared. She was seen twice while you were in Rome. Leo, tell her your bit."

Leo straightened up

"Yesterday we were at Nico's with Elena and other friends. We still have the habit of walking her home. I know there are no problems now, but we still like to do it if we have time. On the way, Elena shared with us that Aunt Deborah and Lottie Alcan had seen somebody dressed all in black, with shoulder-length blond hair."

Leo noticed his mother was opening the 'young baker' folder. He smiled, pleased with himself.

"Aunt Deborah thought she had a very masculine face for a woman. She could see that face with a beard and moustache, a sort of blond D'Artagnan. Mario remembered Alex telling us about somebody dressed in black, wearing trousers, and with shoulder-length blond hair being seen outside the art gallery of the father of Diana's friend Isabella the day he was murdered. We thought you or the police would like to know Aunt Deborah and Lottie Alcan might have seen her."

Rachele wrote, '*Talk to Aunt Deborah about blond D'Artagnan.*' It was now Roberto's turn to speak.

"Tommaso Tron told me he saw somebody who met the description of the person who the cashier at the café in Campo San Polo saw the morning his father was murdered. I told him to repeat the description to Alex. Listening to Leo, I realise everybody thought it was a woman, but it could also be a man with unusually long hair."

Rachele wrote '*Talk to Tommaso Tron*'. Alex had been taking notes, patiently waiting his turn. He took a sip of the coffee the receptionist had brought when Leo was talking.

"Leo and Mario dropped by last night before dinner. They insisted they had to talk to me. They shared the story and asked me if it was important. I realised that whomever Aunt Deborah and Lottie Alcan saw matched the description of whomever Tommaso Tron and the cashier saw. We have had two sightings of that person in the past three days. I rang Umberto, and he told me to tell you he was organising a sketch artist to talk to Tommaso Tron, Aunt Deborah, and Lottie. He asked me to ask you if he could organise it here. It would be less intimidating than having them at the police station."

Rachele couldn't help but laugh at the idea of Countess Deborah and Lottie Alcan at the police station. The meeting room overlooking the Grand Canal was better. She leaned back, her index fingers joined, touching her lips. Everybody else knew she was thinking. Alex waited a while before continuing.

"By the way, Umberto told me to tell you he will drop by tomorrow morning on his way to work."

Rachele sat straight, opened her eyes, and closed the meeting.

"Well, that means I have to be here early. Thank you, gentlemen, for the information. Leo, find out if your father is ready to go home. Tell him I need ten minutes with Franco, and then I will be ready. By the way, it would be great if you fetched my suitcase and carried it home."

~

Alain de Lothringen woke up early. He wanted a leisurely breakfast on the terrace overlooking Rialto Bridge. He was aware he was being the typical tourist, but he had not been in Venice since 1938 and felt entitled to be a typical tourist while he could. After breakfast, he returned to his room, rang Bill Campbell, and arranged a meeting. He then rang Vice-Commissario de Antoni but was told he was not in the office yet. The third call on his list was to Rachele. When he rang the law firm, the receptionist told him she was in a meeting with Vice-Commissario De Antoni. Alan apologised but wondered if the receptionist could interrupt them to ask when he could see them both. After a few minutes, the receptionist came back on the phone; they could meet him at the law firm if he were available first thing the following morning. Alan agreed. He found it intriguing that two of the three people he had to see in Venice were connected, but he did not know that the third person was connected with them and his close friend. He looked at himself in the mirror and thought he had better change to go to the station to meet Bernard Alcan's night train from Geneva. He had not seen him for almost two months.

Tommaso Tron was in Piazza San Marco after his morning walk. A friend of his fiancé's father stopped him outside Caffe Florian, on the other side of the square from his shop. He extricated himself from him as fast as he politely could. He had to open the shop. As he was crossing the square, he noticed two people looking at the Cividali through the grid of the shop's shutters. They were leaning forward as if they had been studying it. When he arrived close to them and was about to speak, they pulled themselves up straight and walked away. From a closer distance, he noticed that the one with shoulder-length hair wore black trousers. Tommaso dismissed the thought one of them was the same person who was outside their gallery the morning his father got killed.

After all, there was more than one woman in the world with shoulder-length blond hair. He could not know they had walked to get a coffee somewhere less expensive than Caffe Florian and planned to return later when the shop was open.

Half an hour later, a blond lady walks into the shop. Once they had established a common language, she started talking about the Cividali in heavily accented English.

"That painting was in the living room of a friend's tenant a few years ago. He was a very kind man, and we were all fond of him. I just remember it being bigger. I understand he sold it, but I was surprised to see it in Venice."

Tommaso Tron became very alert. He had to get her name and where she was staying, but he had to do it without her noticing.

"A French client commissioned Cividali to paint five versions of the same scene. Two of them were larger than the one we have in the window. I am afraid you remember a different painting. If you are interested, I know somebody who has seen one of the larger versions. Maybe it is the one that was in your friend's tenant's living room. If you give me your contact details in Venice, I will ask him if he knows who bought it or where it is."

Tommaso took out pen and paper. The lady was not sure what he had asked her.

"What do you mean by contact details?"

Tommaso was not sure that the question was genuine, but he played along.

"I mean your name and the name of the hotel where you are staying here in Venice. "

The woman moved towards the door.

"That will not be necessary. I was just curious. Thank you for the information. Goodbye."

The woman left in a hurry, just when Isabella Tron was coming in

"Why did the blond lady leave in such a hurry?"

Tommaso was on his feet

"Quick, go back out and see if you can figure out where she is going."

Isabella complied. She started looking around until she spotted a woman with a blond ponytail wearing a floral dress very similar to the one worn by the woman who almost ran out of the shop when she arrived. She followed from a distance until she lost her when she hopped on a vaporetto. When she entered the shop, her brother was on the phone.

"… when I asked for her contact details, she ran out of the shop, bumping into my sister, who was coming in. Isabella rushed out again and started following her. She just got back. Wait a second…"

He turned to his sister

"Well?"

Isabella would have never admitted it, but she enjoyed her ten minutes of playing detective.

"I followed her up to the San Zaccaria vaporetto stop. She got on the vaporetto to Giudecca Island, but I suspect she got on because it was the first one that arrived. I guess I have not been as discrete as I thought. She must have realised I was following her and hopped on the first waterbus to lose me. "

Tommaso was disappointed.

"…did you hear it? Yes, I can describe her face. Meeting a

sketch artist is no problem. One more thing, who is telling Avvocato Modiano?"

The person on the other end of the conversation reassured Tommaso that he would take care of it. Tommaso ended the conversation in a friendly way and turned to his sister.

"I was talking to Vice Commissario Umberto De Antoni. He'll tell Diana's mother. Can you do me a favour? When you meet Diana, can you ask her to ask her mother if Umberto told her?"

Isabella sat behind the small desk next to her brother

"Why? Don't you trust Vice Commissario De Antoni?"

Tommaso put away the pen and the notepad

"I trust him, but I want Avvocato Modiano to know everything so she can protect me."

Isabella realised her brother still had not got over being suspected of murdering their father.

"I do not think you need to worry about being protected from the police. I think you are on the same side now."

Alan de Lothringen and Bernard Alcan were having lunch in a small restaurant away from the most beaten track. They had not seen each other for a few months. They were very happy to be in each other's company. Alan did not know how to bring up the subject of the painting. Bernard still had not got over that he had to sell it.

"So, you say that somebody here in Venice bought the painting. Didn't you sell it to an art gallery in Sanremo, just on the other side of the border?"

Alan was trying to be as reassuring as possible

"I did, and I followed your instructions. A month after the sale, I received a letter from a lawyer in Venice. Her client had bought it and wanted to check that we still had our Cividali. He saw it in a book about Venetian paintings in French museums printed in the 1930s. The book did not show the dimensions of the painting. He was worried that he had bought art looted by the Nazis from a museum in Europe. I reassured him. "

Alan could see that he had not reassured his companion of over twenty years. He continued

"The other three Cividali are all in Venice now. An American art dealer, Bill Campbell, wants to organise a temporary exhibition. Also, the lawyer who contacted me and a vice-commissario of the Venetian police want to talk to me about some accidents involving the Cividali paintings."

Alan knew some mystery associated with the Cividali would trigger Bernard's interest.

"A great-uncle commissioned five identical paintings of different sizes. It was one of the stories I heard when I was a child: how his first wife stopped to see the painter sketch details of the scene and how he fell in love with the image when he went to Cividali's studio. He commissioned five copies. Cividali signed the back of each copy with a number to differentiate those from any future reproduction. Do you know what happened?"

Alan was relieved that his friend had stopped brooding about the sale of his painting.

"Not really, but I'll find out tomorrow morning."

Bernard smiled

"So, what else do you have to do today?"

"I meet Bill Campbell at four in a café by the Rialto market. After that meeting, we can celebrate our reunion after two months. By the way, the hotel apologised they did not have a twin room left, so they put us in a room with a double bed."

Bernard smiled again

"The things I do for you."

Lottie, Charlotte, and Rachele were in the blue sitting room in Countess Deborah's home. Many generations had loved that room. Rachele had asked them to meet her in a more relaxed environment because she wanted to ask a few questions about the Alcan family. She thought meeting outside the law firm or the police would lead to a more relaxed conversation. She was also concerned that meeting in public could make them less willing to discuss touchy subjects. Her honorary aunt volunteered the small sitting room, knowing that her new friend and guest had also fallen into the spell of the blue upholstery and the blue walls with a window overlooking an internal courtyard, a stark contrast with the large formal sitting room overlooking the Grand Canal. Once small talk and refreshment were out of the way, Rachele took out a notepad with her notes.

"I apologise, but I must ask questions about your family; some may intrude into private matters. I think the mystery of how the version of the painting that Israel Alcan commissioned for his father ended up in Sanremo is important to understand why Ludovico Tron lost his life, who owns the jewels hidden in the frame and other things."

Charlotte put down her cup, took a napkin, and cleaned her mouth.

"Your daughter's patisserie makes the most wonderful things. Countess Deborah is very proud of her niece. Anyway, I am not sure I can help. I know very little of the Alcan family, and most of what I know comes from Aunt Lottie."

Lottie Alcan was busy eating a slice of pistachio cake. She swallowed the last piece, cleaned her mouth, put down her plate, and picked up a napkin. Rachele recognised a delaying tactic.

"I am not sure how much I can help, but I took the liberty of asking Pierre Alcan to join us. He may fill some of my knowledge gaps."

They heard the doorbell. Five minutes later, Tonia knocked, then opened the door announcing Pierre Alcan. When they told her they were expecting him, she went back to fetch him.

He sat down. Rachele offered him a piece of cake and a drink and started her preamble.

"We know that Israel Alcan commissioned Emanuele Cividali to paint five versions of the same scene. They were of different size. The largest one, the one Lottie remembers, is now in the Museum of Metz. The other four found their way to the Venice area. Somebody vandalised the frame of three versions. Maybe the same person killed Ludovico Tron. We know what they were looking for, the Jewels we found hidden inside the left side of the frame of the version bought by my client from a Sanremo-based art dealer."

Pierre Alcan stopped eating the cake

"Do you mean the one I thought was sold in 1930, and the letter you found states it was sold in 1938? "

Rachele smiled, undeterred. She was not dealing with hostile witnesses, but she was sure they were aware of something important, but they had no idea they knew. It was up to her to pull it out.

"That one. Later, Pierre's mother told him that his uncle Bernard took it as compensation for being cut off from his father's will."

Pierre had his mouth full of walnut cake. He just nodded.

"I have a theory. Whoever wrote the letter needed to establish an ownership trail. Maybe there was a letter or something else confirming that Raphael Alcan had given the painting to his son Maurice; Bernard Alcan needed some piece of paper that showed that he was the legitimate owner rather than somebody who took the painting from his brother's living room because he was furious their father had cut off his eldest son from his will."

Lottie stood up straight. Her memory for details made her try to correct Rachele.

"If I remember correctly, a Maurice Vernier sold the painting to the art dealer."

Rachele smiled. Her preamble was getting too long.

"I think whoever wrote the letter stating that Maurice Alcan sold the painting to the Vernier family in 1938 needed to establish the alleged Maurice Vernier had the legal right to sell the painting."

Lottie may not have been a source of information, but she would check every detail of the story.

"Why? Why not create a letter stating that Maurice Alcan gave the painting to Bernard Alcan?"

Rachele did not have an answer.

"That is one of the things I am hoping to find out. The real question is why Bernard Alcan could not or did not want to be named as the seller of the painting?"

Charlotte had looked almost disinterested in the conversation; now, she perked up.

"So, you think the Maurice Vernier who sold the painting to the art dealer in Sanremo was not Maurice Vernier?"

Pierre intervened.

"We have already established he was not. "

Rachele was ready to ask the personal question

"Do you have any idea why your grandfather cut off your uncle Bernard from his will? That would be the first step in figuring out the reason behind the confidential nature of the sale. I do not think that Bernard Alcan knew precious stones were hidden in the frame. We may get closer to the owner of the diamonds, emeralds, and rubies once we figure out why somebody felt the need to create a false identity to sell the painting."

Pierre was almost apologetic

"I only know that my uncle Bernard exists. My parents never spoke of him. Maybe my aunt Chantal might know. She is not well at the moment. I wonder if one of my father's cousins remembers."

Countess Deborah chose that moment to enter the room

"Rachele, I am sorry if I left you to play the hostess. I had to write a polite letter to somebody who wrote me asking to source a dozen decent copies of Canaletto's paintings. I had to find a diplomatic way to tell him I only deal in originals. The best I could do for him was to source works from the school of Canaletto. He should commission a young artist in London to create copies of the Canaletto paintings in London museums."

As usual, the countess became the centre of attention for a short time. They introduced Pierre Alcan to her. It took a while for the conversation to settle. Rachele was trying to keep a straight face. She had seen her honorary aunt in her best interpretation of the perfect hostess several times. She continued.

"Pierre, do you mind coming to the office to use the phone to call your aunt? Do you have time tomorrow afternoon?

Umberto De Antoni and I are meeting Alan de Lothringen from the Metz museum tomorrow morning."

Pierre nodded. He had now moved on to a slice of the pistachio cake. Charlotte added.

"Bill is meeting him this afternoon. I hope you do not mind Countess Pesaro De Bonfili, but I asked him to meet me here afterwards."

"Of course, I don't mind. Please, call me Countess Deborah."

The countess knew Rachele did not appreciate the interruption. She gave her an apologetic look and asked her to continue.

"Lottie, do you know why you had no contact with your cousins? Charlotte, did your father talk about his family much?"

"My father only talked about Aunt Lottie and his parents. I know he had an uncle and aunt; therefore, there could be cousins, but I do not remember him ever mentioning them. Aunt Lottie?"

Lottie was not of much help

"I met Daniel Klein, Pierre's cousin, and Jules Levy, the grandson of Aunt Ruth when he came looking for relatives who had survived the war. I remember meeting Aunt Ruth and Uncle Samuel when I was a child, but never met their spouses or children until I met Pierre and the others."

Rachele was disappointed but somehow sensed she was on the right track.

"Pierre, I think your Aunt Chantal or one of your cousins may be our best source of information. Please come to the office tomorrow afternoon."

Rachele started collecting her things. Her meeting was over. The doorbell rang. Charlotte smiled and said it could be her husband. She had already told Tonia she was waiting for him. Five minutes later, Bill entered the room. The countess introduced him to Pierre. Rachele was thinking how long her manners would require her to stay when Bill threw a metaphorical hand grenade into the room.

"I met Alan de Lothringen. He likes my idea of a temporary exhibition of the five versions of Cividali's young baker and the idea of including the story of Israel Alcanthe meeting with Cividali during his honeymoon in the show's catalogue. He came with a friend, Bernard Alcan. Is he a relative?"

Bill could not understand why the others were staring at him as if he said he had just met the man from the moon.

The countess broke the silence.

"Rachele, you may have answers to your questions straight from the horse's mouth, not that I am comparing Bernard Alcan to a horse!"

# Chapter Fifteen

## June 1950

Bernard Alcan and Alain de Lothringen were in the law firm's meeting room overlooking the Grand Canal with Rachele and Umberto De Antoni. They sat on the sofa and armchairs rather than around the table because Rachele thought it was more friendly and less official. They had just arrived, having coffee and pastries while waiting for Alex and Franco to join them. Franco had put together a family tree of the Alcan family, and Alex had become an expert on the five versions of Cividali's young baker. Rachele observed the two men talking. She could see that Bernard Alcan was related to Lottie, Charlotte, and Pierre. She also noticed the dynamic between the two friends and wondered what their actual relationship was. Could they be a couple? She was determined to think of a tactful way to find out. The need to explain some Italian words or phrases occasionally interrupted the flow of the conversation. Rachele would tell Alain the German equivalent, and Alain would translate them into French for Bernard.

Alex and Franco entered the room, holding notepads. Rachele waited for them to settle down before she started.

"As I mentioned earlier, I hope you can help us answer many question marks we have, but I would like to start from the sale of the painting. Who took it to the art dealer in Sanremo, and why did you hide a copy of the letter in the frame?"

Bernard's Italian was worse than his friend's, so Alan translated it into French. His friend looked at him and nodded, giving him permission to answer on his behalf.

"Bernard knew that the Vernier family were his brother's closest friend, so he wrote a letter saying that his brother sold the painting to the Vernier family in 1938. He thought it would be useful one day. When he hid it in the painting's frame, the left side could be removed and put back like a drawer. When he went to retrieve it, he found that somebody had nailed the left side of the frame to the rest of the frame, and it could not be opened again. So we wrote another one."

Umberto took out his notepad and picked a pen from the table. Franco passed him a copy of the Alcan family tree he had put together.

"Why did he need to create a sale to the Vernier family? Couldn't you just say that his brother sold him the painting?"

Alain looked at Bernard. Rachele sensed Umberto had touched on a sensitive subject; after a brief silence, Bernard asked if he could answer in German. His German was better than his Italian, and he noticed that Rachele was helping Alain find the correct Italian translation of German words. Rachele told him she was fluent in German and would translate for the others. Bernard continued.

"It has a lot to do with the rest of my family. When my father cut me off, he told me he would make sure I would get nothing from him, either directly or indirectly. My brother Maurice was unhappy about it, so he gave me the Cividali our father had given him. He told the rest of our family that he had received a very good offer and sold it. Our father was never fond of that painting."

Rachele translated for the other and shared with them what she would ask him. She noticed Alex was taking notes and continued in German.

"I apologise if it is still a delicate subject, but why did your father cut you off from his will?"

Bernard had a very sad face. Alain was sitting close to him and put a hand on his thigh. Rachele did not miss the intimate gesture of support.

"I told him I would leave my wife and young daughter because I had fallen in love with a man. Please translate."

He looked at the faces of the others after Rachele had translated what he had just said. Alex and Franco did not change expressions, and Umberto smiled; when Rachele turned back to him, she knew he was checking her facial expression for any reaction. She was sure that her professional training would make sure she had none. She hoped she sounded sympathetic. Bernard could provide answers to many more of their questions.

"It must have been very painful for you."

Umberto asked why he needed to hide the fact that he was selling the painting. Rachele translated; Alain looked at Bernard and answered in his place.

"Bernard has always been very secretive about his family. When he asked me to sell his painting and told me to introduce myself as Maurice Vernier, I did not ask questions. I just did it."

Bernard looked at his friends with a very warm smile. He turned to Rachele and continued.

"I knew that my brother's business partner was a Monsieur Vernier, so I decided to use his name. I tried to retrieve the letter I wrote from the frame of the painting, but I could not open it. So I wrote another one. I feared that some relative might try to stop or invalidate the sale. I am paranoid about my family."

Rachele translated. She then asked Umberto if it was the time to mention the diamonds. Umberto nodded. Alex noticed that the mention of diamonds baffled Alan de Lothringen. Rachele continued in German.

"Did you know about the diamonds, emeralds, and rubies hidden in the frame?"

Bernard and Alain were both surprised. They were silent for a few minutes. Bernard recovered first.

"You mean there were precious stones hidden in the frame? I did not know. I sold the painting to fund my move to Switzerland, a long story. I would have kept the painting if I had known about the diamonds."

He paused for a moment, then smiled as if he had just realised something.

"That is why somebody nailed the left side of the frame to the rest of the frame. It used to be like a drawer. I thought I could hide my real papers there but did not. When I tried retrieving the letter, I couldn't open the drawer anymore."

Before translating, Rachele had another question:

"Do you know who might have put it there and when?"

Alain took Bernard's left hand, looked at him, and said something in French; Franco translated. Alain was telling his friend it was time to be open; a person was murdered because they were trying to recover the diamonds. Bernard sighed, Alain nodded, and he continued.

"The painting has always been with me. I returned to France in 1938. I had already established a network of suppliers of typical Moroccan furniture. My ex-wife was my partner in France. The arrangement I had with her included the commitment never to tell my daughter that I was her father. She was two when I left. When the Germans invaded France, I hid near Deauville; I became a tenant in what was the holiday home of my ex-wife's parents, which they had sold to some non-Jewish neighbours. I used the name Alain Bernard. It was my way of being near Alain. I hung the painting in my living room."

Rachele stopped him to translate. Bernard noticed that Alex and Umberto were taking notes. He did not like the situation, but someone killed a man to recover the diamonds, so he had to do everything he could to help.

"I found a job working as a concierge in a hotel. I had paid a doctor to give me a certificate that I had heart problems and could not be drafted into the reserves. I was not always home, so I gave the keys to somebody active in the resistance, just in case they needed to hide something or somebody in my home while I was at work. If they hid the diamonds, I cannot understand why they used the painting as a hiding place. They knew it was mine, and I would have taken it with me when I moved out."

Rachele translated; Umberto wondered aloud that they had to find who had the keys to Bernard's flat in Deauville.

Bernard understood and answered that he did not know where they were now. Umberto showed Bernard and Alain the sketch of the blond with shoulder-length hair described by Tommaso Tron, the countess, and Lottie Alcan. He only asked if the face looked familiar. He did not explain the circumstances behind the sketch. Bernard looked at the sketch, his face betraying his surprise. He then turned to Rachele.

"He looks like a friend of my landlord's son. Where does this come from?"

Rachele, Umberto, Alex, and Franco looked at each other. Rachele was the first to recover.

"A police sketch artist drew it based on four people describing the person they saw. He is here in Venice. By the way, there are other members of the Alcan family here in Venice. They do not know what you told me, and we will not tell them. Would you like to meet them?"

A day later, Rachele and Umberto bumped into each other as they were leaving court. They sat at a table in a nearby café to have coffee and exchange their views on the Alcan family, the murder of Ludovico Tron, and the two break-ins that resulted in the frames of two Cividali's young bakers being vandalised. They had to be careful because the other café patrons were mainly locals. The smell of fish from the market was enough to discourage even the most tired of the sightseers. Umberto took out his notepad.

"The most important thing we found out yesterday is the identity of the person with shoulder-length blond hair, the friend of the son of Bernard Alcan's landlords. I hope Albert Dornier is his real name, not the name he was using in the resistance."

Rachele put down her coffee and used the paper towel to wipe the sweat from her face.

"The countess referred to him as 'The blond D'Artagnan'; she would not be surprised to know he is a man. Anyway, you assume he is staying somewhere official. What if he has rented a room in somebody's private home? You know as well as I that often, people who rent a room of their own home are not licenced, and their guests escape police registration."

Umberto was optimistic. The court case where he testified had ended up as he hoped it would; Rachele could not dampen his good mood.

"We'll cross the bridge when we get there. So far, I am not accusing him of anything. If he is the person the café cashier saw outside Ludovico Tron's art gallery the morning he was killed, he may have seen something that interests us. If he agrees to a fingerprint test, we shall compare his prints with what we found in Tron's art gallery and, more specifically, the one we found on the frame of the painting and on the left side the killer took out and accidentally used to harm Ludovico Tron. Until then, he is just a witness."

Rachele took a sip of water

"Why do you say accidentally?"

"Alex has the theory that Ludovico Tron surprised his killer as he, or she, was removing the left side of the frame. If he is right, the murder was not premeditated. It just happened."

Rachele took out her notepad from her briefcase.

"That is the spirit! Keep an open mind. Meanwhile, I am still trying to figure out who put the precious stones inside the frame of Count Contarini's version. Here is where Bernard Alcan could be very useful. It was somebody with access to his living room in the place he was renting in Deauville."

"From what he told us, it could be Albert Dornier."

"I wonder if fingerprints resist that long. Somebody hid the two bags with the stones in the frame sometime between five and ten years ago. Bernard Alcan told us he moved in 1940 and moved out less than six months after the war ended. Therefore, somebody must have used the frame as a hiding place between 1940 and 1945, but who and why?"

Umberto was not letting doubt dent his optimism.

"I wonder if we'll ever know unless the same person is trying to recover them now."

Rachele finished her coffee, looked at her watch, and started collecting her things.

"I have to go. I must be back at the law firm to prepare for a meeting with a client after lunch. I wonder whether the person trying to recover the two bags is the person who put them inside the frame or somebody who knew they were inside the frame. Anyway, let's concentrate on catching Ludovico Tron's killer first."

She stood up, and Umberto stood up as well.

"The only thing I can do now is figure out where Albert Dornier is staying."

They left the café. Before parting company, Rachele told Umberto that Gabriele would get in touch that evening to organise dinner together.

After she left Umberto, Rachele crossed the Rialto bridge to catch the vaporetto back to the office. She had lived in Venice for almost thirty years, but she loved what she called her 'Canaletto moments,' so she stopped at the top of the bridge and spent a few minutes looking at the Grand Canal and the traffic of taxis, commercial boats, and waterbuses.

When she arrived at the office, the receptionist told her that Alain de Lothringen had called earlier. He had a favour to ask and would wait in the lobby of his hotel until half-past twelve. He would call again before going out to lunch if Rachele had not called. It was not twelve yet, so Rachele called him back. She was intrigued by what Alain might ask her.

Alain started the conversation in German, probably in the delusion of being more private.

"Thank you for calling me back. Bernard told me to ask you if you do not mind organising a meeting with Lottie, Charlotte, and Pierre. He wants to meet them. I have to thank you. Bernard has seldom talked about his family. In the past few days, he is catching up."

Rachele smiled at the phone.

"May I ask my daughter Diana to organise the meeting and let you know? She is Charlotte's friend, and I can tell her how to reach Pierre. I'll ask her to leave a message at your hotel when she is ready. If she has time, she might even let you know tomorrow. How long are you staying in Venice?"

"I am staying for five more days. Bernard may stay for two more weeks depending on what happens with his relatives and the case."

Gabriele and Rachele were walking home for their lunch break. Rachele was lost in her thoughts; silence was never heavy between them. After almost thirty years of marriage, they felt each other's presence and could read the other one's mood very well. Gabriele knew his wife would share her thoughts at some point or maybe on their way back to the office after lunch. They had just crossed Ponte Bembo when Rachele stopped, adjusted her hat, took her sunglasses off, and looked at her husband.

"I just do not understand families who don't talk to each other."

Gabriele took off his sunglasses as well.

"Care to start from chapter one?"

Rachele smiled, put her sunglasses back on, grabbed her husband's arm, and started walking again.

"I come from a very large family, but we never stop talking to each other. We are also very aware of our extended family."

"Your mother must spend two hours a day writing to relatives spread all over the world. She remembers all the names and how they are related to her. She remembers all the marriages, the births, etc. Sometimes, she mentions relatives I did not know I had, and that is my family, not yours. What brought this up?"

"I don't understand how Lottie Alcan's father cut all contact with his siblings or why Bernard is so afraid of his family. I hope his meeting with Lottie, Pierre, and Charlotte goes well. Diana will organise it."

They had arrived in Campo San Giacomo Dall'Orio. Gabriele put an arm over his wife's shoulder.

"Maybe we are just fortunate to have the family we have."

They had to cross the Campo, and then they would enter the Mendes family bubble. The rest of the world would stay outside, at least for a few hours.

# Chapter Sixteen

## June 1950

Diana had started her task by contacting Charlotte, which triggered a chain reaction that ended up with the countess ringing Diana, suggesting her home. She had already discussed it with Lottie; Bernard, Lottie, Charlotte, and Pierre would be in the red sitting room while she would entertain Alain de Lothringen and Bill, talking about paintings and painters. Elena might be available to help if Diana had to play hostess. She was also a friend of Charlotte Alcan.

Alain did not expect things to move so quickly. He was looking forward to spending time with a well-connected art dealer and a young art buyer who was also a budding temporary exhibitions curator. A very nervous Bernard, Lottie, and Chantal were sitting in the red sitting room overlooking the Grand Canal, waiting for Pierre Alcan to appear. Small talk never relaxed him, so after a few minutes, he stood by the window looking outside at the boats while Lottie and Charlotte talked amongst themselves. They were relieved when they heard the doorbell. A few minutes later, Pierre Alcan appeared, followed by Elena carrying a tray of pastries; she put them down on one of the sideboards, asked people what they wanted to drink, told them to help themselves and that Tonia would be back with the drinks in a few minutes. Nobody would disturb them until they had finished.

Lottie sensed Bernard's nervousness

"Bernard, we are related, so we shouldn't stand on ceremonies. Maybe the person with more questions is Pierre. Charlotte and I have never met you or your siblings; therefore, it is less emotional for us. I would like to understand why my father, Charlotte's grandfather, never had us meet you, your siblings, and your cousins and never discussed your grandfather and your great-aunt. After all, they were his siblings. Pierre may have more questions."

Pierre almost acted as if he did not expect his name to be mentioned. He nearly dropped the plate with the slice of cake.

"I would love to understand why my parents told us they had sold the painting rather than making up a story about why my father gave it to you."

Bernard stood up and started pacing the room.

"You must understand that this is difficult for me; I seldom thought about it in the past twenty years. I locked the memory of my family away in some remote part of my brain and never thought about it. I just wanted to meet you; please be patient. These are the early stages of a journey for me. I would be more comfortable if I met you separately to answer your questions. Let's just say that my father cut me off his will when I told him I was leaving my wife because I had fallen in love with a man."

Bernard paused, stopped walking, and started inspecting the faces of his cousins. He was relieved that nobody got up to leave the room or looked shocked. Lottie was the first one to react.

"I understand your nervousness; perhaps it is easier for me and Charlotte. We have met you for the first time. There is very little we can say other than it is not our business whom you love. Would you feel more relaxed to discuss why my father had few contacts with his brother and sister?"

Before Bernard could answer, Pierre stood up and hugged him.

"Uncle Bernard, as Lottie said, whom you love does not concern me. I would like to know you. I am happy to spend as much time with you as you like. We can discuss anything you feel free to tell me, or we can discuss the weather and how beautiful Venice is. I would like to know more about your life."

Bernard sat down, overwhelmed and fighting tears. Lottie moved closer to him and hugged him. He started crying.

"I was steeling myself for a different reaction and cannot even begin to tell you how relieved I am. I have just got rid of an enormous weight on my shoulder. Maybe I was not as fine without my family as I thought I was."

Lottie had an arm around his shoulder

"Maybe you and the painting are not the only family secrets we must uncover. I still do not know why my father never tried to make us spend time with his siblings and their children."

Bernard smiled

"Maybe the story of the Alcan family is like one of those miniature Chinese cupboards where you open a door and find a chest of drawers or maybe other smaller doors. Lottie, we may have to compare notes to figure out how many doors we need to unlock to understand all the Alcan family secrets."

Lottie was relieved that Bernard was beginning to relax.

Pierre and Charlotte exchanged smiling glances. Pierre was excited for all the right reasons.

"Uncle Bernard, let me know when you want to meet me. I can't wait to write to your youngest brother and tell him I have met you. We talked about you a few weeks before I left for Venice."

Bernard stopped smiling.

"Maybe you'll wait until we have our conversation. You may change your mind."

Lottie reacted quickly, trying to make Bernard relax again.

"Maybe you stop worrying about it. We need to discuss our secrets to figure out whether we can help the police find who killed that poor art dealer, who vandalised the frames of three versions of the young baker, and who hid jewels in the frame of the fourth."

The countess loved the café past Rio Della Senza, where she still had regular coffee and cake sessions with Rachele. She loved it so much that she had turned it into an obligatory stop whenever her early morning walks with Lottie took them to that part of Venice. Lottie loved the quality of the refreshment. She convinced her niece, Charlotte, to try them. So, they were having coffee and perhaps too many cakes in the Courtyard under the trees, an uncommon setting in Venice, where few leafy public places existed. They had the tasting tray, twelve small pieces of several cakes. Charlotte had just eaten a piece of a pistachio pie; she put down her glass of water.

"We cannot come here every time. I'll turn into a balloon. Next time we go to a café near our new home in Venice. Coming back to what you just told me, you are going to meet Bernard and his companion."

Lottie put down her cup of coffee

"Yes, we have agreed to meet tomorrow morning. I am not sure whether Alain de Lothringen will be there. Based on what we know, we want to see if we can reconstruct why my father, your grandfather, stopped talking to his siblings. When Bernard was young, he spent a lot of time with his grandfather. He may remember something. I have always thought that any relationship broke down when my father re-married after the death of his first wife. I am not sure why, but that seems the most logical explanation."

Charlotte was inspecting the pieces of cake left on the tray, unsure what to try next. Her aunt suggested the almond and chocolate cake. Charlotte found it in her tray, picked it up, but waited before eating it.

"Why do you think it has to do with Grandpa marrying Grandma? I only have a vague memory of them, but I understood he waited a few years before marrying her. I understand you were born about a year after they married. So, he almost waited four years. If I remember correctly, Uncle Philippe was six months old when his mother died."

Lottie was working her way through the tasting tray. She stopped figuring out what piece to try next.

"What else can it be? I do not think that his siblings knew about the letter. Bernard had the painting where it was hidden, and he did not know."

"Grandpa Israel knew; maybe he kept contact to a minimum so they would not find out they were entitled to a third of the bank. "

"Yes, but when the French financial authorities insisted he had to sell the bank, it stopped being a problem. The authorities set the sale price, he did not. Your grandfather kept saying that the bank was stolen from under us."

Lottie picked up two other pieces from the lasting tray, called the waiter, ordered another coffee, and continued.

"Well, I am having coffee with Bernard and Alain near Piazza San Marco tomorrow. Maybe we can figure it out between the two of us. That may or may not bring us closer to figuring out who put the jewels in the frame, but it would help clear the air. Once we have figured it out, we'll discuss it with Pierre. It is silly to spend so long ignoring each other."

They dedicated the rest of their time to the critical task of finishing their tasting trays. After a reasonable amount of time, they got up, paid, and walked to the Sant'Alvise vaporetto stop.

They both got off at Riva de Biasio; Charlotte walked home, and Lottie waited for the vaporetto that would take her to the Ca D'Oro stop, from where she would walk to Countess Deborah's home. Lottie did not have far to go. By now, she felt like a local; she did not sit outside like most tourists but sat inside in one of the first rows. She noticed a young man with a large Panama hat on the other side of the aisle. He looked familiar. At the first stop, the penny dropped.

"David, David Klein, what are you doing in Venice?"

"Bonjour Madame Alcan, I am on holiday."

He nearly took his hat off but stopped as if he remembered something. Lottie remembered Pierre telling her that David Klein was not his cousin; it was his cousin's cousin. She decided not to engage with him. David, however, felt the need to explain himself.

"It is not a holiday. I got married last week, and I am here with my wife. We arrived three days ago. She is having her hair done, and I seized the opportunity to go to the station and sort out our bookings for next week. We are going back to Paris on the night train."

Lottie thought it was bizarre that David felt the need to justify why he was on that specific waterbus. She talked about how beautiful and romantic Venice was until she arrived at the Ca D'Oro stop.

Lottie, Countess Deborah, Elena, and Joshua were having dinner. Elena was discussing an outing to Torcello with Leo, Mario, and their entire class to celebrate the end of the school year. Next year, they would have to study for the tests at the end of the Italian high school system[1]. Joshua was saying what a pity and relief it was that Italian schools did not have a prom night when Lottie put down her cutlery and covered her mouth. That was not lost on the countess.

"What happened? What did you forget? Or, what did you remember?"

Lottie smiled.

"Do you remember the person with shoulder-length blond hair we saw one morning near Fondamenta Nove?"

"The one we nicknamed the blond D'Artagnan?"

"The very one. Tomorrow morning, I need to call Vice-Commissario Umberto De Antoni and ask to see the sketch. I may be wrong, but I think he is the man I know as David Klein."

She then told how she bumped into David Klein in the vaporetto. She concluded the story by saying.

_______________

1. Up to the early seventies, high school leavers in Italy had the so-called "Esami di Maturita' "(Maturity exams), a nightmare for all who remember them. Teenagers would spend Mid May and the whole of June studying the whole curriculum of 12 subjects with written and oral tests in all subjects, keeping them busy for the first three weeks in July.

"I wonder if he did not remove his hat because his shoulder-length hair was hidden in it. I did not see the back of his neck, so I can't tell. "

Joshua remarked that a haircut could also have taken care of the shoulder-length hair. The countess added that the shoulder-length hair could have been a wig.

The following morning, the two friends discussed the blond D'Artagnan during their morning walk. Deborah Camerini thought they should inform the police that Lottie recognised the blond D'Artagnan as David Klein. Elena, however, had already discussed the evening conversation with Leo and Mario outside the school. As they were waiting outside for the door to open, Leo went into a café nearby, bought a phone token, and called his mother to tell her.

Umberto de Antoni was surprised that Rachele had already heard about David Klein when he called her to share that information. He had the last word, though.

"I do not think we have shown Lottie the sketch of the blond D'Artagnan. She is coming to the police station to see if she can recognise David Klein in the drawing. I'll let you know what happens."

Rachele was looking at her diagrams, trying to figure things out. Bernard had recognised the face in the drawing as a friend of his landlord's son. A Jew would have used a made-up name in occupied France. It would have been challenging to link the friend of Bernard's landlord's son with David Klein unless Lottie would confirm the identification. She also thought that if she were David Klein's lawyer, one of the first things she would do would be to infer that Bernard and Lottie did not recognise a photo; they saw a sketch of a face; it was not as tight evidence as she would have liked. She wrote in her diary to call Umberto De Antoni in the afternoon to check if Lottie had identified the drawing and went back to her analysis of changes in a contract that a client's client had requested.

After Lottie left the police station, Umberto tried to figure things out. She had identified the drawing as the person she knew as David Klein and told him she knew little about David Klein. The man with shoulder-length hair, the blond D'Artagnan, had a name; was it his actual name? If the countess was right and the blond hair was a wig, why did he feel the need to wear a wig?

Whenever he had questions without an answer, he checked if Rachele was available. He rang her and was told she was not available but would be free around 4.30. He left a message saying he would be there at 4.30 to discuss the Tron-Cividali case.

At 4.30, he was at the law firm's door. Rachele was waiting for him. They both valued time and were doing their best to be punctual. As usual, the conversation was social while they were having coffee. When they entered Rachele's office, and she closed the door, they switched to business; by then, they had known each other and co-operated for almost seven years.

Rachele took out the notepad

"So, what is the bit that does not add up?"

"It is simple and complicated at the same time. Lottie Alcan recognised the blond person we know as Alain Dornier, except she told me his name is David Klein, the first cousin of Daniel, a son of her cousin. Let us assume for a minute it is David Klein. How did he know that the Cividali paintings were in Venice?"

"He may have visited the art gallery in Sanremo where Count Contarini bought his painting. I could call them tomorrow and check if anybody asked for the Cividali after Count Contarini bought it. If they ask, I'll just say that my client asked me to investigate the previous owner of the painting. I will not share any information about the case."

Umberto stood up and started pacing around the room

"We have sorted that, but why did he have to wear a blond wig? Lottie said David Klein had short, dark blond hair when he saw her in Menton. The other sightings of the mysterious person with shoulder-length blond hair all agree it was more like a platinum blond."

"The sort of colour you get when you die your hair. "

Rachele was looking at her notes and her diagram.

"Let us backtrack for a minute. Bernard Alcan said that the face reminded him of a friend of his landlord's son. We are talking about a period when Jews were hiding their identity, and people could have been involved in clandestine activities. If we want to link David Klein to the jewels hidden in the frame, we need to figure out if he could have access to the painting that was hanging in Bernard's living room."

Umberto stopped pacing.

"Bernard told us he gave the keys to a member of a resistance group, just in case they had to hide something in his flat. They could have figured out when he was on duty at the hotel and therefore unlikely to come home unexpectedly."

When Umberto and Rachele were discussing David Klein, Bernard and Alain were crossing Piazza San Marco to go to the café where Bernard and Lottie had agreed to meet. The tourist season had just started, and the square was crowded. They were very careful; they were likely to be overheard by somebody who could understand what they were saying, whatever language they spoke. When they reached the café, they found her sitting at a far table alone. She looked as if she was sleeping. When Bernard tried to wake her, she almost fell off the chair. They checked whether she was breathing. Bernard stayed by his cousin; Alain went inside the café and asked if they could call an ambulance. They had to inform her hostess, but he had no contact details for the countess. He asked for a phone token to call the law firm, left a message with the receptionist, and then went back to wait for the ambulance with Bernard.

Meanwhile, at the law firm, the receptionist knocked at the door of Rachele's office.

"I am sorry to interrupt, but Alain de Lothringen called with an urgent message. Something happened to Lottie Alcan. They are at Café Al Todaro, waiting for an ambulance. He did not know how to inform Countess Pesaro De Bonfili or Charlotte, so he called here."

Rachele and Umberto looked at each other. Umberto reacted first.

"You call the countess. I go to the hospital. I'll call you as soon as I have news. It is not good."

Back at the café when the ambulance arrived, Bernard insisted he stayed with her. He used any words in any language he knew to explain that he was her cousin. He would stay with her until somebody else arrived. Alain said he would find his way to the hospital and join them there. In Venice, even an ambulance is unusual, so a group of tourists gathered to watch the paramedics take Lottie into a speedboat with a red cross to the sides. Once Lottie was inside the ambulance and Bernard sat beside her, they told Alain he could get on. There was room for him, but he had to sit outside.

Lottie opened her eyes in the ambulance. She saw Bernard, smiled, and started saying something, but only a whisper came out. Bernard approached her. She clearly said, "David Klein," and closed her eyes. The paramedic checked her pulse and said she had lost consciousness. He added that the hospital was not very far. Outside, Alain was reluctant to admit that he enjoyed the speedboat ride among the narrow canals. He was also concerned that whatever happened to Lottie meant that other members of the Alcan family were at risk, especially Bernard. Rachele had mentioned jewels hidden in the frame. Could they think Bernard found them, whoever "they" might be?

Rachele had also called Paolo Mondani, who told her he would go down to A&E as soon as he could and find out what they thought happened to Lottie. Then she called home and talked to Diana, telling her what had happened and asking if she could tell Charlotte. Her last phone call was to Count Contarini. After the shortest possible small talk her manners would allow, she came straight to the point.

"Something happened to Lottie Alcan. I may be paranoid, but I would feel so much better if you could be very careful in the next few days until we determine if there is a link between whatever happened and the jewels we found in the frame."

"Thank you for letting me know. Do not worry about Mila. She and my granddaughter insisted on sharing a room, so she is not staying with us."

Rachele smiled

"I knew you would keep Mila safe as you keep your grandchildren safe; thank you for telling me, anyway."

Rachele went looking for Gabriele and told him she would not leave the office until she spoke to Paolo, or Anita told her he tried to call her at home.

# Chapter Seventeen

## June 1950

In Venice, walking is often the fastest way to go from one place to another, so if you are in a hurry, you try to walk fast, and if you really are in a hurry, you run. Countess Deborah Pesaro De Bonfili's upbringing and age prevented her from running. Taking a vaporetto to the hospital from her home would have wasted time because a vaporetto did not use the narrow side canals. It would just take too long. She knew that Strada Nova would be crowded; it was part of the route from the station to Rialto; she had to grin and bear it. Any alternative route would have been longer because of the location of the bridges. She walked as fast as she could, trying to avoid tourists taking in the scenery, walking in groups, and taking too much space. Her anxiety had two reasons: Lottie was her guest, and they had bonded, so she was worried about her, but she was also relieving the moment a couple of years earlier when she was rushing to the hospital after somebody attacked Joshua Schwartz[1]. She became less anxious when she reached the point when her path diverged from the route to Rialto and Piazza San Marco. It was easier

---

1. This episode is described in Elena's memory, see 'By the same author' section.

for her to walk as fast as her age, fitness level, and dignity would allow.

When she arrived at the hospital, she introduced herself as a relative of Lottie Alcan. The receptionist could not locate her. She insisted she knew an ambulance had been called about an hour earlier from a café in Piazzetta San Marco; they directed her to Accident and Emergency. She found Bernard Alcan sitting outside in the waiting area with Alain de Lothringen. They stood up when they saw her. She hugged Bernard, who was the more distressed of the two.

"I came as fast as I could after Rachele called me. I think Diana, Rachele's daughter, was told to tell Charlotte."

Bernard's Italian was not up to explaining what happened, so he pointed to Alain

"When we arrived, I thought she was asleep. She did not respond to our greetings. When Bernard touched her left shoulder, her head dropped to the right in a way I did not like. I checked her carotid, and then I ran into the café to call an ambulance. I also called Rachele, asking her to call you and the police. We have been here for half an hour, and they are still examining her."

The countess tried to say something in her limited French. Bernard smiled and thanked her. They sat down, and Alain told her that Lottie had woken up in the ambulance and mentioned the name David Klein before losing consciousness again. The countess thought that Vice-Commissario Umberto De Antoni ought to know that. She was about to say it to Alain when she saw Umberto and a policeman in uniform enter the waiting area. The Vice-Commissario told the uniformed policeman to stand outside the room where they were examining Lottie. She stood up, mentioned to Bernard and Alain that the police had arrived, and walked toward the Vice-Commissario.

"I arrived about ten minutes ago. They have been examining Lottie for more than half an hour. Alain de Lothringen was telling me she was unconscious when they arrived at the hospital, but when they were in the ambulance, she opened her eyes, smiled at Bernard, whispered 'David Klein', and closed them again. Bernard Alcan is very distressed; language aside, Alain sounded more reliable."

Umberto felt like his boss had just given a summary of the situation.

"I am not sure what is happening, but I am not taking chances. As you might have noticed, a uniformed policeman is outside the room where they are examining her. I need to talk to Alain de Lothringen."

The countess sat next to Bernard and explained that since Alain spoke Italian, Umberto would talk to him, but she had told him what happened in the ambulance.

When Charlotte and Bill appeared, Umberto de Antoni was still talking to Alain in a corner of the waiting area. Charlotte hugged Bernard and told him they had called Pierre's hotel. The countess was not sure how fluent Charlotte's French was, so she took it upon herself to update her. They sat in silence for what felt like an eternity but, in reality, was less than twenty minutes. As Umberto and Alain joined them, a doctor came out of the room. They all looked at his face, trying to assess the seriousness of the situation before he spoke.

"She is still unconscious. All her bones are OK. We found a sign of an injection that might have triggered a reaction. Her blood test will tell us what they have injected and when. Hopefully, she will regain consciousness and tell us more. At the moment, all the vital signs are there. Her heartbeat is regular, and her blood pressure is at an acceptable level for a woman above sixty. Before we have the results of our tests, we are only concerned she might need help breathing."

Charlotte raised her head and simply said,

"She will be seventy-two next month."

"Well, in that case, she has aged very well. I would not have thought she was over sixty-five, and I base my judgement on her clinical data, not on how she looks."

The countess took over

"Do you know when they will move her to a proper bed? Whom should I talk to arrange a private room for her?"

"We are waiting for the results of the tests before deciding where we should send her; also, if she is still unconscious, you do not get a choice. She needs to be where nurses can monitor her all the time."

Charlotte translated to Bernard; then she turned to the countess

"I am not sure if there is anything to pay, and I do not know how much money Tante Lottie has with her…"

The countess stopped her with her right hand.

"Nonsense, she is my guest. I'll take care of any expenses. When she is out of here, we may or may not have that conversation."

The following morning, Umberto was on his way to coffee with Rachele. Lottie had not regained consciousness, and the doctor in charge had been vague about what could have happened. He had organised more tests and hoped to make a diagnosis once the results were back. Meanwhile, they were monitoring Lottie. Umberto kept thinking of Lottie whispering 'David Klein' to Bernard. He needed Rachele's help. Brainstorming the whole situation with her would hopefully clear the fog in his brain. Like every commuter, his journey from the mainland to the vaporetto stop was the same every morning. He did not have to be awake or pay attention; he just had to remember that he had to get off the second stop, Riva De Biasio, and not stay on till his usual stop.

After coffee and pastry in the kitchen and five minutes of socialising with Gabriele, they were in Rachele's office. She could tell that Umberto was navigating through thick fog and was very uneasy about that. She found a clear page of her notepad and started drawing lines.

"Let's look at things from a clear page. Given what we know now, it will help figure out what we do not know."

Umberto reluctantly sat down at the table.

"Sometimes between 1942 and 1945, somebody hid precious stones in the frame of Bernard Alcan's version of Cividali's young baker. After the war, Bernard Alcan asked his friend Alain to sell the painting on his behalf. Alain takes it to an art gallery in Sanremo; why?"

Umberto had an answer for that.

"He was afraid that somebody in his family might find out about the sale and block it. He thought that having it sold in Italy would have been a safer option."

"Alain De Lothringen brought the painting to Sanremo and sold it to an art dealer pretending to be Maurice Venier. In January, Count Contarini buys the painting and organises its shipment to Stra; the art dealer only knew the courier's name and destination. In March, somebody kills Ludovico Tron in his art gallery in Venice and removes the left side of the frame of his version of the young baker. A few days later, the warehouse of the auction house was broken into. Nothing was missing except they removed the left side of the frame of the Auction house version of the Cividali. Let us assume the persons who hid the precious stones are connected with the murder and the break-in; how did they know they had to come to Venice?"

Umberto smiled.

"That is the first question that needs an answer. We need to talk to the art dealer in Sanremo."

Rachele was smiling as well.

"Count Contarini has approved the costs. Franco Cantoni will leave for Sanremo on Sunday. He will talk to the art dealer on Tuesday. Let's move to the mysterious person with shoulder-length blond hair."

"You mean David Klein…"

"We do not know yet. Remember how we all fell for Bruno Heber when he was impersonating Joshua Schwartz[2]."

"Yes, that led us to an interesting path to nowhere."

Rachele smiled and started another line.

"The blond person with shoulder-length hair first appeared outside the Tron art gallery an hour before the earliest time Ludovico Tron could have been killed; he then was seen again entering Santa Lucia railway station, coming out of a vaporetto in Fondamenta Nove, and outside the Tron shop in Piazza San Marco with a blonde woman who went back asking questions about the Cividali."

Umberto felt better because he could contribute.

"Bill Campbell had a good look at the person's face. He could speak to a sketch artist, and we now have a sketch of the face. When we showed the drawing to Bernard Alcan, he said it

_______________

2. Another episode from "Elena's memory", see 'by the same author' section.

looked like a friend of his landlord's son. Later, when we showed it to Lottie Alcan, she recognised it as David Klein. Pierre Alcan told us David Klein is a cousin of his cousin Daniel Klein."

Rachele stopped drawing.

"If we accept that identification, we have several questions. Lottie told us he had met a Daniel Klein. We know from Pierre Alcan that he is his cousin, the son of his aunt, and David Klein is his cousin. If David had paid her a visit, how would he have found out about her? Pierre did not know. Is David the one who hid the jewels? Do they belong to him or somebody else? In those days, many people had reasons to hide valuables. How did David Klein know he had to come to Venice to retrieve the jewels?"

She checked her notes.

"Last but not least, Tommaso Tron told us he saw the person with shoulder-length blond hair with another woman. Later, that woman walked into his shop and asked questions about the Cividali's young baker. She said that she remembered a larger painting, which would point to Bernard Alcan's version. Who is she?"

Umberto was taking notes. He stopped writing.

"Bernard Alcan identified David Klein as a friend of his landlord's son. Could that be the key to the identity of the blond woman?"

Rachele leant back on her chair and closed her eyes, both index fingers to her lips. Umberto knew she was thinking.

"Bernard Alcan and the art dealer in Sanremo may help us establish a connection between David Klein and the precious stones. Franco will go to Sanremo. You can talk to Bernard Alcan; do we have a way to contact Bernard's old landlord?"

"We could check with the International Criminal Police Commission[3] , but it will take time."

Rachele closed the notepad with the diagrams.

"Do we have an alternative?"

Umberto took out his diary from his briefcase and checked his contacts.

"I have a contact in Lyon. We can ask him if the Commission is slow. I also wonder what Lottie can tell us when she wakes up."

"Do we know what happened to her?"

"The doctors told us they would have the test results this morning, and they hope to understand better what was wrong with her by the afternoon."

Rachele looked at her notes and summarised the actions they had decided to take. Umberto agreed to call her once they had any information from the doctors, but he thought Paolo Mondani or Countess Pesaro De Bonfili might call her first. Rachele smiled at the idea that Deborah Camerini had the last word, metaphorically speaking.

The countess and Bernard had taken turns being by Lottie's bedside. They agreed her niece Charlotte should not be there by herself. The countess had just taken over from Bernard Alcan when a nurse told them that there was a blond woman at reception that wanted to see Lottie Alcan, she only told the receptionist that she was sitting close by at the café when she saw the ambulance arrive, would they allow a visit? Charlotte looked at the countess, who pointed her to the policeman that

_______________

3.  The name was changed to Interpol in 1956

was sitting near the nurse's station. The policeman thought she might provide useful information about what happened, but he would move to Lottie's bedside just in case. Charlotte agreed. The nurse went back and rang reception.

A short time later, the blonde woman appeared.

"Nice to see there are people here. I came because I thought she was a tourist who did not know anybody in Venice. I thought a visit would make her feel less lonely."

Charlotte reacted in French.

"I am her niece and I live in Venice. But thank you for your consideration. Did you see what happened? We do not know, we are waiting for lab tests."

The countess thought that the woman did not expect to see people. She asked the lady if she spoke Italian because her French was not good. When she shook her head, she asked Charlotte to translate.

"Do you know what happened? Her cousin Bernard found her already unconscious."

The visitor was not expecting to be questioned. The countess was happy that the plainclothes policeman was there; there was something in the woman's insistence in seeing Lottie that did not convince her. She took a good look at the visitor to be sure she could describe her, beyond what she was wearing.

The visitor only stayed a few minutes. She was very vague about what she saw and where she was sitting in the café. Her story did not convince the policeman as well; he asked to use the nurse's phone and called Vice-Commissario Umberto De Antoni.

"We had a strange visit. I wonder if you could send a sketch artist while our memories of the visitor are still fresh."

"Who else is there? Is Lottie Alcan still unconscious?"

"Her niece and Countess Pesaro De Bonfili are here. The countess also thinks there was something that did not add up in the woman's demeanour. Lottie Alcan is still unconscious and the doctors have not appeared yet. The nurse said they are will make a round in two hours."

Umberto De Antoni agreed to send a sketch artist as soon as possible. Then he called Tommaso Tron and see if he could drop by the shop in Piazza San Marco later that day with a sketch of the face of a blond woman he might recognise. They agreed to meet around six.

Umberto dropped by the shop on his way home, he showed the sketch of the blond woman to Tommaso who thought she looked like the blond woman who came into the shop asking information about the Cividali, unfortunately she did not say her name and had been very vague where she was staying. Before leaving the shop, Umberto asked if he could use the phone. He called Rachele, asking if he could drop by on his way home. Rachele was about to leave the office but told him she would wait.

Pierre Alcan had decided to stay in Venice longer to help in any way he could. His dream of playing with the children in the painting when he was hiding almost turned into reality. Joshua Schwartz, Dante Bembo, and Alex Modiano had drafted him to be the fourth oarsman on their early morning rowing trips. What Pierre lacked in experience, he compensated with unlimited enthusiasm. It was the age-appropriate version of playing with the children in the painting. He wrote to his mother begging her to send money to allow him to stay in Venice longer, explaining about the painting and Lottie. Somehow he thought it would be better not to mention Bernard. Pierre's mother relented when she read he had not had one of his nightmares since he arrived in

Venice and organised more money than Pierre expected. She could not believe the renewed zest for life, which had transpired from his letter. She used to describe her son as 'a bright light that was switched off during the war and had not found the sparkle yet'. When she read the letter, she saw a hint of a sparkle.

Besides learning to row like a Venetian, Pierre also helped the law firm and the police by contacting family members who could have some information. That morning, he was at the Questura to ring one of his Klein cousins. Umberto was hoping to find out more about David Klein. They had agreed that he should talk to his cousin and a police interpreter would listen in, so the court would not doubt Pierre's account of the conversation if it became material for a trial. Pierre was on the phone with his cousin, Daniel, reading from Umberto De Antoni's list of questions. He had already told him why he was in Venice and what happened to Lottie, and that she had mentioned David Klein before losing consciousness. He looked at the interpreter before asking the first question.

"The police asked me if I knew who David Klein was. I told them that the only David Klein I know is your cousin. Do you know if he ever visited Lottie Alcan in Menton?"

Daniel was silent for a short time before replying.

"I went to see her. I had been to Metz and looked up the Cividali at the museum, and wanted to know if she had an idea what had happened to the other versions of the Cividali. I got her address from Jules Levy."

Umberto passed a note to the interpreter who wrote it in French and passed it on to Pierre.

"Ask him if he knew whether David Klein went to see her in Menton."

Pierre asked, and his cousin's answer did not surprise him.

"He asked me for her address. I think he went to see her, but I am not sure."

Umberto pointed to the second question.

"Do you know where David Klein was during the war? Another person involved in the Cividali case identified him as 'a friend of his landlord's son'. That person spent the war years in Deauville."

Daniel asked Pierre something in French. The interpreter shook his head. They had agreed not to talk about Bernard. Pierre nodded.

"I am not sure who else identified him. Things have been hectic since Lottie lost consciousness. I only met her here in Venice, but I like her. I do not want to take too much of your time, so could David Klein have been in Deauville during the war?"

The interpreter sensed Daniel had become weary because he changed the tone of his voice.

"He might have been. The only thing I know for sure is that he had a role in supporting the landing in Normandie. Deauville is not very far."

Pierre translated Daniel's answer and Umberto's face lit up.

Daniel summarised the conversation.

"Whatever is happening in Venice and whatever role David has in it, I think he could have visited Lottie in Menton and could have been in Deauville during the war."

At the end of the conversation, the police interpreter intervened.

"On behalf of the Venetian Police, I would like to thank you for your co-operation. I would also like to stress that your cousin Pierre is helping us. He is not implied in anything."

Then he hung up. Umberto thanked Pierre and promised to keep him informed. Pierre told him he would be in Venice for another month. He hoped everything will be clarified by that time.

Once he was alone in his office, Umberto took out his version of the circle diagram Rachele had taught him to use. He ticked two questions and wrote 'possible' next to them. The only thing left to figure out is how they knew that the Cividali they were looking for was in Venice. He hoped that Franco Cantoni would be back from Sanremo, with information that could provide an answer to that question.

Rachele put down the phone and took out the notepad with the diagrams and the notes of the Cividali's young baker case. She updated a few things based on the conversation she just had with Umberto, then stared at the diagrams with the list of questions in mind, turned the page, looked at the list for a few minutes, and added one about the identity of the blond woman and her role in the murder. She hoped Franco would return with an answer to the most critical question in the theory that was slowly taking shape in her head. How did they know to come to Venice?

The circumstantial nature of the evidence that brought them to David Klein bothered her now that they knew he was the person with blond shoulder-length hair. Somebody saw him outside the Tron art gallery the morning Ludovico Tron was murdered; that, in itself, was not enough to accuse him of murder. She hoped they would get hold of his fingerprints to compare them with those found on the piece of frame used to murder the art dealer. In a way, Lottie whispering his name before sinking back to unconsciousness was a more substantial evidence of David Klein's role in the entire story.

They only had Bernard Alcan's word; could he have a reason to make it up? She dismissed the thought mainly because Bernard was in Venice to spend time with his friend and companion. The timing was pure coincidence, or at least that is what it looked like.

Gabriele interrupted her thoughts. He knocked at her door to clarify her billing instructions.

"Am I interrupting something?"

"No, it was perfect timing. I just decided that we must wait for Franco to return from Sanremo and for Lottie to regain consciousness unless something else happens."

Gabriele walked into the room, holding the paperwork.

"Do you think something could happen?"

Rachele collected all the notes she wrote on odd pieces of paper and put them inside the file marked "Cividali's young baker."

"Not really, unless Count Contarini rings us to tell us they had broken into his study and helped themselves to his version of the Cividali's *young baker*."

The phone rang. Gabriele and Rachele looked at each other and smiled nervously. When Rachele picked it up, she listened for a short time, and then she smiled. She thanked the caller and put the phone down.

"It was Charlotte Alcan Campbell. Lottie just woke up. She is still confused and weak, but the doctors say that her vital signs are good. She may be up to talk to the police in a couple of days. I am relieved."

Charlotte had also rung Countess Pesaro De Bonfili to inform her of Lottie regaining consciousness; the countess picked up the call when she was almost ready to go out; a client had asked to inspect a painting in a home that was on her way to the hospital. The good news had put a spring in her step. She was on her way to the potential seller, who lived close to the hospital in Calle del Console. Like many Venetians, she had a map in her head and rarely asked for directions. She did not know where the specific street was but had written the instructions they had given her when they spoke on the phone. In typical Venetian style, the directions used shops, restaurants, and hotels as signposts. She had to turn left when she reached a specific shop, so she paid attention to her surroundings and did not miss the woman who paid the weird visit to Lottie in hospital coming out of a hotel on the street where she was walking. She decided that the best thing she could do was remember the hotel's name and call Vice-Commissario Umberto De Antoni as soon as she could.

Once she reached the hospital, she asked for phone tokens at the reception, found a phone box, and called Rachele first and then Umberto, as planned. She then took the lift to the floor where her guest was. Charlotte was standing in the corridor because doctors were with Lottie; the policeman had insisted he could not leave the room but was convinced to go when a doctor told him he was a very close friend of the countess. They were part of the same extended family. Deborah Camerini immediately realised that Paolo Mondani was with Lottie. She turned to Charlotte, smiling.

"Paolo is there, Paolo Mondani, there are no risks."

Charlotte smiled. The countess told the policeman and Charlotte what she had seen. After all, they were there when the blond woman paid that weird visit. She also told them she had already rung the Vice-Commissario.

~

Umberto De Antoni immediately called Rachele. They agreed he would go to the hotel and then drop by the law firm on his way home. He left Rachele's phone number with his assistant, put the sketch of the blond woman and his notepad in his briefcase, and left for the hotel. A police boat was available, so he used it instead of walking to the hotel. They dropped him by a bridge close to the hotel, Ponte Minich. He showed his police card to the receptionist and took out the drawing. The receptionist's reaction made him smile inwardly; he tried to have a professional demeanour but would celebrate with Rachele later.

"Vice-Commissario De Antoni, the drawing looks like a French guest we have here. Her name is Brigitte Fontaine; she has been here for three weeks. She booked her room for another week."

Umberto still wanted to be sure she was the right person.

"I need to make sure she is the right woman. Can you possibly find out when she has breakfast in the morning? Is there a way I could take somebody here who could confirm or deny whether she is the person they saw? We ought to do that without her spotting us."

The receptionist was very cooperative.

"It is very doable. A room next to the kitchen is only used when we have large groups. The doors between that door and the dining room do not have glass. There is a grid instead of glass to keep the room ventilated. You can be on the other side of the grid, and nobody in the dining room could see you. The problem is, you should probably stay there between 7 am and 10.30 to make sure you see her."

Umberto was almost triumphant, but he thought he hid it.

"There is no cause for concern. We think that Brigitte Fontaine may be the witness to something we are investigating. I can arrange my side relatively quickly. How much notice do you think the hotel would need to accommodate us?"

"Probably 24 hours because I, or my colleague, would have to tell the owner and make sure we can easily smuggle you into the room."

Umberto told him he would be in touch the following morning. The receptionist should share the plan they had just put together with whoever was working in the morning. Then he left to go to Rachele.

# Chapter Eighteen

## June 1950

Gabriele was in his aunt's study doing her bookkeeping for June. He was almost done when Countess Deborah burst into the study.

"Do you know if Rachele is available? I have just come back from the hospital. Charlotte, Bernard, and I spoke to the doctors. It was very nice of them to include me as well. I need to talk to Rachele as soon as possible."

Gabriele was used to the whirlwind created by Deborah Camerini's entrances, so he barely lifted his head from the ledger.

"As far as I know, she does not have client meetings. Paolo and Sofia invited us to dinner. She will come here around six thirty, and then we go together."

The countess sat down in one of the chairs on the other side of her desk from Gabriele's

"I can't wait till six thirty. I have to talk to her now."

She got up and picked up the phone, dialled the number of the law firm, and spoke to the receptionist. Gabriele guessed that the silence meant that Rachele was available. After a brief pause and the minimum level of small talk her manners would allow, she came straight to the point.

"Can you believe Lottie was poisoned? They knew it almost immediately from all the tests they did when she arrived at the hospital, but they were not sure how the poison got into her. Now they know. A nurse started washing her when she was still unconscious and noticed a red patch on the back of her neck. She looked more closely and noticed the sign of a puncture, almost as if she had been stung by an insect. She called the doctor, and, to cut a long story short, they now are confident that the puncture was where the poison entered her body."

It was very hard to stop Deborah Camerini, Countess Pesaro De Bonfili when she was in full flow. Somehow, Rachele managed it.

"Umberto should be with her right now. He is supposed to drop by tomorrow morning. Do they have a theory about how it happened?"

The countess knew when she was about to provide a coup-de-théâtre.

"They think somebody used a blowgun, and either the tip of the arrow had the poison or they had soaked a pin in poison. They reckoned it must have happened half an hour before Bernard Alcan appeared. By the way, I do not understand why his family cut him off. He is such a nice man and very caring. What does it matter if he is not of the marrying kind?"

Rachele smiled but couldn't help herself

"Would you think the same if he were your son?"

The countess could not easily be fazed

"Considering that I only have one son, my immediate reaction would have been the title would go to my late husband's horrible cousin and his sons. Other than that, I could not care less whom he loves. It is his business, not mine."

Rachele could not help herself. She loved to tease her aunt each time she could.

"Are you saying that just because your son is married to a nice Jewish lady, and you have three grandchildren, so there is no immediate risk to the title?"

The countess thought about it. Rachele could picture her adjusting her skirt to gain time.

"Yes, but I like to think that I would have given the same answer, anyway."

Then she closed the conversation after another small amount of small talk, as her manners required.

It was only 8 am, but the weather was already very hot and humid. Vice-Commissario Umberto De Antoni's shirt was already soaked after half an hour on the bus that took him to Venice from his home in Mestre every morning. He hopped on the vaporetto at Piazzale Roma, standing outside without leaning on anything always made him feel like a true Venetian. He got off at Riva De Biasio, looking forward to coffee and the high-quality pastries available at the Cantoni-Mendes-Modiano law firm. Today, he was also looking forward to a large ceiling fan in the back meeting room.

As expected, he and Rachele withdrew to the back meeting room after the social side of his visit. Rachele had all her notepads.

"Yesterday, the countess told me about the poison. Do you have any idea what happened?"

Umberto had just started recovering from the heat and humidity. At 8.30 in the morning, the ceiling fan was helping.

"Can anything be kept secret in Venice?"

Rachele smiled back

"You can slow down the speed at which news travel unless you have an indignant or concerned Aunt Deborah or when she is on her metaphorical high horse about something. Anyway, I assume you spoke to Lottie."

"I did. She bumped into David Klein and a blond woman in Piazza San Marco when she was on her way to the café where she was supposed to meet Bernard Alcan. She did not know why, but she did not share whom she was going to meet, but just said she had half an hour."

"So, she mentioned David Klein to Bernard because…"

"David and Brigitte were about to go. They were standing, saying their goodbyes and planning to meet again while they were all in Venice when David saw somebody with a blowgun; they thought it was strange to see a grown-up man playing a children's game."

Rachele was writing on her notepad. She gestured for Umberto to wait a minute.

"Sorry, I have a question, but I wanted to make sure I took a note of something else that I just thought. So, David Klein and the mysterious blond woman could be witnesses. Did Lottie think David could recognise the man?"

Umberto raised his eyebrows, and his shoulders

"She did not say, but he could be our only hope. We just have to find him. At the moment, Brigitte Fontaine is our best hope of finding him. We need to talk to her."

"Assuming the Brigitte Fontaine that stays in the hotel near the hospital is the woman we are looking for."

The last line took the smile out of Umberto's face.

"Well, thanks to the cooperation of Tommaso Tron and Charlotte Alcan Campbell, we'll find out tomorrow morning."

It turned out that Brigitte Fontaine was the woman they were looking for. She was sitting at a corner table, removed from the rest of the guests. Tommaso left after the identification, but Charlotte stayed to help Umberto; initially, Brigitte was reluctant to cooperate; her reluctance faded when she realised Umberto knew where the precious stones were. They had to speak through Charlotte, who had already introduced herself to her as Lottie's niece.

"I am so relieved your aunt has woken up. David and I thought he was the target, so when something happened to her, David was afraid, and he left, trying not to run so he would not draw attention to himself."

Charlotte translated but did not wait for Umberto to say anything.

"And you left my aunt there? She could have died."

Brigitte replied with an apologetic tone of voice.

"I did not want to leave her, but in the end, I followed him. We stopped in the gardens nearby; I was determined to ask somebody to call an ambulance. David was afraid. When I saw an ambulance arrive, I concentrated on him. We bought a stupid hat from one vendor outside the Giardini and boarded the first vaporetto that arrived."

This time, Charlotte translated and waited for Umberto to ask a question

"What or whom is David afraid of?"

Brigitte took a sip from her tea before answering.

"He is afraid of the man who killed the art dealer a few weeks ago, but there is a long story to explain why."

Charlotte raised her eyebrows and opened her mouth to translate but could not speak for a few seconds. Umberto had a similar reaction but wondered whether Bernard Alcan was at risk. He decided to reveal as little as possible until he knew more.

"If we organise plainclothes policemen to protect David, do you think he will speak to us?"

Brigitte started showing signs of anxiety

"He might. He kept saying he promised my brother he would protect my family but did not want to tell me whom he saw. I need to go to him. Is there a place that is not a police station where we can continue this conversation?"

Charlotte translated and then suggested the Pesaro De Bonfili home; Umberto had a better idea, the law firm.

"We work with a law firm based in Riva De Biasio. We could all meet there, and there is no need to arrive together. However, if David is so afraid, I would rather give him some police protection. Having plainclothes police officers with him could be a good idea. We can be very discrete."

He smiled. Charlotte translated and threw in a few words to reaffirm how good and discrete they were. She told Brigitte that 'the cousin' who was at Lottie's hospital bed when she paid her a visit was a policeman.

Brigitte reluctantly agreed to the police protection; Umberto stood up, telling Charlotte to translate that she should wait for him to return. He went to the reception, showed his ID, and asked to use the phone. Half an hour later, two plainclothes policemen appeared at the hotel. One of them had some French. Brigitte left them with a message for David to be at the law firm the following morning at 10 with Brigitte. Umberto thanked Charlotte, and after she left, he rang Rachele.

"I'm afraid I have made use of the law firm as if it were a police station. David Klein and Brigitte Fontaine will be there tomorrow at 10. They are too afraid to be seen entering a police station."

Rachele was eager to cooperate.

"That is not a problem. I will organise a meeting room. Do you mind if I join you?"

"I was hoping you might."

Before leaving, Umberto also rang the hotel where Bernard and Alain stayed. He asked the receptionist to pass on the message to wait for him; he did not say why.

Vice-Commissario Umberto De Antoni had spent the rest of the previous day organising the meeting with David Klein and Brigitte Fontaine. He had cleared his plan with his boss because he wanted to deploy several police resources and with the law firm's partners; after all, the police were taking over both meeting rooms for the morning. Everything depended on David Klein and Brigitte Fontaine showing up; he hoped that the offer of a police escort for David would be enough to make him leave the shelter of his room during the day.

When he arrived at the law firm, he was confident about his plan; over coffee, he thanked Roberto Mendes and Alvise Cantoni, the other two partners; Rachele was not there yet. She wanted to help Anita organise a day at the beach for all the Mendes children; it was not easy to get a bunch of teenagers out of bed and ready to leave early in the morning. She would be in the office by 9.30, which should give them plenty of time before "their guests" arrived.

When Rachele arrived, she was not surprised to find Vice-Commissario Umberto De Antoni sitting at the small meeting table in her office; he was going through his notes and lifted his head when he heard the door open. Rachele smiled as she walked in and came straight to the point. They did not have much time.

"Good morning; what do you hope to achieve this morning?"

Umberto smiled back

"Good morning to you; I hope to have a better idea of the man who used a blowgun. I am also hoping to figure out why David Klein thinks he was the target and the shooter could not aim properly and hit Lottie Alcan. Just to be on the safe side, I also organised fingerprint people to check that David Klein's fingerprints are not one of those forensic people managed to isolate from the side of the frame that was used to kill Ludovico Tron."

Rachele had reached her desk and was busy retrieving things from her handbag or her drawers.

"Where do I come in?"

"I value your opinion and your assessment of people, and this time, I want to reassure David Klein that we are not planning any trick. Although he is not your client, or at least not yet, I would be grateful if you could act as if he were whenever he might be afraid that what he has to say might make him a suspect in the murder of Ludovico Tron. Of course, you are welcome to ask any questions."

Rachele was going through things on her desk to ensure there was nothing confidential, given that her office would be used as an extra waiting room that morning.

"Thank you. Do you have a report on what poisoned Lottie?"

Umberto took the report out of his briefcase and gave it to Rachele.

"Do you know if this poison can be found somewhere in Venice?"

"I just found the report on my desk yesterday afternoon. I read it on my way home."

Rachele stood up and moved to sit opposite Umberto

"We still have no idea what made the murderer come to Venice. If the poison is not easy to find here, the murderer came to Venice planning to kill."

Umberto moved to the window to see if he could see David Klein, Brigitte Fontaine, and the plainclothes police officers arrive.

"I thought about it… they are here. I asked Alex Modiano to be with us and help bring other people to the meeting when needed. I cleared it with Roberto and Alvise."

Umberto went to the reception area to meet "his guests," and Rachele and Alex inspected the meeting room to make sure that nobody had left anything confidential lying around.

David Klein and Brigitte Fontaine were very nervous. Rachele and Umberto thought of sitting everybody on the sofa and armchairs rather than around the meeting room table. They reckoned it would have created a more relaxed atmosphere. Before he started asking questions, Umberto asked David Klein if he could get his fingerprints just to exclude him from the list of persons who grabbed the left side of the frame to kill Ludovico Tron. Rachele asked the interpreter to introduce her as a solicitor on his side and explain to him that the police could interpret a refusal as an admission of guilt; it was better to cooperate. David accepted, and Alex left the room to return with a policeman who was an expert in fingerprinting. Once that was over, Umberto asked the first question.

"Why do you think you were the target and Lottie was the accidental victim?"

Rachele noticed David had relaxed after the policeman took his fingerprints. She could see the sign that he was now ready to speak and tell them everything he knew.

"Because the day Ludovico Tron was killed, I saw him enter the art gallery. He had an appointment with his victim."

Umberto sat upright and asked Alex to fetch the sketch artist. He looked at the interpreter and told him to ask whether David Klein minded describing him so the sketch artist could draw a realistic image of his face. David did not mind. Umberto breathed a sigh of relief. Less than an hour later, he had an image of the face of the man who could be the killer of Ludovico Tron. Umberto looked at the picture.

"Do you know his name?"

"He is Jean-Claude Ferrand. During the war, we knew him as *Serge le-Norman.* "

Rachele looked up from her notes

"What is your connection with him?"

The need to go via an interpreter frustrated Rachele; she tried to focus on all the non-verbal clues when David or Brigitte were talking and relied on the interpreter for the content of what they were saying. She noticed that David and Brigitte exchanged looks, and David looked as if he was trying to organise his thoughts.

"The short answer is that he was in our team in the resistance. We met in the workshop attached to the house where the owner of the painting used to live. He must have seen me and Brigitte's brother hide the precious stones in the painting's frame."

Rachele noticed that David Klein looked more relaxed once he started talking. Unfortunately, the need for an interpreter interfered with the pace of the interaction. She had to remind herself that she was not in court. She was not facing a hostile witness, just a very nervous one.

"Why did you hide the jewels in somebody else's home?"

David smiled when he heard the question repeated by the interpreter

"It was a safe place. We did not want to bury them, and we did not want to hide them somewhere obvious. Alain Bernard, the tenant, was the concierge at the hotel in Deauville where high-ranking German officers used to stay. He was an important source of information on the movements of the German army or the SS."

Rachele looked at Umberto, who nodded, happy to leave the questioning to her. At least for the moment, the interpreter was also an annoying necessity for him. Rachele wrote "Alain Bernard = Bernard Alcan?" in her notepad and passed it to Umberto. After the interpreter had finished translating, David continued.

"He was also out of his home most of the day. He allowed us to go through his home to access a shed from the back entrance. We kept our radio in that shed. Most of the time, it was me, Brigitte's brother, or the landlord's son going through his home. One morning, we saw him take off a side of the frame of the painting, one of the few things he had with him when he arrived, and retrieve what looked like a letter.

Months later, when Brigitte's brother told me he wanted a safe place to hide something, I thought of that frame."

David paused for the interpreter. Umberto had a simple question.

"Why?"

David understood

"It seemed a good idea. We trusted Alain, and nobody would have thought of looking there. We were hiding something significant for the Fontaine family. Brigitte's father had a pivotal role in the local resistance. He was afraid for his family if something happened to him. Jean-Claude Ferrand must have heard us discuss it or seen us hiding the bag with the stones."

Rachele noticed that David Klein was getting more and more relaxed while Brigitte was getting more and more tense. She thought it had to do with the memory of what had happened after the war. Her question had been in her mind since they discovered the bag with the diamonds and the other precious stones.

"Why were the jewels still there?"

This time, Brigitte answered

"The SS arrested my father three weeks before the allied army liberated Deauville. Somebody betrayed him; David and others suspected it was one of them because they came at night when they were all busy somewhere else. My mother and I did not know that my father had asked my older brother to hide the jewels. A week later, my brother was also killed. When David came looking for us after the war, we found out about the precious stones. By then, Alain Bernard had left Deauville, taking the painting with him."

After the interpreter translated, David continued the story.

"I loved that painting. Two years ago, I talked about it with my cousin Daniel Klein. He mentioned the story of Israel Alcan and his five versions of the same painting. He also said that a cousin from London had told him Israel's daughter Lottie had survived the war and lived in the South of France. I found out the painter's name and that one of the five paintings had been donated to the museum in Metz when Lottie's father died. I wrote to the museum, and they told me that Ludovico Tron was the leading expert on Cividali and he could have information about the other versions of the painting. After all, if somebody wanted to authenticate one of them, they would likely ask him. So, I came to Venice and looked for Ludovico Tron."

David looked at Brigitte, then he added.

"It was important for me to find the painting and the jewels; after Brigitte's father was arrested, her brother asked me to protect his family if something happened to him. I had to find the painting and the jewels for their sake and his memory."

As she was listening to the interpreter, Rachele observed the non-verbal interaction between David and Brigitte. She was getting more tense. Maybe they were getting close to an unpleasant memory or something that bothered her. She was about to ask a question when Brigitte started talking.

"David wrote to us he had information that may lead to us finding Alain Bernard and the painting. We know Jean-Claude Ferrand. He came to the shop after we received David's letter, and my mother told him that David might retrieve the jewels. She was excited about it and trusted Jean-Claude because he was part of my father's team. When he asked her for more details, my mother told him about Cividali, Ludovico Tron, and Venice."

By now, they were all used to the need to translate what they were saying, so David waited to interject until the interpreter had finished translating.

"What they did not know then was that we suspected that Jean-Claude had given up Brigitte's father because the SS had arrested his brothers, and they were threatening to deport them. We did not act on our suspicions because we had no evidence, just that Jean-Claude's two brothers were arrested and released after three days. Somebody saw Jean-Claude's mother talking to the wife of the SS commanding officer in Deauville."

At this stage, Rachele had one last question to ask:

"So, Jean-Claude Ferrand knew he had to come to Venice because Brigitte's mother mentioned it. How did he know Ludovico Tron had a version of the Cividali?"

"Maybe he didn't know. I came because the curator of the Metz museum told me that Ludovico Tron was the authority on Cividali, and if anybody knew anything about the paintings, it was him. So I decided to come to Venice to talk to him. Walking around one morning, I found out where his gallery was. I was thinking of a good time to return, introduce myself, and talk to him when I saw Jean-Claude Ferrand meet another man outside the Tron's art gallery. I did not want him to see me, so I moved somewhere where I could see the art gallery without being seen. I saw Ludovico Tron, or at least I think I saw Ludovico Tron, open it, and they walked in. When I came back later that day, I saw the police. I found somebody who spoke French and asked her what had happened. She told me they had found the body of Ludovico Tron, the gallery's owner. I thought that Jean-Claude Ferrand had killed him and left. I did not want to risk being seen by him."

Umberto and Rachele exchanged glances. Rachele had discovered the legitimate owner of the precious stone; Umberto now had an actual suspect for the murder of Ludovico Tron. His problem now was to identify him. Rachele wrote, "Where is Jean-Claude Ferrand?" and passed another note to Umberto. The Vice-Commissario looked at her, shrugged his shoulders, and stood up. He turned to the interpreter and told him to tell David and Brigitte to wait because people wanted to meet them. He left to fetch Bernard Alcan and Alain de Lothringen, who were waiting in the other meeting room.

# Chapter Nineteen

## June-July 195

Count Contarini arrived in Venice with his sons; he felt more comfortable travelling with his personal bodyguards, his sons, because he carried the bag with diamonds, emeralds, and rubies they found in the frame of his version of the Cividali. During the short vaporetto ride between the station and Riva de Biasio, he kept his briefcase between him and one of his sons. When they got off the vaporetto, he walked between his sons for the short distance between the waterbus stop and the law firm. He did not know whether they were in danger; he felt anxious walking around with a small bag worth so much money.

Gabriele and Rachele met them at the door. Count Contarini started relaxing in the meeting room facing the Grand Canal. He took the bag from his briefcase and put it on the table. His sons had already started enjoying the refreshments; the count smiled and shook his head. They might have been grown-up men in their thirties and early forties, but they were still acting as children when there were cakes around. Gabriele noticed it and smiled at him. Rachele entered the room with notepads and a couple of folders.

"We are waiting for Brigitte Fontaine, the sister of the man who hid the precious stones. She came to Venice hoping to find the painting. Tommaso Tron and the police found her as part of their investigation of the murder of Ludovico Tron."

The younger of the two count's sons stopped eating the cake

"How did she know to come to Venice?"

Rachele was surprised that anything could come between him and one of her daughter's cakes.

"It was an interesting coincidence. She did not know whether the painting was the right one; a family friend read an article and contacted the museum in Metz, who mentioned our letter and Ludovico Tron as the leading expert on Cividali. He came to Venice, hoping to find more information about the paintings. She followed a few weeks later. The sad thing is that Vice-Commissario de Antoni and I think that the man who killed Ludovico Tron is also after those precious stones. Therefore, they are coming with a police escort, and Umberto will be here in about fifteen minutes."

The Count checked his briefcase to make sure that nothing had slipped out of the bag during their journey from Stra. His eldest son had already finished his slice of cake. He took a sip of his coffee.

"How did Ludovico Tron's murderer know he had to come to Venice?"

Rachele did not like sounding powerless, but she felt powerless.

"The killer knew Brigitte and her mother. Brigitte's mother told him about David Klein's trip to Venice to find more information from an expert. That's all we know. We are not even sure how he looks like. I am sure the Vice-Commissario will find out when he catches him."

They heard the doorbell. A few minutes later, Vice-Commissario De Antoni appeared with David Klein, Brigitte Fontaine, two plainclothes agents, and the interpreter. By then, Rachele was used to an interpreter. Count Contarini surprised his friends with his fluent French. Brigitte looked at the bag and hugged the Count. She somehow did not dare to pick it up yet. It was almost as if she had waited for permission. She looked at the count.

"Thank you for returning it. It represents more than money to me, my mother, and my younger brother. It is almost as if my father and older brother guided you from heaven."

The count looked at her.

"I think they also guided you here to Venice. "

Brigitte was visibly touched. She could barely speak.

"To tell the truth, they guided David to Venice, but that would be a long story. Now I can go back to France."

The interpreter was translating for Umberto and Rachele. Umberto asked him to translate what he was about to say.

"We still need David Klein here to testify as and when we catch Jean-Claude Ferrand."

He then looked at Rachele, smiled, and added.

"Assuming he is the one who killed Ludovico Tron."

Rachele nodded as if she had approved whatever her children had just done or said. Nobody else noticed the silent interaction between them. The interpreter conveyed David Klein's response.

"I have no problem staying in Venice for longer, but the guest house where I am staying told me they have no room for me in August."

Count Contarini did not need the interpreter,

"If it comes to that, you can stay with us. Rachele and Vice-Commissario De Antoni know how to reach us. We have a room for you."

Umberto had been thinking of a way to find Jean-Claude Ferrand since he left home that morning. He had a name and an image of his face drawn by a sketch artist. Agents were checking the hotels in Venice, but that was a long and slow process. His main concern was finding where his suspect had been staying. He got off the bus at Piazzale Roma and walked to the vaporetto stop to begin transitioning into the Venetian bubble. A place where people still walked, where every *campo* was the centre of a small community. Residents, business owners, and everybody who walked through the area regularly were all familiar faces. He got off the vaporetto and stopped to get his second coffee of the morning. People vaguely familiar were discussing the front page news and stopped to greet him; the bartender greeted him when he walked in, started on his coffee, put the croissant he usually had with his coffee on a plate, and placed the plate and the cup of coffee on the counter, pointing to Umberto where he would find them. In a way, he had become a local, at least a daytime local. The regular patrons of the café would have remembered a stranger. Few tourists ventured into that part of Venice.

David Klein was staying in a guest house in a part of Venice seldom visited by tourists, which was more likely to cater to out-of-town relatives of hospital patients than people who were visiting the Most Serene City. David Klein had been staying there for at least a month and would have become familiar with residents and local businesses. At least he could find out if somebody had seen Jean-Claude Ferrand in the neighbourhood.

Once sitting at his desk, he thought it better to check with a 'real Venetian,' so he called Gabriele, who pointed out that a plainclothes agent that sounded local would have more chances of success. People may not talk to a police officer in uniform. If he had an accent from other parts of Italy, people would consider him an outsider, and not everybody would share information with an outsider. Umberto thought he knew whom to ask.

～

At the same time, Vice-Commissario De Antoni briefed two agents who had grown up in Venice. Rachele was in her office, talking to Franco Cantoni, who had returned from Sanremo the previous evening. He had exciting news for her.

"I think you'd better take out the notepads. You will have notes to update."

Rachele took out the two notepads with 'Cividali's young baker' on the cover, opened both, and nodded. It was a silent invitation to start.

"The art dealer had sold other Cividali paintings in the past. That is why Alain Lothringen contacted him using the name of Maurice Vernier. He knew the story behind the five authentic versions of the same painting, so he had every reason to believe the painting was real. The letter that Maurice Vernier gave him provided the evidence."

Rachele was listening and looking at her diagram; she pointed her pen towards him

"Therefore, he did not think to remove the backboard to check if there was a signature on the back of the canvas."

Franco's face lit up.

"When Count Contarini bought the painting, he took care of shipping it himself, so the art dealer did not know the count's address beyond the hotel where he was staying in Sanremo. He knew that the Count was from somewhere near Venice. A few days after the sale, a man asked him about the Venetian scene he saw in his window a few weeks earlier, so he told him a gentleman from Venice had bought it."

Rachele looked at her diagram, putting some notes next to one circle

"So, that's how the murderer knew to come to Venice. We still do not have a reason for him to contact Ludovico Tron. I wonder if he had read his name in a Cividali catalogue or just walked past and saw a version of the Cividali inside the art gallery."

"We can only know that when we ask him."

"Umberto De Antoni must find him first. I'd better ring him to share this information."

Franco picked up his notepad, put it on the tray with the two empty coffee cups, and left the office. Rachele picked up the phone, called Umberto De Antoni, and told him that Franco had found out how the murderer knew to come to Venice, but they were still missing the specific link to Ludovico Tron.

David and Brigitte had arranged to meet Bernard Alcan and Lottie at a café by the Giudecca Canal. Two plainclothes policemen were with them. Vice-Commissario De Antoni did not want to lose the only person who could identify Jean-Claude Ferrand. Brigitte was not eager to travel back home by herself. David was trying to reassure her.

"The bag with the precious stones can fit inside your large handbag. You have nothing to worry about."

"Except I'll be nervous. So somebody might guess there is something worth stealing in my handbag."

"I have to stay in Venice longer. Once the police have caught Jean-Claude Ferrand, I need to make sure they can use my testimony as evidence, at least for the attempted murder of Lottie Alcan. The lawyer we met, Rachele Modiano Mendes, told me my statement that I saw Jean-Claude-Ferrand entering the art gallery with Ludovico Tron may not be enough to charge him with the murder of Ludovico Tron."

They were so engrossed in their conversation that they ignored the world around them. The two policemen had only a vague idea of how Jean-Claude Ferrand looked and relied on David Klein to identify him. They could only look out for anybody trying to approach them. Therefore, they paid little attention to other people waiting once they reached the waterbus stop. They were among the first to board, their escorts behind them; nobody suspected somebody was following them. They sat outside at the back of the vaporetto, the two plainclothes agents sitting near them. One of the two agents had some French; as they were getting closer to their destination, he told them they had to get up to be ready to get off at the next stop. They walked through the seating area of the vaporetto and paid little attention to those sitting there, much to the relief of a French gentleman seated at the front, ready to stand up and get off after them. When the attendant was about to close the gate of the vaporetto, a man walked towards the exit.

"*Attendez, attendez*[1]."

The plainclothes policemen, Daniel and Brigitte kept walking. That man would not be the only tourist who had realised almost too late he had to get off.

---

1. French for 'wait, wait'

They walked to the café where Bernard and Lottie were sitting. The two policemen sat at a nearby table to give them some space. David Klein and Bernard had not seen each other since the end of the war. David had a problem adjusting to Bernard's real name.

"So you are Bernard Alcan, not Alain Bernard. You swapped your initials."

"You did not even keep your initials, Monsieur Albert Dornier. "

They were both smiling, but it did not last long. Bernard became serious.

"So, if I understood correctly, this mess started when this young lady's brother hid diamonds, emeralds, and rubies in the frame of my painting after you saw me check the letter I already hid in the same frame. We were both using Isaac Alcan's secret compartment."

Lottie intervened

"A compartment that had been used to hide compromising documents when my grandfather left Metz during the Franco-Prussian war."

Bernard looked at his cousin and almost smiled. He still felt very protective of her. After all, it was only her second outing after she recovered from the poisoning that was most likely aimed at David Klein. That thought made him look at David with a stern expression. Brigitte figured she'd better say something to defuse the tension.

"My brother thought it was a safe place, and it was a shame he did not share it with us, David knew. It turned out it was a safe place because we have recovered everything. So, thank you."

Bernard did not lose his stern expression

"Yes, but somebody else knew as well, and somehow that person found out you hid precious stones. Unfortunately, that person decided he had to find the painting and retrieve the bag at all costs, even if it meant killing somebody. By the way, do you have any idea who this person could be?"

"Do you remember Serge-le-Norman?"

"I think so. He used to work at another hotel in Deauville. I think his name was Jean-Claude… what's the matter?"

Bernard stopped talking because suddenly David Klein looked alarmed. He put one hand on the back of his neck just when the two policemen sprung up and started running. Brigitte inspected the back of David's neck. Before she could do anything, Lottie intervened.

"Don't. You may get poisoned as well."

She stood up, grabbed a waiter, and told him to call an ambulance; she then picked up her handbag, opened it, took out gloves, wore one on her right hand, used the second as a handkerchief, and removed the pin from David's neck.

The two policemen had thought it odd that a grown-up man would take a blowgun out of his pocket. Then, they realised that something had happened to David Klein and started walking towards the man who had just got up to leave. When Jean-Claude Ferrand realised two men were coming towards him, he ran. The agents began running after him.

Very often, visitors find it challenging to navigate Venice streets and alleyways; it is common for tourists to get lost. A visitor running to escape two police officers chasing him would find it difficult to lose his pursuers. Jean-Claude Ferrand made the mistake of taking the wrong turn. He ended up in a dead-end sottoportego with nowhere to go. The two policemen caught him and arrested him. As they were walking him back to the main road, they realised he had thrown away the blowgun. They walked past a shop, and one of them asked the staff to use the phone to summon a police speedboat and inform Vice-Commissario De Antoni.

Meanwhile, at the café, the ambulance had arrived, and David Klein was about to be transferred to the hospital. Brigitte and Bernard were going with him; Bernard had decided that Lottie should go home.

"Lottie, there are already two of us with him in the ambulance. You can go back to Countess Deborah's home."

Lottie was not convinced

"But you only know basic Italian. I am fluent in Italian. I can help."

The paramedic who had been injecting something into David's arm intervened, not on Lottie's side. His French was basic but not bad.

"The hospital has interpreters. The French interpreter is there all the time in the summer."

Bernard smiled despite himself

"You see, you can go home. "

Lottie was not happy about it but sort of understood. On the way to catch the Vaporetto at the Accademia stop in the Grand Canal to return to what had become her Venetian home, she noticed the plainclothes agents waiting for the police speedboat with Jean-Claude Ferrand between them. She had a message for them.

"My name is Lottie Alcan. Vice-Commissario de Antoni knows how to reach me. The others have taken David Klein to the hospital in the ambulance."

When she was halfway to the Vaporetto stop, Lottie changed her mind and went to the hospital to be with Bernard and Brigitte. It might have been faster to walk, but she only had a vague idea of the route, and therefore the vaporetto was a safer option. She retraced her step back to the Zattere to catch a vaporetto that would take her to the hospital and would call the Countess from there and explain why she would not be back in time for lunch and they should not wait for her.

Vice-Commissario De Antoni left his office with an interpreter, heading for the hospital. Jean-Claude Ferrand could wait. He arrived to find Lottie Alcan already there, so he sent back the interpreter. Bernard was consoling a crying Brigitte. Lottie approached him.

"Did they tell you what happened? I have kept the pin I removed from David's neck. I used one glove to do it and the other glove to store the pin and gave them to the hospital so they could test the poison. "

Umberto De Antoni was impressed. This lady was cut from the same mould they used for the Countess and Rachele.

Lottie gave him a summary of what happened at the café. David Klein was in a coma. Lottie wondered whether it was a more potent dose of the poison that almost killed her. Vice-Commissario De Antoni left the agent with Bernard and Brigitte and went looking for a doctor to talk to. He had to ask them to check if David Klein had been poisoned and if it was the same poison found in Lottie Alcan's body when she arrived at the hospital unconscious a few weeks earlier.

Lottie's call alarmed Countess Pesaro De Bonfili. She decided to go to the hospital to support her guest and see if there was anything practical she could do to help. Before she left home, she called Rachele and told her what had happened. She took a longer route, doing her best to avoid the bridge where her honorary great-nephew, Joshua Schwartz, had been attacked a few years earlier[2]. Walking along Fondamenta Nove, she could see the mainland in the light mist of the summer heat. The view made her shift her thoughts from Lottie and Bernard Alcan to David Klein and Brigitte. She did not know what they had planned to do; but she was certain that those plans had been disrupted. Maybe there was something practical she could do to help.

When she arrived at the hospital, she found Lottie, Bernard, and Brigitte talking to the Doctor and Vice-Commissario De Antoni. Somebody came to ask her if she needed help. She pointed to the group and said she was here for them and was waiting until they had finished talking to the doctor. When the doctor left, she approached the group. Brigitte was crying on Lottie's shoulders, and Bernard was looking at them with a concerned face. Vice-Commissario De Antoni still had a few things to ask, but he was giving Lottie and Brigitte some space. She put a finger to her mouth to tell Bernard that he should not say anything, at least for the moment. Umberto De Antoni noticed her.

"You'll find out from Rachele, anyway. It was the same poison they found on Lottie."

"Did you catch him this time?"

Umberto always felt he was talking to his boss whenever the countess was in her 'woman with a mission' mood. He nodded. Lottie was still talking to Brigitte, who was talking and crying. She asked her to wait so she could ask if the countess could help.

"Brigitte does not want to leave Venice until she knows what happened to David. Unfortunately, she cannot stay at her

---

2. The episode is included in "Elena's memory", see "by the same author" section.

hotel past tomorrow night. Do you know a jeweller in Venice who might buy one of her precious stones?"

The countess looked pensive for a moment, then she smiled.

"I have a better idea. Brigitte could come and stay with us if you do not mind sharing a bathroom. She shall use the old-guest room. It will be ready by tomorrow."

Lottie had another idea

"Do you mind if we share a room tonight? Brigitte is very distressed, and I'd rather she is not on her own tonight. I know she is a perfect stranger, but I would love to offer her to move in tonight. "

The countess did not hesitate

"Of course, maybe if we all give Tonia a hand, the room could be ready tonight. Elena speaks French. You will not be her only interpreter."

Lottie translated for Brigitte, who accepted. The countess thought that coming to the hospital had been a good idea. She now knew what she could do to help and had to go home to organise it.

"I'd better go now and tell Tonia. If Elena is around, the three of us can sort out the room Brigitte will use."

She hugged Brigitte, Bernard, and Lottie, then turned to Umberto de Antoni.

"I called Rachele before leaving home and told her what Lottie had told me."

Umberto realised that there was a not-so-hidden hint to call Rachele.

"I will call her before I go back to the office. I need a sounding board to make sure I have a watertight case and there is nothing I missed."

The countess nodded, shook his hand, and left. Umberto thought that 'his boss' had just given him her silent approval. He told Lottie he wanted to ask her a few questions. Lottie excused herself with Brigitte and stopped hugging her to focus her attention on Umberto.

"Did you see Jean-Claude Ferrand use the blow gun?"

Lottie tried to recall the scene.

"We did not even notice him. David just stopped mid-sentence and touched the back of his neck. The two plainclothes agents must have noticed him because they ran after him when he got up and left."

Umberto then asked Lottie to ask Bernard whether he could identify the man.

"I did not look at him until he started to run when he noticed that the two agents had got up and told him to stop. Yes, I can identify him."

Umberto hoped that Jean-Claude Ferrand did not use gloves, likely in the summer, and they could lift his fingerprint from the blowgun. He thanked everybody and left them with an agent; on his way out, he stopped to call Rachele, who expected to receive his call since the countess had already informed her.

"Aunt Deborah told me what happened. How is David Klein?"

"In a coma, and the doctors are not hopeful. He has more poison in his blood than Lottie had. "

"How can I help?"

"I need a sounding board, a legal sounding board. I want to make sure we have a watertight case, so I would like to have a confidential chat with you after I questioned Jean-Claude Ferrand. "

"Come tomorrow morning first thing. "

Umberto agreed, told her to give Gabriel his best, and hung up. As he was walking back to his office, he started thinking of the questions to ask Jean-Claude Ferrand. He realised that his starting point was not very strong. His agents saw a man with a blowgun. They could tie him to the attempted murder of David Klein and Lottie Alcan, but if he wanted to charge him with the murder of Ludovico Tron and the break-in into the warehouse of the auction house, he had to have his fingerprints. It would help if they had the blowgun he used. He decided that whatever happened, he would arrest Jean-Claude Ferrand as a suspect. After all, he had 96 hours to charge him. He would question him that afternoon and he had the chance to ask him further questions after his conversation with Rachele.

When he arrived back at the police station, he stopped by his office to cool off and drink some water. He was about to leave the room to go where they were keeping Jean-Claude Ferrand when the phone rang. It was the agent who had stayed behind at the hospital.

"A doctor told me the poison used for David Klein and Lottie Alcan comes from a plant that grows around Normandy. It is impossible to find in Italy. The man they arrested must have brought it to Venice in his luggage."

# Chapter Twenty

## July 1950

For once, Vice-Commissario Umberto De Antoni was not paying any attention to his surroundings while standing on the vaporetto during the journey from his home in Mestre, mainland Venice, to Rachele's office. By now, it had become one of his two commuting routes, and he could negotiate buses, walks, and vaporetto like commuters everywhere in the world who navigate their route to work like a migrating herd of wildebeests.

He kept going back to his questioning of Jean-Claude Ferrand the previous afternoon and wondered whether he had missed anything. He was hoping to solve Ludovico Tron's murder and the warehouse break-in, as well as the attempted murder of Lottie Alcan and David Klein. His case had to be watertight, and he had three days and a few hours to build it. He needed Rachele as a sounding board.

He got off the vaporetto and bumped into Gabriele, who was leaving to run some errands, but did not pay attention to anything that Gabriele told him during the brief conversation. He climbed the steps to the first floor of the building and found the receptionist at the door.

"I was standing by the door when you rang the bell. Avvocato Modiano is in the kitchen."

He had no memory of ringing the bell. He was sure that the door downstairs was already open. On his way to the kitchen, he reminded himself to be more in the here and now. After all, he could not let his thoughts distract him if he wanted to make the most of using Rachele as a sounding board. He stopped at the kitchen door and greeted Rachele, Roberto, and Alex, who were talking while having a second breakfast. Rachele passed him the plate with the pastries, and Alex started making coffee for him. Roberto excused himself and left. Umberto picked a pastry and sat down, waiting for his coffee.

"Alex, are you free for the next hour? If your aunt does not mind, I wonder if you could join us. You may help me with your recollection of the day Ludovico Tron was murdered."

Alex smiled and looked at his aunt, Rachele nodded; they put the coffees, some water, and a few pastries on a tray and moved to the meeting room facing the back. The firm did not have any client meetings that morning, and Rachele had booked the room for two hours because it was cooler than her office, thanks to the ceiling fan.

Alex and Umberto left the kitchen to go to the meeting room. Rachele excused herself, saying she wanted to get all the relevant notepads from her office. When she joined them in the study, Alex was discussing Franco's visit to the art dealer in Sanremo. Rachele coughed to alert the other two that she was in the room, sat down, and took over the meeting.

"Why don't we start from what Umberto has established so far? We can discuss the art dealer, the Alcan family, and anything else later."

Umberto felt reprimanded. He looked at his notes.

"The hospital has confirmed that the same poison sent David Klein and Lottie Alcan into a coma; David had much more in his blood, which is why they were pessimistic. So we could charge him with David and Lottie's attempted murder."

Rachele could not hide her surprise.

"Could?"

Umberto felt as if he had failed his friend.

"Jean-Claude Ferrand threw away the blowgun, so we cannot use it for fingerprint. He is under arrest on suspicion of poisoning David Klein and Lottie Alcan."

Rachele was aware of the complication.

"I do not need to tell you that without the blowgun, you do not have watertight evidence."

Umberto was prepared for that.

"The hospital laboratory told us that the poison comes from a plant that only grows in the Normandy area. We are trying to find out where Jean-Claude Ferrand is staying. We hope that if we search his room, we find the poison and, if we are lucky, we can also find other makeshift arrows for the blowgun."

Umberto took a sip of water.

"My guts tell me he also killed Ludovico Tron, implicating him in the murder and the break-in at the auction house warehouse is more complicated."

Rachele went through her notes. She lifted her head and poured herself some coffee.

"Can we establish if the killer used the detached piece of the frame to murder Ludovico Tron?"

It was Umberto's turn to look at notes.

"The doctor said that the pattern of the injury on his back is consistent with that specific piece of the frame. We are confirming whether the fingerprints on the piece of the frame match Jean-Claude Ferrand's."

"Do you realise that even that would not be conclusive? Jean-Claude Ferrand can say he picked up the painting earlier. We need to place him at the scene, or near enough, at the right time on the right day. Did he get in touch with Ludovico Tron before coming to Venice? That is the other weak spot in building a watertight case. David Klein told us he found the Tron gallery walking around Venice. It looks as if Jean-Claude Ferrand had an appointment."

Umberto felt like a schoolboy who did not complete his homework.

"He said he followed Brigitte Fontaine."

Rachele checked her notes.

"She arrived in Venice a week after Ludovico Tron was killed. "

Alex seized the moment.

"What about asking the art dealer in Sanremo?"

Rachele and Umberto looked at him.

"If he can identify Jean-Claude Ferrand as somebody else who came in and looked for the painting and was told that he sold it to a gentleman from Venice, then we may have enough to build a circumstantial case while you look for better evidence."

Rachele could see Umberto's brain thinking. He was silent for a few minutes and smiled before he started talking.

"We can keep him in custody for three days and two hours. Technically, we have time to question the art dealer in Sanremo."

Rachele was going to dampen Umberto's enthusiasm.

"Placing him in Venice would make a better circumstantial case but would not represent watertight evidence. You would have an even better case if a member of the Tron family would recognise him as somebody who has paid a previous visit to the Tron gallery close to the day Ludovico Tron was murdered."

Umberto wrote something in his notepad.

"So, finding the poison and talking to the Tron family are my top priorities. "

Alex felt he had to add something.

"Witnesses saw David Klein near the art gallery the day Ludovico Tron was murdered, nobody else. But, if I remember correctly, many people heard David Klein say he saw Jean-Claude Ferrand enter the Tron gallery that morning."

Umberto sounded deflated.

"So, if David Klein doesn't recover from the coma, it is hearsay and not as strong evidence as David Klein could say it himself. Unfortunately, yesterday, the doctors were very pessimistic. He has too much poison in his blood."

Rachele tried to sound more upbeat…

"Lottie recovered."

…but it did not work.

"Yes, but the forensic pathologist had a theory that since she was not the target, the poisoned pin just scratched her skin. David Klein was the target, and the poisoned pin got into his blood vessels. His blood has ten times the level of poison they found in Lottie's bloodstream. If Jean Claude Ferrand does not cooperate, we must ask around all hotels, guest houses, bed-and-breakfast, etc., to find out where he stays. I think I can have the people. After all, he is a suspect for a murder, a break-in, and two attempted murders."

Umberto started putting his notepad and diary in his briefcase when Rachele had another idea.

"What about fingerprints? If you can match the fingerprints with what you found at the Tron gallery or the warehouse of the auction house, you have reasons to charge him, and that will give you more time to find more evidence for the two attempted murders."

That did not improve Vice Commissario Umberto De Antoni's mood. He looked at his watch.

"I have three days and three hours. Wish me luck with the fingerprints."

Diana Mendes and Charlotte Alcan Campbell were sitting in a café near their homes; it was a quiet corner of the city, away from the tourists. Isabella Tron had joined them, because there was something she wanted to ask Charlotte. It was Diana's turn to speak English, so Isabella tried her best.

"We are going through my father's correspondence at the gallery. There are still conversations he had with potential buyers or sellers, which we know very little about. Can your aunt Lottie help us with a few letters written in French? We do not know if they are genuine enquiries or not. Three of them even mention Cividali."

Diana stopped discussing their order with the waiter.

"Are you sure? Does Vice-Commissario De Antoni know? Maybe you ought to give them to the police. It may help them solve the mystery of your father's murder."

Isabella was about to say something when Charlotte intervened.

"Maybe if we ask my aunt Lottie to look at them, you may have a better idea whether you should give them to the police."

Diana had an even better idea.

"What if you take them to the law firm, and Charlotte's aunt reads them in my mother's office? My mother has been discussing your father's case with the police. She can tell you whether those letters can help them."

The waiter brought them their drinks. After the pause, the conversation continued, discussing Charlotte's problems in setting up a household in Venice and Diana and Isabella's plans for August.

When Diana told her mother about the letters Isabella Tron found, Rachele realised the urgency of finding out if one had any relevance to the police investigation; after all, time was ticking. She also contacted Lottie, and when the Countess replied, she had to explain the urgency, so Deborah Camerini decided to join her guest. Curiosity may kill cats, but nobody ever said anything about curious countesses.

Rachele had decided she would let Vice-Commissario De Antoni know if there was something relevant to Jean-Claude Ferrand. They had gone through at least eight letters when Lottie picked up the next one and smiled.

"This one is signed Jean-Claude Ferrand."

Rachele could tell that her honorary aunt had been bored but was still too curious to excuse herself and leave; Lottie's excitement sort of woke her up.

"What does it say?"

Rachele was more pragmatic.

"We do not know what Ludovico Tron replied, but see if there is any reason why Jean-Claude Ferrand knew he probably had to come to Venice."

Lottie was now reading the letter; it was not very long.

"There may be another letter before this one. This one reacts to Ludovico Tron's reply to another letter, but it confirms that he is interested in one of the five authentic versions of Cividali's young baker."

The Countess had found something to do. She was now looking through the remaining letter to see if she could find another one with the same signature. Rachele was less interested; she had a reason for Jean-Claude Ferrand to travel to Venice. She stood up and moved to her desk where she could call Umberto De Antoni.

"Umberto, I think we have found the evidence that ties Jean-Claude Ferrand to Ludovico Tron. He wrote a letter asking Ludovico Tron to put a hold on the Cividali until he had time to travel to Venice two weeks later."

Umberto did not sound excited.

"When was the letter dated?"

Rachele wondered why his voice did not show the same excitement she felt, yet she knew she was about to share important information, the beginning of the decisive evidence.

"Sixteen days before Ludovico Tron was murdered."

Rachele could not see that Umberto was smiling. He had important news to share with his friend and ally.

"That is something we can add to everything else."

As Umberto expected, Rachele was silent for a minute. The other two ladies did not miss her reaction and stopped going through the letters. Rachele could not hide the surprise in her voice.

"What do you mean by everything else?"

Umberto felt like a student who was doing better than the teacher expected. The excitement he had hidden was now apparent in his voice.

"Well, we got incredibly lucky. We found the hotel where Jean-Claude Ferrand is staying yesterday afternoon. This morning, we searched his room and found the poison. Once we charged him with two attempted murders, there was no objection to taking his fingerprints, and they matched! They matched those we found in Ludovico Tron's gallery and the warehouse. We have enough evidence to lock him up."

Rachele was smiling.

"Well, the letters are further evidence. They prove that his trip to Venice was not a random occurrence. We have to make sure we have statements from those who heard David Klein explain why he and Brigitte's brother thought of hiding precious stones in the frame of Bernard's copy of the young baker. Also, they have to give us statements they heard David Klein say he saw Jean Claude Ferrand walk into the Tron art gallery on the day Ludovico Tron was murdered. Then you have a watertight case."

They made vague plans for a celebratory dinner and ended the conversation. Rachele put down the phone and turned to the two ladies.

"We still need to find the original letter that Jean-Claude Ferrand wrote to Ludovico Tron. That would be the icing on the cake. We have him."

She was interrupted by the receptionist, who came to tell them that Elena Pesaro De Bonfili had an urgent message for her mother and Lottie. The receptionist noticed that Rachele's telephone call had ended. She went back to put the call through Rachele's office.

When the phone rang, the Countess picked it up. She had a brief exchange with Elena that ended with,

"I'll leave immediately. Lottie will come as soon as she can."

She put down the phone and turned to Rachele and Lottie.

"David Klein died two hours ago. Brigitte is devastated. I go home to see what we have to do. Lottie, you should finish going through the letters before you come."

Lottie was not sure staying was the best option.

"You do not speak French."

The Countess was not prepared to start a conversation about what she had decided.

"Elena does; you stay here. It is now two murders and one attempted murder. We need to provide the police with as much ammunition as we can in the shortest time. Elena has told me she will call Pierre and Bernard."

# Chapter Twenty-One

July 1950

Death creates many administrative problems, and dying abroad generates even more complications. Pierre Alcan contacted his Klein cousins, who contacted David Klein's parents. They contacted Lottie Alcan to tell her it was simpler to bury David in Venice. The Countess was determined to help them navigate the bureaucracy and the practicalities associated with the funeral.

Brigitte was adamant she had to pay.

"It is not a problem. Thanks to Count Contarini, I have retrieved precious stones worth a fortune. I can sell one and pay for David's funeral. He would not have come to Venice had he not helped me retrieve what he and my brother hid in the frame."

They were having breakfast. Elena translated to her mother, and Lottie tried to reassure Brigitte.

"You should not feel guilty. Jean-Claude Ferrand decided that David Klein had to be eliminated because he saw him leaving the Tron gallery after he killed Ludovico Tron."

The Countess waited for Elena to finish translating. She had an idea to help Brigitte pay for David Klein's funeral.

"I want to buy something important for Elena's eighteenth birthday. I know a jeweller near the Rialto bridge who is also a goldsmith. We pay him a visit together; he will value the emeralds, and I commission him to make a pendant for Elena. When we come home, I'll give you the difference between everything I have paid for David Klein's funeral and the value of the emerald."

Elena was lost for words. She did not know that her adoptive mother wanted to give her 'something important' for her forthcoming birthday. Lottie translated. Brigitte smiled for the first time in days.

"It is the perfect solution. An emerald will go well with Elena's green eyes."

After breakfast, they left for the station to meet David Klein's parents, who had travelled from France for the funeral.

Jewish customs envisage a seven-day period where mourners receive friends for condolences, share memories, and provide support in the transition toward life without the deceased[1]. There are many logistic complications when the funeral happens in a different place from the usual residence. Countess Deborah offered David Klein's parents to organise meals and prayers in her home for as many of the seven days as they wished to stay in Venice.

The whole Mendes/Pesaro De Bonfili clan was out in force the first evening. During dinner, Elena, Lottie, and Charlotte placed themselves around the table to interpret whenever

---

1. This period is usually called "sit shiva". "Shiva" in Hebrew means seven, "sit" because the mourners sit in low chairs and do not do any work like preparing food or even opening the door to visitors. Friends and relatives who are not direct mourner (parents, children, siblings) perform all these tasks.

required. David's mother was from Strasbourg and was fluent in German; Rachele, who was also fluent in German, sat next to her. Their conversation started with David's mother asking Rachele about her children and soon turned to the events that led to David's death. David's mother was emotionally exhausted but was not ready to stop thinking about her son.

"When I packed to come here, I put the book I was reading in my bag. When I was in our sleeping car compartment, my husband pointed out that I was reading Thomas Mann's Death in Venice. That is when I emotionally realised that David was dead. My husband took Pierre's call. I heard the news from him and started thinking about what we had to do. When I picked up the book, I admitted to myself that David was dead."

Rachele did not know what to say. Once more she thanked everyone and everything, from the Almighty to her lucky star, that, until then, all her children were alive and well. She forced that thought away from her mind but concentrated on David's mother. She did not want to challenge her good fortune.

"I cannot even imagine what you are going through. I am very sorry."

David's mother was not after sympathy; she had a different agenda. Pierre Alcan told her that Rachele knew almost everything and could find out what she did not know. David's mother wanted to know what happened. She was not sure she could understand it but was determined to find out.

"Pierre Alcan tells me you can explain everything. Can you tell me what happened?"

Rachele expected that question. She did not expect it during the first dinner after they were back from the cemetery.

"I understand. I just wonder if now is the best time to go through everything that led to David's death. Do you mind waiting until tomorrow? I asked my secretary to free my afternoon to make myself available for any question you or your husband might have."

David's mother could accept that but was not ready to change the subject.

"Is it so complicated?"

"Well, the short story is that David was killed because he could identify the person who killed Ludovico Tron, the owner of an art gallery. The killer was after something that David and Brigitte's brother hid during the war. That makes it complicated."

David's mother put down her cutlery, took a sip of water, and grabbed Rachele's arm.

"Brigitte already told me that David was in Venice to help her recover something precious that would allow her family to save their business. I understand the story could be long, and I am prepared to wait."

Rachele nodded. She asked whether she could hug David's mother. Unfortunately, the hug did not happen because the waiters that the Countess had hired for the evening were trying to retrieve their plates, thinking they stopped eating that course. The two ladies stopped them. They had not finished. David's mother smiled for the first time.

"We are not used to this formality,"

Rachele reassured her.

"Neither are we. It is just that Aunt Deborah hired waiters that work at the Gritti, one of Venice's top hotels."

～

Countess Deborah decided that her red sitting room was a warmer environment than the law firm, so several people assembled in the large room facing the Grand Canal the following day. Elena Pesaro De Bonfili and Charlotte Alcan Campbell were there to help Lottie translate into French what Rachele was going to say; Lottie, Pierre and Bernard Alcan, Bill Campbell, Tommaso and Isabella Tron were there because of their connection to the story. Diana was there to support her friend Isabella, and because she was curious, Dante Bembo was there because his family owned one version of Cividali's young baker. Rachele also asked Umberto De Antoni to be present in case David Klein's parents had questions she could not answer.

Alex Modiano, Elena and Diana were helping with the hosting, making sure that everybody sat down with refreshments. They knew it was going to be a long explanation. Before everybody arrived, they had helped Tonia and the maid place chairs, armchairs, and sofas in an amphitheatre layout. The countess had placed Rachele centre stage. Elena sat near Bernard Alcan, Lottie sat behind David Klein's parents, and Charlotte Alcan Campbell sat behind Pierre Alcan and Brigitte Fontaine. Deborah Pesaro De Bonfili, in her perfect hostess mindset, thanked everybody for coming and invited Rachele to explain. Elena and Diana looked at each other, smiling. Whenever the Countess was not sure how to behave, she was always very formal. Rachele also understood it and played along; formality could be an excellent way to start.

"First, I would like to thank Aunt Deborah. This magnificent room is a much better environment than the meeting room in the law firm. It is a long story, and you must allow me to start from the beginning. It took me a long time to understand how everything unfolded. "

Rachele looked around, waiting for a nod from Lottie, Elena, and Charlotte before continuing.

"It all started when a gentleman from Metz, Israel Alcan, loved a painting so much that he asked the artist, Emanuele Cividali, to paint five versions of different sizes. He wanted to give one to his parents and one each to his two siblings, and he wanted one to pack in his suitcase to take home with him to show his family while they waited for the four larger versions to arrive from Venice."

Pierre, Bernard, Lottie, and Chantal smiled. They had all heard the story before.

"When the Prussian Army was about to encircle Metz, Israel's father left Metz with his eldest son's family and joined his daughter in Paris. They took the paintings with them, but Isaac Alcan had planned to use his version of the painting to hide documents. He had the second largest version of all five, so he commissioned a different frame, one where the left side could be removed and was hollow, with enough space to hide things. "

Rachele noticed that Bernard Alcan was saying something to Elena. She waited for Elena to translate.

"Bernard did not know he had his grandfather's version."

"He did. We now move to World War II. Bernard Alcan fled to Deauville before the German Army entered Paris. He rented a flat and found a job in a hotel under an assumed name. His landlord was the leader of a resistance group. They met in an outbuilding that used to be a storage place for barrels of wine."

Rachele knew that this was only the introduction. Allowing time for translations allowed her to observe the people gathered around her; nobody looked bored yet.

"Bernard knew about the left side of the frame. He heard the story from his grandfather. One evening, he was hiding something in the frame of his big picture when David and Brigitte's brother walked past the window. He did not notice they had seen him take out the side of the frame. When the SS arrested Brigitte's father, her mother gave her brother a small treasure in precious stone to hide."

Once again, Elena translated Bernard's comment.

"They never told Bernard."

Brigitte lifted her head and said something, which made David's parent shake their head, almost smiling.

"They meant to, but the following day, my brother was killed. David barely escaped arrest and hid in our cellar until the Americans arrived."

After Charlotte translated, Rachele resumed.

"Brigitte's brother did not know where to hide the bag with the precious stone. David Klein thought of the painting. The landlord's son gave them the key to Bernard's flat. Bernard was working at the hotel when they hid it; they nailed the side to the rest of the frame to be sure that nobody would remove it until they were ready to do so."

Umberto De Antoni had asked to join the party just in case he might hear something he did not know. He was enjoying Rachele's performance. The ornate sitting room of the Pesaro De Bonfili home made him picture her addressing the rulers of the Most Serene Republic, knowing full well that a woman could not do it in those days. After the translation, Rachele was ready to continue.

"They did not know that Jean-Claude Ferrand saw them. He had overheard the conversation about the precious stones, so he knew what they were hiding and where. Meanwhile, the war continues. Brigitte's brother is killed, David is hiding, and Jean-Claude Ferrand thinks he has time to retrieve the precious stones from their hiding place."

Once again, Bernard spoke.

"But I left immediately after Paris was liberated."

Rachele smiled. She was about to say that.

"When Brigitte's mother and David came to retrieve the stones, you had already left. Everybody considered the diamonds and the other precious stones lost. Two years later, an article appeared about how the museum of Metz had hidden 'depraved art' in the basement and saved it from the Nazis. David Klein and Jean-Claude Ferrand read that article with a picture of the large version of Cividali's young baker."

This time, Rachele would have paused even if she did not have to allow time for the translation.

"David and Jean-Claude Ferrand wrote to the museum, mentioning they had seen a copy of the Cividali. An assistant answered Jean-Claude Ferrand's letter suggesting he contacted the expert on Cividali, Ludovico Tron, in Venice. David's letter made it to the curator, Alain Lothringen, because he wrote that he was interested in buying one version of the Cividali if it ever surfaced. The curator told him that an art dealer in Sanremo had a version for sale."

After translating, Lottie said.

"For the benefit of the Kleins, I just added that Bernard had asked Alain to take it outside France to be sold."

The others knew that already, so Rachele could continue.

"So, Jean-Claude Ferrand wrote to Ludovico Tron, and David Klein took a trip to Sanremo. Isabella Tron found the letters in his father's archive. We know when Jean-Claude Ferrand arranged to meet Ludovico Tron in Venice."

Tommaso and Isabella Tron looked at each other.

"Our father never mentioned the meeting, not even to our brother."

Umberto De Antoni intervened.

"Why would he? The letters you gave us showed he regularly received queries about Cividali's work. Jean-Claude Ferrand's was just one of many."

"He did not know that the Tron gallery version belonged to Israel Alcan's siblings, smaller than the one he gave his parents. Meanwhile, in Sanremo, the art dealer told David Klein he sold the painting to a gentleman from Venice. So he came to Venice on the odd chance he could track down the new owner of the painting."

Rachele was listening to Elena, Lottie, and Charlotte translate. She almost smiled at the thought that the need for translation interrupted her flow and made her delivery flatter.

"When he arrived in Venice, David started by researching Cividali. He went to the Marciana library where he found, amongst other things, Ludovico Tron's *catalogue raisonné* of Cividali's work. He read about the five versions. The best starting point for his search was asking Ludovico Tron if he had heard of any version of being in Venice."

Rachele noticed Isabella was whispering something in her brother's ears. She couldn't tell Tommaso's reaction from his facial expression. It must have been intense for them since she was now leading to their father's murder. She was lost in that thought and almost missed the nod from Lottie to continue.

"David found Ludovico Tron's gallery and walked past it one morning. He wanted to be sure he would be there as close to opening time as possible. He figured out that Ludovico Tron might not be busy with customers just when he opened the gallery. That was when the cashier at the nearby café spotted him. His long hair made her think he was a woman."

When Lottie translated the last remark, David Klein's mother smiled.

"I told him several times to get a haircut. He told me he enjoyed looking like a blond D'Artagnan since he was 16."

Lottie translated that and looked at the Countess. They had thought he looked like a blond D'Artagnan when they spotted him near Fondamenta Nove and thought he was a woman. The light-hearted interruption changed the mood of the room. Rachele was relieved. She knew her tale was about to get dramatic.

"When he returned, he found the door open and a mess. He just stepped inside but realised that something must have happened. My nephew Alex had the same reaction when he arrived there later that morning. He did not go in. David took a few steps back just when Jean-Claude Ferrand ran out of the gallery."

Isabella gasped, realising that Rachele had talked about his father's killer. When Lottie had finished translating, David Klein's mother gasped as well, realising that her son's killer had just appeared in the story.

"Jean-Claude Ferrand recognised David Klein from his long hair. He stopped running. They looked at each other in silence for a short while, then Jean-Claude Ferrand kept running. David did not know that Ludovico Tron was dead. He thought Jean-Claude had tried to steal something. He thought he would go away and come back later in the day."

Rachele noticed Tommaso had an arm around his sister's shoulder. She continued when she saw that Elena, Lottie, and Charlotte had lifted their head.

"Jean-Claude Ferrand knew David Klein had seen him running out of the Tron Gallery. He knew that there was nothing hidden in that frame. Bernard's painting was larger than the one on the trestle. He had to continue looking, but he also had to get rid of David. Except he did not know where David was staying."

Umberto stood up and whispered in Rachele's ears while waiting for the translation.

"The auction house."

Rachele nodded.

"Jean-Claude Ferrand thought that if he had found the right version before David found out that Ludovico Tron had been killed that morning, he could have left Venice with his loot with no problems. He thought David could only hear of the murder if it became a headline. When he found a notice of an auction that included Cividali's work, he thought he hit the jackpot. However, when he broke into the auction house warehouse, he realised their version was not the right one either."

Tonia came in with a message for the Countess, who did not want to leave the room. She whispered her reply, and Tonia left.

"Jean-Claude Ferrand never liked guns. He thought they were too noisy. A blowgun with poisoned darts was his preferred weapon, and he always carried it with him. So he took to walking around Venice with a blowgun and poisoned darts in his jacket, just in case he stumbled on David Klein. None of us knew that Jean-Claude Ferrand existed until David told us. Several of us had spotted David and recognised him as matching the cashier's description of the person who stood outside the Tron gallery the day of the murder."

Tonia came in with Count Contarini in tow. He had entered the room in the middle of the pause for translation. The Countess and Rachele approached him. Rachele said they had to come to dinner to hear the part he missed.

"The gentleman who just arrived is Count Contarini, the current owner of the Cividali that had Brigitte's family precious stones hidden on the left side of the frame. Anyway, Jean-Claude Ferrand knew David was the only one who could place him at Tron's gallery at the time of the murder. He had to find him and kill him. Therefore, he kept walking around with the blowgun and poisoned dart, ready to strike."

Umberto De Antoni summarised to Count Contarini what Rachele said before he arrived while Lottie, Elena, and Charlotte were translating. He knew most of it already, anyway.

Rachele used the pause for translation to drink water and to prepare herself for what was about to come in her tale.

"Jean-Claude Ferrand thought his lucky day had come when he noticed David Klein sitting at a café by San Marco square with two women, Lottie and Brigitte. He used the blowgun, but David moved. He was standing up to leave. The poisoned dart scraped Lottie's neck but did not cause a cut. Unfortunately, some of the poison entered her bloodstream, but it was not enough to cause her death."

Rachele knew she was almost done. Suddenly, she felt tired.

"Jean-Claude Ferrand left the scene unnoticed. He did not know what had happened to the woman who almost got the poisoned dart. However, he kept following Brigitte, the woman he knew in 1943 as a teenager. He found David. By then, the police had drawings of his face, so when they saw him in the same café where Lottie, Brigitte, Bernard, and David were sitting, they recognised him."

This time Rachele was almost tempted to ignore Elena and Lottie waving to remind her to pause so they could translate, but she waited.

"They could not stop him using his blowgun with a poisoned dart. This time, he hit David's neck. Lottie realised what had happened and tried to get the dart out. Luckily, she used gloves, so we have Jean-Claude Ferrand's fingerprints on the dart. Unfortunately, Lottie was not fast enough, and a lot of poison entered David's bloodstream."

After the translation, David Klein's mother asked a question in German.

"Was David the only one that could testify that Jean-Claude Ferrand killed Ludovico Tron?"

Rachele translated the question and looked at Vice-Commissario Umberto De Antoni to invite him to answer. Umberto smiled and took over.

"Once we had Jean-Claude Ferrand and took his fingerprint, David Klein's testimony was useful but not indispensable. We had his fingerprints. Once we found the poison in his hotel room, we had enough evidence to arrest him for David's murder and Lottie's attempted murder. The poison is not available in Italy. Once we had him in our custody, we took his fingerprints. So, David's death helped us arrest a murderer."

Bernard Alcan stood up.

"I used to work with David Klein and Brigitte's brother during the war. His wish to help Brigitte recover the gems shows his character."

He turned to David's parents and held his mother's hands.

"I did not know they hid anything in the painting. I feel privileged I knew him."

Bernard spoke French, so David's parents understood. The Countess stood up, thanked everybody, and told them she had organised dinner after prayers in memory of David, and they were all invited.

Pierre Alcan had become a rowing partner of Joshua Schwartz, Dante Bembo, and Alex Modiano. He loved the atmosphere of early morning rowing in the lagoon in the summer. There was hardly anybody around, so there were few waves. The heating had not yet become oppressive.

He knew he and Alex were not as fit as Joshua and Dante, but they were getting there at their own pace. Rowing with his friend was the closest fulfilment of Pierre's dream to play with the children in the painting. His mother sent him money to stay in Venice for August, but he did not like the idea of leaving the city and the lagoon.

That morning, they had reached Murano island before turning back. By the time they reached the Island of San Michele, where the cemetery is, Alex and Pierre showed signs of exhaustion. Joshua and Dante adjusted the pace. When they arrived at the rowing club's pier, a sigh of relief came out of Pierre's mouth.

"I am not sure I could have kept rowing for another meter. I thought somebody had moved the pier."

Alex was silent. He was out of breath as well. Joshua gathered the oars, and Dante helped Pierre get out of the boat.

"We have gone a bit too far for you this morning. Don't be discouraged; it will get better as you get more used to it."

"I have no intention of stopping. I only wish I could move to Venice."

Alex and Pierre went to the club café to grab a table while the other two checked out the boat. They had their coffee and a drink to recover from the hour spent rowing Venetian style. Once they had changed into their everyday clothes, they left the club, walking towards Fondamenta Nove to start their working day. Dante would take a vaporetto to Murano. Joshua and Alex would go to the law firm because Joshua was meeting his lawyers. Pierre had offered to help Franco go through papers in French for a client. They spoke English because Pierre's Italian was improving fast but wasn't good enough yet.

On the way, Joshua let Alex and Pierre chat. He was formulating a plan that would help him and may allow Pierre to stay in Venice if he agreed.

By the time they had climbed the two flights of steps to the law firm, he had a clear vision of what he wanted to do. He hoped it was feasible. They greeted the receptionist, who was on the phone, and just waved at them. Joshua knew the way to the meeting room, and Pierre followed Alex into the room he shared with Franco.

A few minutes later, the receptionist appeared, asking Joshua what he wanted to drink, followed by Alvise Cantoni and Roberto Mendes. Joshua listened to them, giving him an update on the actual recovery of possession of the assets seized by the Fascist state in 1944. Joshua took a sip of the cold lemon and mint drink always available at the law firm.

"I can't believe we are done. It took almost two years. May I run past you the plan I have just formulated in my head?"

Roberto got up to take a notepad from the top of a cupboard and sat back down. Joshua waited for him and Alvise to nod before he continued.

"Between my father's inheritance from his parents and what he inherited from Aunt Sylvia and Uncle Raffaele[2], there is a variety of investments, real estate, one industrial company in Treviso, one in Monfalcone, and hotels. I want to rationalise everything, create one or more holding companies."

Roberto looked up from the notepad.

---

2. The story of that inheritance is in "Elena's memory" the first book of the series "Rachele Modiano Mendes investigates"

"That seems a sensible opinion, but who would take care of that?"

Joshua took another sip of the drink.

"This is heaven on a day like this. Well, you would take care of the legal side. I would like Gabriele to be available to advise on some financial aspects. I will need my father to approve of the plan. He is the leading shareholder."

Alvise opened the folder with the lists of assets.

"Between assets your father owns as an individual and the various legal entities, you have forty-eight items to include in the holding group, some based in the Free Territory of Trieste, which adds to the red tape. You need somebody who works at it on a day-to-day basis."

"I think I found it. Pierre Alcan has finished university. He would like to stay in Venice. The group will be based in Venice. He can manage the entire process, and once we are done, we'll see what role he might have in the group."

Roberto stood up, saying they would need to ask Pierre. He left and, less than five minutes later, returned with Pierre Alcan. Joshua stood up.

"Pierre, would you like the opportunity to move to Venice and work here? I have an opportunity for you, but you must improve your Italian."

Pierre looked at him as if he had just seen an angel.

"You are not having fun? Are you?"

Joshua shook his head.

"I am not joking. Of course, this is subject to my father's approval; he is the real owner of everything, not me. So far, he always agreed with what I wanted to do."

Pierre stood there speechless for a few minutes.

"Would I look too much like a child if I jump up and down? Of course, I am interested!"

It was the end of July, and the whole Mendes household was preparing for their holiday in the Dolomites. Everybody was looking forward to some respite from the heat and humidity of a Venetian summer. They were moving a family of nine for a month, which had to be planned with military precision; Anita was in charge, as usual. Rachele was helping her pack jumpers when the doorbell rang. Neither of them welcomed the interruption. They had just a few days to organise everything, and there was a lot to organise. They looked at each other; Anita put back an unfolded jumper in the pile of clothes they had decided to take with them and went to see who their unexpected guest was.

Rachele heard the unmistakable voice of her honorary aunt. She knew somebody in her family would spend time with her, so she finished sorting out the younger children's clothes and then went to the sitting room to greet the Countess and whoever was with her. Lottie Alcan, Elena, and Aunt Deborah were talking to Diana, Leo, and Mario about holidays. When they noticed her, they stopped. The Countess had seen her first, so she stood up and walked towards her.

"Lottie is leaving tomorrow, and she couldn't leave without saying goodbye. We won't stay long. Diana told me you are in the middle of packing for the Dolomites."

Rachele sat down as Anita came in with cold drinks and biscuits.

"We are. I cannot wait to have some respite from the humidity and an evening without worrying about mosquitos."

Lottie took a sip of the lemon and mint drink that was popular in the Mendes clan.

"I can understand that. I am not going home yet. Bernard has invited me to Switzerland. We want to make up for the time we never connected because of our parents' issues. Pierre's mother and his uncle invited me to visit as well. We are thinking of organising a gathering of the descendants of Isaac Alcan. Maybe we buried the past."

The guests stayed a little longer. When they left, Rachele went back to packing. The military-style operation of moving three adults and six young people under twenty to the Dolomites for a month was in full swing.

# Epilogue

## October 1950

B ill Campbell and Tommaso Tron were very busy checking everything. The opening of the Cividali exhibition was only a few days away. The initial idea of showing the five versions of the young baker together for the first time in seventy years had morphed into putting together a collection of the best work of Cividali. In a short time, they secured the cooperation of other museums and Venetian private collectors. Alain De Lothringen had arrived with the large version that Israel Alcan donated to the Museum of Metz. Ca Pesaro had reserved four rooms for the exhibition. The first two rooms had about 15 paintings lent from museums, art dealers, and private collectors. Some were marked for sale with the details of the art dealer that was handling the sale; the two rooms led to a third room that showed the story of the five versions of the *young baker*, why they were five originals, not one original, and four copies, and how the Metz museum saved its version from destruction when Nazi Germany annexed Lorraine. The last room had all five versions on display, together for the first time since they left Cividali's workshop in 1863. Under each version, there was a photograph showing the signature on the back of the canvas, with the number between the first and last name.

They had organised a preliminary viewing for friends, family, and owners. There were a lot of expectations among art dealers and art historians. Cividali was the only modern painter who had painted five versions of the same painting. There were a lot of requests for access outside opening hours to examine the five variations, looking for different details or signs that would differentiate each version other than size and the number in the middle of the signature in the back.

The exhibition was also the launch of Tron Art Publishing, a separate company owned by the newly formed Tron art group. Isabella convinced her eldest brother that splitting the business into three companies would be a good idea: Tron Art, Tron Antique, and Tron Art Publishing. Isabella was going to manage the financial side of the three companies. Her eldest brother ran the art gallery and the antique business, and Tommaso was in charge of the publishing company. Tommaso had his dream. The catalogue for the exhibition was the first new book published by Tron Art Publishing. Tommaso and Bill had dedicated it to the memory of David Klein.

Bernard Alcan intercepted Count Contarini and his wife as soon as they arrived.

"Thank you. You started a chain of events that reunited me with my family."

"I just bought a painting. My wife and I love it very much."

Umberto De Antoni and his wife arrived at the same time as Joshua Schwartz and Dante Bembo. Joshua greeted Pierre, who introduced him to his family. Dante made a beeline for Isabella Tron without talking to anybody else. The Countess noticed Dante's entrance. She stopped Diana, who was sharing hosting duties with Charlotte Alcan Campbell.

"Do you know why Dante has hardly noticed us and went to talk to Isabella Tron?"

Diana smiled. It did not happen every day to be more informed than her honorary great-aunt.

"Aunt Deborah, I am not sure they are ready to make it public yet, but they have been going out together for a few weeks."

The Countess smiled at her great-niece.

"I think it is a brilliant match. The two families represent two sides of Venetian art life. I could not have organised a better match myself if I had invited them to dinner."

Diana decided somebody was trying to talk to her and moved away from her honorary great-aunt. She was not ready to be invited to dinner by Deborah Camerini and find a suitable young single man among the other guests.

The Countess joined Elena, who was talking to Lottie, Bernard, and Charlotte when Pierre joined them with his mother and siblings. Rachele noticed that Pierre's family greeted Lottie and Bernard warmly. She was talking to Alain de Lothringen and told him to turn around. He looked at the scene with a huge grin.

"I think Bernard is reconnecting with his family. He seems to have stopped being afraid of his shadow. His daughter is now an adult. He is even talking about trying to contact her."

Rachele was about to comment when the Countess and her older daughter joined them.

"Elena has gone with Charlotte to fetch me a drink from the waiters. We have left the Alcan to themselves. They seem at ease with each other. It took them long enough to bury whatever reason they had to be estranged from one another."

Elena appeared with a glass of champagne for her mother. The Countess took one sip and continued.

"I have to talk to Bill or Tommaso. Somebody bought the

Cividali's version that the Tron Art Gallery was selling. I hoped I could buy it. Do we know who the buyer is?"

Rachele looked like the proverbial cat who ate the canary.

"Gabriele and I bought it. I convinced him. You will see it every time you come to see us."

The Countess did not expect that, but she recovered faster than her daughter and niece expected.

"Well, I will have to come and see you more often. It is the price you and Gabriel have to pay for stealing the *young baker* away from me."

# Rachele Modiano Mendes

I shamelessly borrowed from my mother's family to create the series Mendeses, the Modianos, and other fixed characters. My maternal grandmother's family was the inspiration for the Modianos, a family made of very strong characters who were all very close and got along very well; or, at least, if they didn't, they kept it to themselves and showed a united front to their children and grandchildren.

My maternal grandmother was the inspiration for Rachele Modiano Mendes. I hope I managed to convey her strong character, empathy, and unconditional love for her family and close friends who had become part of her family.

In Italy, women do not change their names. In the old paper identity cards, where men had 'married', women had the last name of their husbands. Rachele had two legal signatures: Rachele Modiano, and Rachele Modiano Mendes. She could be introduced as Mrs Modiano Mendes, or Mrs Mendes. Professionally, she would be 'Avvocato Modiano' (Avvocato is lawyer in Italian, and it is also used as a title, like Doctor in the Anglo Saxon World) because she was not married when she graduated.

It was uncommon for women born in 1897 to attend University, but the real-life Rachele did. My grandmother always refused "to be a handbag in her husband's arms", as she used to say to anybody who asked. She would also add that she was lucky to have a supportive husband and working environment, something not at all common in pre-WWII Italy.

# Venice street names

Venice is one of the characters in the book. The characters in the story walk around Venice, and their route is often described in detail.

Venice streets and squares have unusual names. There is only one 'Piazza' (Square in Italian), Piazza San Marco. All the others are called *Campo* (Field in Italian), or, if they are small, *Campiello*. Streets are not called *Via* (Street in Italian), but *Calle, Ruga*, and sometimes even *Sottoportego* if they are under arches or start after an arch.

Sidewalks on a canal can be called *Riva* (usually where boats could moor) or *Fondamenta*.

*Salizada* is a slightly larger alleyway, sometimes referred to as one of the earliest paved roads in Venice. Salizadas often curve, just like most canals, so most likely, they were canals or ditches filled in to create a road.

*Rio Tera* is a street resulting from a canal that has been filled with earth sometimes in the past. There are over forty streets in Venice that used to be canals. Most of them were filled in the nineteenth century. The most recent was filled in 1915, the oldest in 1774.

There are a few exceptions. Two are the results of projects started when Venice was part of the Austrian empire (Between 1815 and 1870), and one happened during Fascist Italy

*'Strada'* in Italian means 'road' – **Strada Nova** (new road). Once the railway arrived in Venice in the 1830s, there was a need for a way to walk from the station to the Rialto area. The Austrians filled in narrow canals and demolished a few houses, resulting in **Strada Nova**.

**Via** – There is only one 'Via' in Venice, called **Via Garibaldi**. It used to be a major canal, but the Austrian rulers decided to cover it up and create a wide road with outdoor cafés like Vienna.

**Piazzale** in Italian is a large open square. When the fascist regime built a road bridge into Venice alongside the Austrian-built railway bridge, they demolished an area to create a bus terminal and multi-level parking. **Piazzale Roma** is now the connection between Venice and the ordinary world of roads, buses, cars, taxis, etc.

# Reference to other books

Rachele Modiano Mendes, her family, and many other characters are featured in other books I have written. After I published *The Dressmaker's Parcels*, I thought I could turn Rachele Modiano Mendes into a cosy detective, unravelling many crime riddles. Here are some references to other stories:

I started two series

- Rachele Modiano Mendes The early years – Novellas that take place in Venice between 1921 and WWII (So far, I have published two)

- Rachele Modiano Mendes investigates - Novels that take place in Venice from 1947 onwards. This book is the second in the series.

Samuele Mendes (Gabriele's father) was caught in the first round-up of Jews in Venice towards the end of 1943. He died on the train that was taking him to the camps.

Emanuele Mendes, Gabriele's brother, and his wife were shot while trying to escape after being arrested in 1943. Their children, Mario and Paola, survived because a neighbour took them in before their parents were arrested. Since the end of World War II, they live with Gabriele and Rachele. Emma Mendes, Gabriele, and Rachele's eldest daughter, married Roberto Sonnino in 1946 after he started working for an oil company. During the time covered in this story, they lived in Venezuela.

The Mendes family left Venice in October 1943 and found refuge in Stra, on Count Contarini's estate. They used fake identities. Rachele started working for Guido Orlando under the name Rina Von Moden Conti.

More information about what happened to the Mendes clan during World War II can be found in my other book *The Dressmaker's Parcels*

Elena Pesaro de Bonfili and Joshua Schwartz's story can be found in the first book in this series, *Elena's Memory*.

Umberto De Antoni met Rachele in Stra when they both were in the Resistance. He now works in Venice. Married with one daughter, wife, and daughter are mentioned in the story but never named. You can find him in *The Dressmaker's Parcels* and *Elena's Memory*.

Alain De Lothringen saved version 15 of Cividali's *Young Baker* (the largest one donated to the Museum when Israel Alcan died) from being destroyed when the Nazis annexed Lorraine in 1940. Cividali was Jewish, and therefore his work was considered 'depraved art' by the Nazis.

# Acknowledgments

I'll never tire of repeating it. Writing may be a solitary endeavour but it takes a village to create a book. Let me start by thanking my beta readers Rose Kemps, Andrea Rosen, John Sloggem, Alli McKenzie, and Jennie Cook. Their feedback has been invaluable. You owe it to them if you do not fall asleep reading this book!

Rose Kemps also suggested the title of this book. Nobody was happy with the original title, including myself. The original title will stay a secret between me and the beta-readers!

The London Writers' Salon (LWS) makes writing less solitary. You are one of several squares on a Zoom screen up to four times a day (so far). We all write "alone but together". It's magic. Try it if you do not believe it. LWS is also a source of friends who provide encouragement and, by talking about our books, we bounce ideas from each other. The Gold coaches Katryn, Niamh, Eimar, and Anna support you and help you get unstuck or recover your motivation on bad days. Fellow gold members are a group of cheerleaders who support you and cheer you. Whether the journey has been long or short, I would not have been able to do it without them.

Family and friends provided encouragement, listened (or acted as if they listened) when I let off steam, when I bragged, and when I bored them. Thank you Alessandra, Alessandro, Maria Vittoria, David, Michelle, Eyal, Moshe, Jonathan, and Sam.

I am also grateful to the librarian of the Biblioteca Marciana in Venice, my invaluable source of information for anything about Venice in 1950. I was not born then and most of the people who were are no longer with us.

Last but not least, thank you Venice. It is a city vilified by overtourism, but the magic is still there. If you move away from Instagram locations and the hordes of visitors, you can still find magical corners. Writing stories that take place in Venice takes me back there and make me relive the magic from the comfort of my home in London, by the river Thames.

# About the Author

Silvano Stagni is a multilingual citizen of the world, a father of four, and a cosmopolitan character with a long and varied life. In his youth, he was blessed to have many storytellers, people from different cultures and walks of life. He heard stories from the Imperial Court in Vienna, stories from the Kenyan bush, stories of seafarers, stories of survivors, and stories of fighters. He started writing articles, white papers, and opinion pieces during his previous professional life as an expert in the implementation of financial regulations. Now, it is his turn to tell stories.

Silvano doesn't have a website yet. It will happen one day, but he is not sure when. Meanwhile, he can be reached by leaving a comment on the 'books' page of his Substack Blog:

https://authorsilvano.substack.com/

www.ingramcontent.com/pod-product-compliance
Lightning Source LLC
Chambersburg PA
CBHW020652120726
47906CB00001B/240